THE SEARCH FOR HANNAH

CJ KNAPP

DEDICATION:

This is for the two women who led the pack before anyone knew there
was a pack.

My grandmother – Annina Fappiano

Born 1901

She always told me, "Forget about the boys… get an education."
She eschewed brassieres, deeming them cruel and unnecessary,
and had three husbands.

My mother – Erminia Amelia Mongillo

Born 1921

Her oft repeated observation about me,
"Give her a book… she's happy."
She learned to drive while six months pregnant with a broken arm. She
had three husbands.

Tough women who raised survivors.

I'll love them always.

CHAPTER 1

Mandy Rose shivered as goose bumps gathered on her naked arms. Was the A/C up too high? Nope, she was nervous.

She swung the white T-Bird into a "Visitors" parking spot and frowned. Not too many visitors. Mostly empty spaces.

Her shoulders produced one more shiver as she pulled the emergency brake. These buildings were dirty red, turned-to-brown brick. They crowded together, not bothered by a lack of air or green grass. Not a single tree.

Mandy knew this was where Clyde was being kept. That's all she knew.

If you weren't a spouse or family, information was withheld. Held with pit bull insistence. Confidentiality, of course. And she agreed. But what about the people who want news concerning their loved ones? They're shut out, left to worry and feel the pain of not knowing.

Rummaging around in the past, she acknowledged that finding Bertie's green Porsche saved her from the bullet Felix Guidry meant for her. He'd be away for a long time, not in a mental institution like Clyde.

She climbed out of the low-slung car and shouldered her bulging pocketbook. Would it work; to tell the admitting office she was a social worker, here to help Clyde Boudreaux? She doubted it but had to try. Play it by ear.

She slammed the car door and locked it, then looked up at the grand ancient front entrance. Limestone accents and a slate roof completed the elegant portico. The footpath seemed ignored by comparison. Rain would leave great round puddles to step around. She squared her shoulders and hurried to the massive doors leading to who knew what.

Inside the dimly lit building were high ceilings that did little to mask the musty odor. The lone occupant sat at a huge oak desk, typing. Boney hands paused over typewriter keys and shiny lavender curls bounced as the stiff senior looked up. A questioning expression.

"May I help you, young lady?"

"Uh, yes please. I'd like to know when I'll be allowed to visit someone who's a," she paused, "resident… here."

"Is this person a family member?"

Mandy squirmed at having to tell this curt old woman her business, but she kept her voice even; discarded the idea of impersonating a social worker. "He's the father of my daughter."

"Are you married?" Spoken as though a crime had surely been committed by the girl standing in front of her desk.

Face reddening with anger, Mandy twisted the strap on her purse and her voice cracked. "No, ma'am. We're not married."

Adjusting her spectacles, the woman leaned forward and peered into a wooden file box. The lid squeaked. "What's the name please?"

"Clyde Boudreaux."

The old lady mumbled, "B, B." Then she said, "Are you sure he's in *this* building?"

"No, I'm not. Is there another building?"

"If this man is exhibiting florid symptoms and/or is considered a danger to himself or others, he will be in the back building. Who is Mr. Boudreaux's doctor?"

"I don't know."

The wrinkles smoothed a bit on the aging face. "Let me check elsewhere."

A few steps away at a tall metal file cabinet, she pulled open the top drawer. On her tiptoes, she pushed her glasses down to see into the deep drawer. Her fingers slid the files back until the motion halted.

"Ah yes, here it is. He*'s* in the back building. Doctor Romano is his physician, though he's presently on vacation." The woman's face grew dark.

Mandy had to sit down. A wooden bench leaned against the far wall. She headed for it and fell heavily into it. Her purse swung off her shoulder and hit the floor with a solid thump.

The old woman's brow furrowed as she scurried over and patted her on the shoulder. "It's probably just temporary miss, uh, what is your name?"

"Mandy, Mandy Rose Bokum."

"Your young man's doctor is expected to return within the next day or two. Possibly three. Try calling him again. He's the only one who can arrange a visit for that building. It's typically not allowed."

Mandy sat up straighter.

"Sit there a minute. Your color looks better. Would you like some water?"

"Yes, please."

Mandy was ice cold again and her mouth was desert dry. Her mind whirled, dark thoughts erupting like swollen boils, and the future lost its promise. She soothed herself. "It's just for today, not forever."

"Are you feeling better dear?"

Mandy took the paper cup of water and nodded. "I'm fine. If you'd be so kind as to give me Clyde's doctor's number, I'll contact him."

"Of course, dear. Stay right there. My name's Mabel. Mabel Casner."

The water helped rejuvenate Mandy and so did Mabel's change of attitude. She accepted the folded paper with the doctor's information and pushed it into her pocketbook. Managing a feeble smile, she thanked Mabel and left the building.

Back in her car she headed toward her apartment, her thoughts on fire. She craved some sister talk. She knew Laura didn't approve of her attachment to Clyde; wanted her to make a clean break. Part of her agreed with Laura. It would certainly be easier, especially since right now their daughter, Hannah, was not in the picture. Was not found. Was still missing.

But according to Angus, things were being done to find the children that had been taken. That included Hannah.

It took her less than twenty minutes to get home. Her multi-unit building was dark as she mounted the stairs leading to her second-floor apartment.

A male voice intruded. "Hey Mandy, c'mon over to Jake's. We're doing Hurricanes. Have the official glasses."

"Um, I don't know Mark, I'm kind of tired. Maybe some other time."

The building Mandy lived in was not as quiet as she'd hoped when she signed the lease. In spite of the bloated rent, noise and partying were common occurrences.

Will I ever stop trusting everyone? Wish I had Laura's Watcher.

"Whatever you say, Mandy. I hope you change your mind. You're only young once. We're right upstairs at Jake's."

Mandy knew Mark had a thing for her. "I'll see. Maybe later."

Mark gave her a soft salute and continued to his own apartment on the same floor as Mandy's. She noticed how his faded blue jeans hugged his slim hips.

Each apartment was spacious; occupied by someone single and under thirty. And almost everyone had a cat. No one was poverty stricken, and nobody talked about their families or money.

Mandy keyed into her place and headed to the far end where her bedroom was. The quietest part of her apartment. She muttered to herself, "Maybe I'll go over to Jake's later; maybe later."

Shoes got kicked off before she lay down, fully clothed, and fell sound asleep in minutes.

CHAPTER 2

It was an unusual night. Cassy, Sophie and Laura were all home.

After a full and happy day, Arriona was sleeping in her canopy bed. Her "Princess" bed. She loved her new school and loved her Sophie Grammy and Aunt Laura too.

Sophie and Arriona were inseparable. A love match.

Laura called out, "Who wants a glass of wine and to try the new cheese I found?"

"Me, me," sang Cassy. "I do."

Sophie took longer to answer. She recalled when booze was her best friend, her only friend. "I'll have a glass too, Laura." Then quieter, "Or maybe I'll wait till Angus gets home."

Laura entered with a tray that held a decanter of white wine, three glasses on their heads and a cream-colored block of cheese that looked as though it would melt in your mouth. A little silver cheese knife sat daintily by its side.

"Oh, we need some crackers, Mama. Go get some please."

Sophie left to do her daughter's bidding.

Laura's smile faded as she looked hard at her friend. "Have you heard from Mandy Rose?"

"No. I take it you haven't either?"

Laura pinched her eyebrows and said, "Well, we'll have a meeting with Angus so I guess that'll be soon enough. He has news about Hannah, probably some of the other children too. I think all girls."

Cassandra reached for the decanter then poured the transparent liquid into the stemware. She said, "I wish graduation would hurry up so we can do more to help with the investigation."

Laura took a deep breath and answered, "I know. Almost though. Then we'll be official. Cops at last."

Sophie came in carrying three boxes of gourmet crackers and

plopped them down next to the tray. The spicy scent from the opened boxes was mouthwatering. The decanter was empty. The glasses were full.

They each held their wine glass a different way; Laura by the stem, Cassy between her fingers and Sophie, who'd decided not to wait for Angus, firmly around the bowl.

Sophie lamented, "I've gained back ten pounds." Her face softened as she said, "Teaching Arriona to make sugar cookies is bad for my waistline."

All three women knew Sophie was just talking to fill the space while they waited to hear what Angus would have to say.

Soon the sound of the old pickup pulling into the front parking area made Sophie smile. She recalled Angus's refusal to upgrade his truck he'd owned for ten years.

Cassy and Laura watched as Sophie hurried to the front door to greet Angus. He entered with a well-worn briefcase that appeared full and important. His free arm went around Sophie, and they walked into the sitting area entwined.

Angus dropped the dossier into a clean spot on the wine and snack table. "Whew, it's hot out there. I'm glad you girls are in here with air conditioning."

They waited.

Laura took the lead. "Angus, Mom said you had news. Do you want a snack first or at least a cool drink?"

"Yes, some lemonade would be nice. A tall one please."

Cassandra volunteered to get the drink and then they were all seated.

"Okay, here's what I know. I have information from a guy who drove one of the vans that would've picked the kidnapped girls up from that awful place."

Pause. "The Leprosarium. He'll get a lighter sentence for cooperating.

"He told us that after the vans pick the kids up, they're brought to a bus terminal near Baton Rouge, then bussed to waiting vehicles that take them to holding places. A kind of headquarters. There are three such facilities in our general area. He was very insistent about their treatment, saying they had to be 'in good shape' to be 'placed.'

"He also said none of the van drivers know what the final destination is for each group of kids. He conjectured that some of the people who worked at the Leprosarium did have knowledge of where kids were being 'placed.'"

Angus looked down at his still sweaty lemonade glass and placed it gently on the table. He was quiet for a moment, his forehead creased, and he licked his bottom lip. He lifted his head and gazed at Sophie. She was staring straight at him with her lips pressed together.

He cleared his throat and spoke again. "Some of the children, as we've surmised, would be going up north to be adopted. Black-market babies and toddlers, I've been informed is a very lucrative market. Some younger children are also adopted."

He took a few sips of his lemonade. "New York, Massachusetts, New Jersey and Connecticut have a great need for children to adopt. These folks prefer light-skinned. Dark-skinned children are more difficult to place with families"

Angus swallowed hard. "Now, as we've spoken of before, these kids are given new names. Their adoptive parents never know their birth name. There is a glimmer of hope on this subject though. After they're taken and first arrive at the Leprosarium, some of them find ways to tell each other their real names. Or they hear the abductors talking to each other, using original names. In speaking with some of the children we've rescued from the Leprosarium, we've been able to get some first names.

"In custody now are over one hundred children. However many are so traumatized they can't communicate. We have psychologists working with all of them."

Sophie blew out a puff of air and said, a bit loud, "Angus, we know most of this. What new things did you learn? Please tell us everything. You can't shield us."

"Yes, you're right." He took a labored breath and said, "I hate to hold out false hope."

"Hope?" Sophie yelped.

"Okay, one of the girls, about seven years old, said she remembered hearing the name Hannah. She heard one of the adults say it. And she heard Hannah spoken also by the woman the kids called 'Bertie Hurtie.'"

"Oh my God. That horrible woman Clyde supposedly murdered!"

It wasn't a question, but Angus answered anyway. "Yes, that's her."

Sophie looked at Laura who was biting her fingernails.

She winced with pain but managed to say to her younger daughter, "We have to tell Mandy Rose all this."

Laura stopped mid-bite and said, "Yes, of course we do. Angus, will you find out more tomorrow?"

"Not sure, Laura. The task force is busy already in the field tracking down leads."

Cassy had remained silent. She spoke up now. "Are Laura and I going to be able to join that task force after we get our badges?"

"Well, in an official capacity there will be limitations, but on your own time, that's your business."

Laura cracked a smile and said, "Hey Cassy, look what we did on our own time before."

Angus wanted to be encouraging. "This is not going to be sidelined. It's top priority. Chief Detective Sloane is pushing in every direction possible." He looked around and said, "Has anyone talked to Mandy Rose?"

Sophie answered, "The girls are gonna catch her up. Just need to get ahold of her. Right, Laura?"

"Yeah, Ma. I'll call her, tell her to come over here."

Sophie asked Cassy, "Is Arriona sleeping already?"

Cassy chuckled and said, "Yeah, she was all tired out, told me, 'school exhausted me, Mama.'" Cassy beamed.

Cassandra loved having a family. A life she never would've imagined possible only a few months ago. She felt guilty she'd resented Laura for her charmed life. Now that easy life was hers too.

Cassy looked up to see Laura watching her. She never knew for sure if Laura could read her thoughts. She suspected there was more to Laura than most other mere mortals. Even as close as they were, she knew Laura kept secrets. She was proud of herself for telling Laura that she was gay. Sophie and Angus took it in stride also. She wasn't sure about Mandy. There was another enigma. All this good stuff made Cassy nervous. *Was it too good to last*?

"Cassy, Cassy… Earth to Cassy."

"Mama made po'boys for all of us. Roast beef, shrimp, crawfish and crab and her famous hot sauce."

Sophie said, "Oysters too. After I slide the whole affair into the broiler, we'll eat."

"I wish Arriona was up," Angus lamented.

"C'mon Angus, see her tomorrow or sneak into her room and kiss her goodnight."

Angus reneged. "No, I don't want to wake our little darling. A growing girl needs her sleep."

Cassy's eyes were wet. She wiped the edge of each with her delicate little finger. But she couldn't stop the dark shadow that slid over her chiseled features, leaving her dark brown eyes bone dry.

As for Sophie, she pictured Hannah's tangerine curls and lime green eyes but pushed the vision away.

CHAPTER 3

Both arms were pinned to his sides. His buttocks were shooting firework explosions straight up his spine. The frigid tub he sat in made clanking noises when he jerked his shoulders. His nostrils flared to a familiar smell; scotch on the rocks, without the scotch.

Good God, he was in a vat of ice. It blinded him. Couldn't see a thing. Total black. *Let me wiggle my cheeks; see if that helps. Those fucking bastards blindfolded me. With a rag that stinks like old menstrual blood. I've been trapped here for hours. Wait, what's that?*

A door opened with a clang. *One of those Goddamned dungeon doors.*

"Sam, does he look like he just moved?"

"Nah, he's so pumped full of shit, he prolly thinks he's dead."

"Might's well be."

A low-charged chuckle sent chills through Clyde's brain and body.

Another chuckle, broken up with for sure a smoker's rattle, then a volley of hacking noises. A deep-throated phlegm gathering, then the fucker hurled a hawker into the tub where Clyde Boudreaux sat, wrapped like a Lucky Strike, submerged in icy liquid.

"Throw some more ice in there. He ain't cooked yet."

"Blade, you're one sick fuck," was spoken while more ice was shoveled from the nearby locker, plunking into Clyde's *bath.*

"Whaddya mean? I'm not the sick fuck. This guy is. He murdered a woman, young pretty one too, I'm told. I can't do bad enough to this piece of shit."

Blade continued his diatribe. "Then he has a 'mental break-down.' What a load of bullshit. He knew damn well what he was doing. Never admitted it. Just went whacko. Her nickname was gruesome Gertie or Bertie, or sumthin' like that, as if that made it okay. Sam, you know what those crazy Northerners call the 'lectric chair? Old Sparky," he answered his own question, much to his own delight. "Man, I'd love to pull that fucking lever and watch 'em fry."

Clyde listened intently. He'd emerged from the darkness of the grave, couldn't put things in order. Head pounding, every brain cell was swollen to capacity, might burst.

"Sam, give this Black bastard another shot of Haldol."

"We ain't supposed to give shots, Blade."

Blade quipped, "Ain't never stopped us before. 'Sides I like a hit of Haldol myself on occasion. "Nope Sam, I ain't gonna ease this prick's misery."

Blade kicked the tub, then held the loaded syringe up high, pushed the plunger, emptied the anti-psychotic liquid into the icy water, making sure to pull Clyde's blindfold down to be certain he watched. "Soak that up, fucker."

"C'mon Blade. Let's get outta here. We hafta pull him out of there in a couple of hours. Let's go get coffee with a little of this," he said as he pried a flat metal flask from his back pocket.

The two orderlies left the ice-treatment room.

Left Clyde, minus his shot of Haloperidol, which was just fine with him. He was emerging back into reality, back into present time and space. Was he ready to face it?

CHAPTER 4

Mandy Rose pulled the pitcher of lemonade out of her fridge and poured herself a tall glass. After several swallows, she sat down at her kitchen table in one of the only two chairs. Two, the way she liked it.

Laura had sounded so excited on the phone. News about the investigation. News about Hannah? All from another lifetime.

Mandy Rose hadn't dreamt about Hannah for months. She wondered what her daughter looked like now. More like Clyde? Was she adopted by some fine white family up north? What if they guessed her parentage? Would they reject her?

Mandy felt old tonight. She could hear soft rumblings of the party in Jake's apartment. Mark was probably still hoping she'd show up but knew better than to push her.

That time he showed up at her door at eleven p.m., half in the bag, announced he was getting addicted to her. A stupid thing to say; he hardly knew her. To his credit, he didn't get pissed when she refused to let him in. It did take twenty minutes to get him to leave her doorway.

Tomorrow, she'd try again to see Clyde. His doctor, Romero, was due back soon. He'd have answers for her. She'd ask why Clyde was in that back building. That did not sound good.

The lawyer she'd wanted to hire, wouldn't take Clyde's case. The bigot. If he knew how rich she was, he would've had a change of attitude. Racist pig. She'd enjoyed telling him as she'd left his office that money was no object.

She'd find an attorney who saw people, not skin color.

Her admirer, Mark, was a law school graduate but never bothered to take the bar. He could be of some help. Or not, since he had this crush on her.

Mandy poured some more lemonade into her glass and mentally counted the months until her accelerated human services program would be completed. She wanted to become a social worker, and her studies were important to her. Crack cocaine, AIDS, homelessness and domestic violence; the crime rate was staggering.

She pondered, How could a social worker be a mother and work a job like the one she was planning? Seemed impossible.

She also noted that some of her classmates wanted to escape their own problems by delving into other people's problems. An escape of sorts.

The noise upstairs hit a crescendo.

"What else is Jake serving? Just Sazeracs? Doubt it."

She reviewed her plans in her mind. Need to contact that Dr. Romero. Pretty weird, they don't even know exactly when he'll be back to the hospital. Hopefully she could see Clyde, one way or another. Then later over to Mama and Laura's. Well, now it was Angus and Cassandra's and of course can't forget the daughter.

What was her name? *Keep forgetting it.*

Mandy finished the lemonade and went back to bed.

CHAPTER 5

Saturday morning.

Drinking coffee the way she liked it, half cream, half coffee and three spoonfuls of sugar, was performing its usual magic.

The light tapping on her door was not a welcome event. Neither was the stage whisper of her name.

She grabbed her pink silk shortie robe and shrugged into it, pulling it tight, securing the belt. The long end dangled, skimming her knees. Knowing the answer, she called, "Who's there?"

"It's me, Mark. Can I come in?"

She sighed, then scuffled to the door and swung it open. "C'mon in, Mark. Coffee?"

"Yeah, thought you'd never ask."

His grin was genuine. His teeth perfect, white and even as a new picket fence. His chiseled features a Robert Redford clone.

Mandy tried not to notice how he filled out his faded blue cutoffs but failed.

Quick on the pickup, he caught her glance and a tiny smile made his damn face even handsomer.

"You take it black, right?"

"Yep."

They both sat and plopped their coffee mugs on the little rectangular table at the exact same time.

Double clunk.

Now both grinned.

He said, "No classes; what're you up to today? Thought maybe we could do something?"

"Well, we're doing 'coffee' right now."

His smile faded almost into a pout. It was corrected quickly.

"I want to get to know you better. Maybe I'm wrong, but it seems like you could use a friend. And besides, I could too."

Mandy vacillated. Here was a nice guy who liked her. He wasn't a drunk like Jerry. As far as she knew, he hadn't murdered anyone. Yet all she wanted was Clyde Boudreaux. She shook her head to clear away these confusing thoughts.

He waited.

She answered, "Mark, I have a lot of things going on in my life. Too many to start anything else right now."

"Okay." Pause. "Do you have a boyfriend? I've never seen any. You're not married, are you?"

"No and no. Just circumstances right now that I have to address."

Mark's face looked deflated. He finished his black coffee and put the mug in the sink then turned to Mandy and said, "If I can help with any of this, please let me know. I want to help any way I can."

Mandy recalled those same words from Jerry Walker. She saw how that turned out.

She and Clyde had made a daughter. Clyde would help in the search for Hannah if he could. Right now she'd persevere in helping Clyde. Her path was chosen.

"Thanks Mark. If things change and I need your help, I'll call on you and hope your offer still stands."

"Okay, if that's how you feel, I accept it. My offer has no time limit. I'm not going anywhere any time soon."

Mandy reached out, gave Mark's shoulder a full palm rub then pulled her hand back, making it into a fist, so it couldn't explore any further.

"Will you be home later, Mandy?"

"Not till late. I'm going to visit my family for dinner and spend the evening there."

"You've never mentioned your family."

"And I'm not gonna now. Some other time maybe we'll talk more. Right now, I have to leave."

Mark surprised Mandy when he grabbed her by her shoulders and landed a soft and tender kiss on her mouth.

She shocked herself when she responded all too warmly then felt guilt. Blue cold guilt.

Again she questioned herself. Was she so damaged by Daddy's

molestations that she craved to be abused? Was she doomed for life? Was something that seemed good repulsive to her?

One thing rang true. She had to help Clyde clear himself of the charge of murder. The poisoning and killing of Bertie Bergeron.

Bertie Hurtie.

CHAPTER 6

Saturday's secretary from Temps for Hire chirped, "Doctor Romero's office. Who's calling please?"

"This is Mandy Rose Bokum. May I speak with Doctor Romero?"

The same sing song voice answered, "That isn't possible. It's Saturday, you know. You may try again on Monday."

Mandy frowned into the receiver. *Thought he was coming back from vacation. You'd think he'd want to check in on patients. I'm not trying to get an audience with the Pope.* Her frown deepened.

All she said though was, "Uh, okay, what time on Monday is good to call?"

Squeaky voice being so efficient said, "Not until after his rounds and meetings. You may try after three p.m. Or you may leave your name and number and a message, and I'll be sure and put it with the rest of the doctor's messages."

"I'll try again after three on Monday. Thank you for your help."

Another musical ditty twittered, "Very good. Goodbye now."

Mandy didn't let the brush off bother her. She had another plan.

CHAPTER 7

Mandy hoped her white Thunderbird wouldn't get noticed.

Already sweating like a Georgia fieldhand, her jersey pedal pushers remained stuck between her cheeks. A long-ago favorite line from a poem popped into her head. "Tweaked the material from twixt the peach clefts."

Her mind was seeking refuge from the mission she was hell-bent to perform. An illegal mission. *Wonder what it's like to get arrested. What would the charge be? Trespassing? Could she do jail? Maybe just a fine?*

"God, stop ruminating."

It was easy to follow the road that passed behind the building where she'd met Mabel Casner. The back building.

Saturday, the woman was likely home doing her weekend chores. Not at her desk since the rule was no visits on this day.

So this was the chosen day. To do what she had in mind to do.

Find Clyde.

See Clyde.

Oh nice. She was relieved to see trees, big and full, loaded with moss, enough camouflage there to cover her car stem to stern.

A wave of optimism, then a downhill plunge, drowning her in her own perspiration. She creaked the car door open and pressed it shut as she slipped out.

Mandy crouched low as she duckwalked to where the back building still gleamed from the afternoon's canary-yellow sun rays.

She spotted a hiding place. An attached brick alcove that served as a trash can haven. She snuggled into it. The stink had a life of its own. It would stay with her, she knew, as it buried itself into her hair and burrowed into the gray jersey pants. Shampoo and soap would fix her later, but the pedal pushers and shirt would need to be burned.

She heard voices.

CHAPTER 8

Her breasts were mashed against her thighs as she made herself small. Her breath stopped. There were two voices. One clearly the leader. She trembled.

They must not see her. She pushed her shoulders down between her knees and tucked her head into the smelly jersey pants. She allowed herself a tiny shallow breath as she remembered with horror Felix grabbing her and slamming her on the bed at Clyde's house. The same bed she and Clyde had made love on.

The brute had planned to rape her. Rip her open and leave her for dead.

She still had scars on her heels where they were scraped down the hallway after her sandals had fallen off. Skin sanded off leaving them pink and raw as he dragged her.

Her heels had oozed for a week.

The putrid odor of the decaying matter from the trash barrels made her eyes and nose water. It smelled like Felix.

The two men in the courtyard sounded like Felix too. Poor white trash was what the natives called "those kind of people."

Mandy called "those kind of people" dangerous. Sometimes dumb, but always dangerous.

The voices were closer. Now she could make out what they were saying. "They oughta fry him. Fry the nigger bastard. He murdered a white woman, not one of his own kind."

"No Blade, that's right where you're wrong; she warn't no white woman. She was brown. And if the stories I heared was cor-rect, she was letting him bang her, so she warn't no better."

"Nooo." A long, drawn-out note came from the depths of Blade's belly.

"Yep. Him being colored still don't make it right."

"Shit, what about them calling him mentally ill is right? Goddamn nothing. That's what."

Mandy Rose was frozen. Both legs had gone numb. She reached her fingers down her legs, wiggled them on her shins, tried to rub some blood back into them.

The voices grew nearer. "Well now Sam, I don't see no reason why we can't just take care of this nigger ourselves. We done it before, ain't we? Could do it tomorrow morning. Sunday, no visitors till later. Too late today. I gotta plan it. Tomorrow's perfect."

"I dunnoh. Let me think on it."

"Sam, it's our duty. Our patriotic duty. We gotta take care of this son of a bitch. Him and his high fa-lutin, Goddamn fancy French name. Bordeaux. And first name Clyde. What the fuck anyway."

"But Blade, how're we gonna get back into where the cells are. The main door'll be locked after we punch in the code for locked-down Sunday."

"Dummy, we didn't punch in the code. It's open. Nobody visits these animals back here anyway. We just come back in the morning. No one will find the body till Monday. The fucking head doctor… Rotten Romero hasn't been back here for years."

"I s'pose it could work." Cough, cough. "I'm not feeling so good, Blade."

"Bullshit, you're just yellow. I'm telling yah Sam, it's our patriotic duty."

Sam puffed out a long whoosh through fat pursed lips. "I dunnoh, Blade." Then with a look of hope on his fat, poorly shaved face, he wailed, "Blade, won't the trash collectors be here tomorrow to get those cans?"

"Forget it, Sam. You know Goddamn well they pick up on Monday morning."

Mandy Rose was still frozen in a ball. Her right calf screamed; a painful cramp. The numbness had been preferable. She clenched her jaw, but the knife-like pain brought tears. Her fingers ached to dig into that calf to relieve the excruciating agony.

The voices were louder still as the two vile health aides walked closer to the trash disposal area where Mandy squatted. She bit down on her tongue to keep from uttering any sound.

The men were now within feet from her. Her tongue throbbed as her teeth sliced into it again. She pushed her head closer to the ground, a tormented ball of pain now.

Still, very still, not breathing, she waited for discovery.

The pain in her calf passed and so did the two brutes.

They were walking away as Blade said to Sam, "Tomorrow seven a.m., sharp. No excuses."

Mandy didn't hear an answer; assumed that the more docile Sam nodded.

They were far enough away now to allow her to stretch her leg out from the hunkered down position. She rubbed her tortured calf. "Ahhh."

She replayed what she'd heard and cringed at the need for a plan that had to be executed rapidly. If she wanted to help Clyde, and she did, she'd have to get in there through that open door, find Clyde and hope he wasn't so drugged up he couldn't walk and help himself. She knew she couldn't carry him.

Those two cretins were planning to murder him. And they didn't seem concerned about any consequences. *A repeat performance?*

Their voices were faint now, on the far side of the courtyard where parking was. She could see them from her vantage point and assumed they were making plans. Their heads were close together. Well, as close as possible when one was about five foot six and the other was over six foot five, a genuine giant. Every disgusting inch as big as that lummox Felix.

Her mouth went dry, made the blood pooling in it taste poisonous.

She watched as they planned; hands making wild gestures in the air. Periodically the big and uglier one pushed his overgrown hank of black hair back over the top of his head, only to have it fall down again as he bent toward the shorter conspirer.

Mandy Rose knew she had to get into the building tonight while the back door was left open.

Finally she dared to stretch and pushed both legs out in front of her; didn't believe they would hold her weight yet. She hated sitting on the damp lumpy ground, not sure what the lumps were.

A minute or two passed and she chanced standing. A soft electric charge traveled up both legs, then eased slowly. Finally her legs felt like they belonged to her.

Car engines were turning over. She peeked out. One driver pulled out in a storm of impatience. A black pickup on big tires. The other took some time, backed out of his occupied space, then rolled slowly off in some off-brand ugly yellow car.

Mandy waited for the day to darken.

CHAPTER 9

"So Mama, are you really gonna marry Angus?" Laura's eyebrows jumped up and down a la Groucho Marx.

"Oh Laura, why do you find that so old-fashioned? People still *do* get married, you know."

"But isn't there something you're forgetting?"

"Don't be so cute. I know you mean some *one*."

"Okay, some *one*. What's the law about divorcing someone who's in prison? Daddy will be there a long time. Wouldn't surprise me if he contested it." She paused. "Does he know about Angus?"

"One question at a time, Laura. Of course things would go more smoothly if Daddy doesn't cause problems. It'd be quicker and cost less."

Then Sophie switched tracks. "I've made up my mind to go see him next week and discuss everything. I'll propose a settlement for him to be used however he chooses. For him to spend money on lawyers, probably a waste. He won't get out of there for a long time, but at least he'll have money in the commissary for his needs. I think it's called a canteen. Angus told me there's a limit to how much cash they're allowed. Something about purchasing favors from other inmates who have connections outside to do stuff for the prisoner.

"But I don't see that happening. Many of the people involved in the black-market baby schemes and the sex and organ trafficking have been picked up; at least the ones he might know. Hard to imagine him having any way to profit from any of that scum he was involved with. Well, I know the ones higher up in the organizations don't even know who he is. Plus," Sophie continued, "your father ended up very unpopular with those horrible people."

"You mean hated, don't you, Ma?"

"Well, yes. I guess so dear." Anxious to end the discussion about

Harold, Sophie inquired, "What time is Mandy Rose coming over? I can't wait to see her."

"You know Mandy. Hard to pin her down. I asked her to come, she said yes. That's all I can do. She knows we have news about Hannah. Obviously she hasn't been here much, seems to like her new digs."

"What on earth are *digs* dear?"

Laura kept her mouth from smiling, but her eyes twinkled. "Just a hip name for her apartment. Means where you live. This mansion is your *digs*, Mama." Her face lit up and she didn't hold back the grin.

Sophie made a "get outta here" motion with her hand but also smiled.

Life without Harry in the house casting a pall over everything was decidedly pleasant. Having Cassy and Arriona living here made it quite enjoyable. There was frequent laughter with the giggly little girl sounds Sophie so adored.

There was of course no clear sailing though. Sophie suffered guilt that was sometimes capable of making her want to go back to drinking and spending her days and evenings in the chaise lounge with her gin and tonics. She chastised herself constantly. She should've heard the kidnappers when they came into her granddaughter's nursery and took sweet little Hannah, poor little baby sleeping peacefully.

Where was she now? Was she alive? If she was, would she have forgotten all of us? Forgotten me?

And Harry molesting Mandy Rose. His own daughter. How could she ever forgive herself for not seeing what was going on. *Was she too darn drunk?*

And Laura. Laura was left on her own most of the time. Always so independent. She never needed much care. Then when Hannah arrived, she was ignored even more. Never seemed to mind. Never complained.

Sophie lamented, "How can I feel so happy and so miserable at the same time?"

And Arriona. *Oh Arriona, that child is a delight. So happy all the time and so affectionate.*

"Mama, Mama, Earth to Mama." Laura placed her hand on her mother's arm and gave it a little shake. "Where were you just now?" She bent and looked into her mother's startled face.

"Sorry, guess I was daydreaming. So many changes and still so many things to work through. Laura, did Mandy Rose mention Clyde?"

"No, and I didn't ask either. She'll have to work all that out for herself."

Sophie pinched the bridge of her nose. She hurt for her older daughter. She hurt for everyone. She lifted the tall glass of lemonade, ice cubes all melted now, making it thin and watery, then took a long deep swallow and wished it was laced with vodka.

CHAPTER 10

Mandy closed both eyes and tried putting together the events that led to Clyde's commitment to this state mental hospital.

His release from Bingham Medical Hospital went without a hitch. He recovered quickly from the inflicted gunshot wounds from that pig Felix who left him for dead. And would've killed her too if he was a better marksman. Thank you, Bertie Bergeron, for leaving your Porsche behind at Clyde's house. *Strange to think my escape from Felix was made possible by your little green sports car.*

So much had happened since her return from Santa Ana, California; where Jerry Walker was back employed doing his radio show. Last she'd heard anyway, she couldn't get the station in Louisiana.

This trash can cubbyhole had sunk so deep in the ground it was spongy. Probably vermin, maybe mice might make up some of that sponginess. God, could be rats too. Her whole body shuddered.

She was so thirsty. Maybe a Life Saver would help. Usually some hanging around in her purse. She snapped it open and reached in. *Where was that tasty roll of treats?*

The knuckles of her hand had a dark wisp of something that'd attached itself to her skin. She rubbed them on the sides of her pants, steering clear of the underside, which was damp, almost wet from sitting, and might have more of the same stuff that already clung to her.

She left the lifesavers wherever they were.

She rolled onto her knees and palms and peeked around the edge of the small structure she was in. It was purple dark now. She had to act.

She could see the door of the back building. It looked medieval. What would she find behind it?

Make a break for it. Now or never.

CHAPTER 11

Dusk had drained the Louisiana sky. The back building too on an ominous note. The brick looked dark gray. The black bars on the windows held no reprieve.

Mandy stayed low and ignored the crackles of her disapproving knees. She hugged her pocketbook to her belly and made good time crossing the barren courtyard.

She looked up at the door. Close up she could see it was made of a combination of weathered wood and ancient iron hinges. There were worn marks around a big plate that held what appeared to be a lock from the Middle Ages. The horizontal handle was scratched and worn metal.

"Oh no!" *Was the door locked after all?* She stood straight up. Her heart was thumping wildly, a little rabbit with a coyote in pursuit.

"Get ahold of yourself, Mandy." She grabbed the handle with both hands and jumped when it moved so easily. The door's hinges needed oiling. A high-pitched squeal sounded like a four-alarm fire to her.

Speaking again to calm herself, she said, "Quiet Mandy," before she slipped into the inky black interior of the back building.

It took a minute for her eyes to adjust to this new darkness. The strong musty smell filled her nostrils. *Evil smells.*

She could see a hallway with doors on either side. Placing each foot down flat to make as little noise as possible she felt her way along the wall.

She discovered each door had a metal square of something on it at eye level. They measured about six inches by one foot. After a bit of exploration, these proved to be a panel that could slide open and give the viewer a look inside the room, or more accurately, the cell. There was no glass or grate. Just the rectangular hole. That little window opened to the world of whatever or whoever waited on the other side. Behind the door. In the cell.

"Who goes there?"

Mandy Rose turned to marble.

"Where yah going? Who are yah? Whaddya want? What's yer name?" The voice was high-pitched, like a mountain wind. The words were all linked together as one long continuous song and spoken as though well-rehearsed.

Now Mandy could see what appeared to be an apparition. A long white gauzy gown that had a tiny body inside of it. A flow of long dark hair jutted out from a rather small head with a face as pale as milk. Two round dark eye pockets completed the vision.

The song continued. "I'm yer doctor. Who are yah? Whaddya want? What's yer name? Where yah going?"

Mandy breathed a bit easier as she saw the singer more clearly. The woman, for it was a woman, had the remains of canvas restraints hanging off her elbow. She carried the long straps quite reverently.

This was no doctor.

Mandy stepped over to the tiny lady dressed in white and straps. "Hi, miss. I'm here to visit a friend."

"Is it a good friend or a bad friend?"

"A good friend. What's your name, miss?"

"Rosie. I'm Rosie, always been Rosie, always will be Rosie. What's your name?"

"Oh how nice. My name is also Rosie."

"Well, you can't be me, so maybe we're cousins."

"Maybe. Can you help me, Rosie?"

"Sure can, sure will try. Sure will."

"Can you help me find my friend?"

"What's the name? Gimme a name. I need a name."

"His name is Clyde."

"Clyde, Clyde. Can you abide Clyde. Let's give Clyde a ride."

"Oh Rosie, so you know him. Can you show me where he is?"

"Clyde, Clyde. Let's slide over to Clyde."

The tiny waif floated only two doors down the hallway. She swirled and did a graceful twirl, her white nightie continuing until it wrapped around her legs and mixed with the cruel straps.

She stopped.

Mandy's heart leaped.

"Clyde, Clyde… Clyde's inside."

Mandy stared at the little square rectangle on the door where Rose waited. She wondered how this tiny woman managed to break free of her tethers but couldn't take the time to question her. The little damsel seemed quite content and pleased to be of assistance.

Mandy Rose faced her eager helper. "Rosie, let me see if I can slide the window open and see if Clyde's awake."

Rosie clapped her hands twice and sang out, "Clyde, Clyde, Clyde's inside."

Mandy's fingers trembled as she grabbed the ridge on the ancient slider and pushed. It stuck; wouldn't budge. It was accustomed to stronger hands. Mandy flexed her hands first, then stiffened her fingers and using all her strength, she pushed to the left.

"Ugh." It slid open. She raised up on her tiptoes and looked in. The air that escaped was fetid with human waste.

But yes, Clyde Boudreaux was in there. Clyde *was* inside.

She called his name as loudly as she dared, held her mouth against the opening as closely as possible. Her lips touched the metal rim and she was repulsed. The smell from inside gagged her. She was afraid to speak too loudly. There could be more aides like the two she'd encountered outside.

She tried again. "Clyde, it's Mandy. Clyde." She spoke as loudly as she dared.

The form on the mattress in the corner jerked. Twice.

Even with the scant light available, Mandy recognized the ginger curls.

The body sat up. The head homed in on the door.

"Clyde. It's me, Mandy. Come to the door."

"Oh my God. Mandy!"

He moved amazingly fast. Was at the door in one and half sprints.

Mandy's mouth was over the opening. "Clyde, let's get you outta here."

"Are you nuts. We can't do that. How did you get in here?"

"Never mind about that now. We have to move fast. I heard two men saying they were coming tomorrow to kill you. They weren't just talking. They meant it."

"You must mean Sam and Blade. They're animals. They've killed before. How'm I gonna get out of here though?"

"Clyde, listen to me. I'm counting on you to know what to do. Watch the opening. Right here, Clyde. Watch it. Watch. Be ready."

Clyde was mesmerized by Mandy Rose's tone and message. He watched.

Mandy reached into her pocket and pulled out her secret weapon.

Clyde's deliverance.

Rosie stood there, straps hanging straight down by her sides and watched, fascinated. She stage whispered, "Clyde, Clyde, Clyde's inside."

Mandy repeated her mantra. "Watch the opening. Right here, Clyde. Watch it, Clyde. Watch. Be ready."

Mandy's fingers held tightly to her treasure. It was far too precious to let drop. There could be no mistakes. Her very being held mountains of hope, her stomach tightened as she trusted her instincts. Their future depended on this strange Voodoo totem.

She pushed her fingers through the opening and once they were on the other side, she partially loosened her grip, letting it hang over the edge, hang there waiting for its proper owner.

The emerald-green eyes glittered. The swarthy face produced a new layer of sheen and a soul was captured in a beatific smile.

Mandy saw the colors of the amulet reflected in that shining face.

Clyde raised his arm until four fingers from inside the cell grasped the sacred charm and tightened, bringing a slim strong thumb up to enclose it in a rapturous stronghold.

Mandy said, "Can I let go, Clyde? Is it okay?"

A jubilant voice cried, "Yes, Mandy. Now, Mandy. Let go."

The door shimmied and glowed. It felt warm as though alive. A silver light filled the hallway that Mandy Rose and Rosie stood in.

The cell appeared as a new morning being born.

Rosie laughed, a brilliant garrulous volley of mirth. A clear, clean sound of joy. "Clyde, Clyde, gonna ride."

The heavy metal door moved. A low rumble erupted from unseen depths.

The door made way. Made way for Clyde Boudreaux.

He pressed the gris-gris to his heart, looked heavenward and thanked Marie.

He took one last look at his fetid cell, now in the last stages of a glorious glow. He hoped enough energy would remain for the next poor soul.

A few steps brought him to her.

Mandy hugged Clyde then backed away, not wanting to waste any more time. They had to get out of there.

Rosie clapped her hands, the long canvas restraint straps flying in wild gyrations. She sang out, loud enough to wake the dead. "Go Clyde. Go Clyde. Clyde, not inside."

Time to bolt. Clyde twisted toward Mandy and said, "I see you've met Rosie."

For answer, Mandy just smiled.

The young couple held hands and half-ran, half danced down the short hallway to the doorway that beckoned and helped by letting in some outdoor light.

A full orange moon adorned the deep purple sky.

Their hands stayed connected until they reached the Thunderbird that glowed in the moonlight; glowed with promise.

CHAPTER 12

"Laura, what time did you tell Mandy Rose to be here?"

"Nothing exact, just told her around sixish. You know Mandy, Ma, she'll fly in the door and have a dozen reasons why she's late."

Cassy, ever the peacemaker said, "It's not that late yet. It's barely seven o'clock." Cassy covered her mouth with her hand, then took it away so fast it appeared to be an illusion. "Well, Arriona has new pajamas, in a spaz to get into them. Purple, the color of everything in her world these days. Her new friend has a purple bedroom; waiting for that request for hers."

Sophie, who was all ears for anything concerning Arriona said, "Well, Cass, if that's what she wants, I'll have our maintenance guy show her some colors, maybe some different shades of purple. After all, it is *her* bedroom."

"Sophie, you're spoiling her rotten."

Sophie shrugged one shoulder as if to say, "What's wrong with that?"

Laura was rearranging the hors d'oeuvres, not able to stop them from cooling off. Cajun shrimp, sausage jambalaya and dirty rice were laid out, compliments of the new cook, Portia, and smelled beyond delicious. She'd been given the night off and was already gone.

Almadine was like family, not hired help, and came and went as she pleased. Had her own three rooms, hers for over thirty years.

Almadine didn't approve of the new Samsung microwave. Didn't see how it could do anything but ruin good cooking. She cringed knowing that jambalaya was likely doomed to get reheated, not to mention the shrimp. "Good gravy," she clucked as she took in Laura's attempts to save the repast.

"I didn't see Mandy Rose's car. She's here, isn't she?"

"No, Angus." She paused. "Not here yet." Sophie gave Angus a peck on the cheek.

"I guess we should wait a while longer. Better we discuss everything together." Then he rubbed his stomach like the male he was and said, "I am hungry though and something smells darn good."

Laura saved the moment as she entered with a humongous carafe of chilled white wine and a silver tray loaded with gleaming stemware and tiny cheese cubes stabbed with colorful toothpicks.

They settled down to enjoy the icy cold liquid refreshment as Angus plucked three cheese loaded toothpicks and plopped them in his mouth. He said, "This'll hold me while we wait."

And they waited for Mandy Rose.

And they waited.

And waited.

CHAPTER 13

They'd moved at warp speed across the courtyard behind the back building of Louisiana's Mental Institution. Clyde let his jaw drop as he took one last look at the moonlit back building.

Mandy yanked Clyde's hand down to duck with her under the low branches that hid her T-Bird at the edge of the lot.

The keys jingled noisily, so Mandy wrapped her hand around them, finding the correct one that unlocked the passenger door. "Get in," she ordered.

He folded himself into the shot-gun seat. When he peered up, Mandy had already cornered around the T-Bird's hood and was yanking on the driver's side door.

She jumped in, squeezed the key and the engine roared to life. The vehicle was moving before any words were uttered.

No reverse necessary, a gargantuan U-turn aimed them away from the moon-soaked building.

It was too light for comfort. The moon was a natural floodlight, blasting them with unwanted illumination.

The ill-kept pebbly road was straight until it curved around the main building, which unlike the back building had soft interior lights that peeked out from what was surely Mabel Casner's office.

Mandy inhaled deeply and let the breath out with a somewhat raspy whoosh.

Clyde hunched and looked back at the main building; a frown marred his handsome features. He bowed his head to look at his cupped hand and let his fingers uncurl.

The gris-gris nestled there.

It shone, and he marveled at the colors of its inlayed stones on his pale palm. Ruby shadows. Streaks of gold. His lower jaw dropped as his deep sonorous voice filled the air. He chanted, softly at first.

As the car's speedometer climbed, so did the volume of Clyde's prayers.

Mandy brought the speed down as she arose from the reverie she found herself encased in. Suddenly aware that she harbored a fugitive and it was imperative to avoid any traffic stops, she counseled herself to, "Keep a low profile. Attract no attention."

The inside of the automobile fairly rang with the musical tones of ancient Voodoo chants. The sacred words were foreign to Mandy, but she recognized a few of them. *Mambo… Marie…*

Now she sank into a new kind of reverie. A time and place separate from ordinary life. A place where beingness was all there was. No past. No future. She longed to be able to join in. She craved to experience the peace it brought Clyde. Her eyes shone, a moist heavenly blue. A full throat prevented the tiniest of sounds. She sensed the existence of her heart in her own body. She wanted to meld with Clyde, meld with the sound.

Oh, how she loved him.

CHAPTER 14

The mesmerizing chanting slowed and became cotton soft, the vowels were stretched to infinity, until Clyde was merely making low vowel sounds deep in his throat with no structure at all. "Ahhhhhh, oooooommm. Ahhhhhhh… ooooooommm."

The air was full. There was nothing else. Just the smooth powerful energy without form. An hour later, the only noise was the humming of the Thunderbird's tires on the sleek asphalt highway.

Clyde's head was tilted to his chest, and a soft pleasant snoring broke the silence.

Mandy's eyes felt grainy and her shoulders ached. They'd been on the road for over three hours without speaking. She was aware she had no plans past finding Clyde. Never dreamed she'd be breaking him out. But what else could she have done?

What if those two men just bragged about committing murders in the past. About plans to murder Clyde?

But no. Clyde had agreed. They'd meant it. He had knowledge they'd killed before. *Just more bragging?*

Mandy felt the first painful pangs of remorse for her actions. *What if Clyde wasn't in any danger? But what if he was?* She had to wake him up.

Surprised at her own aggression, she shoved his bowed head that had been lolling peacefully. "Wake up! Clyde, time to wake up."

"Huh?"

"You have to wake up, I can't keep driving forever. We have to make plans. What're we gonna do?"

Clyde hoisted himself up in the bucket seat and shook his head.

"You need to come back to Earth."

"Uh, okay Mandy. You're right. What *are* we gonna do? Maybe you should've just left me where I was."

Mandy's head snapped toward her seatmate, then whipped back to watching the road. "No Clyde. I'd do the same thing over again. Those lowlifes weren't bluffing. They meant every word. They'd convinced themselves they were doing a good deed for society. Total racist assholes."

Clyde laughed, a very agreeable sound in response to hearing Mandy Rose swear. She'd never used curse words before, at least not that he'd ever heard. But then he'd been busy being shot and bleeding to death when that piece of shit Felix attacked her. Maybe she let loose with a few cuss words then. It all seemed like a long time ago. He'd be happy now with his little house. If only he'd known Mandy had given birth to his child. His thoughts drifted to Hannah. His little Hannah. His baby girl. He felt different now. Somehow more of an adult. Sort of.

"Clyde, are you going to sleep again?"

"No, I'm awake. Do we have any money?"

"Yes, plenty of it. I thought I might have to bribe guards in that place in order to visit with you, so I brought lots of cash."

"You're amazing."

Not letting the smile reach her lips, she replied, "Yeah, yeah. Now, what're we gonna do?"

"Let's find a motel and get a good night's sleep. First though, we have to get some food to take in with us, coffee, sandwiches, chips. If possible… toothpaste and toothbrushes too. When we get to the motel, you go in and pay, I'll wait in the car. Tomorrow morning when we're rested, we'll make plans."

Clyde grew serious. "I also think we should get an early start and get out of Louisiana."

Mandy Rose grimaced; could just imagine what her family was thinking right now. Laura would be, "Where the hell is Mandy Rose?" Angus was too new to the game to have much to say. Her heart broke for Mama. "Did Mandy Rose leave us again?"

And Mandy knew she couldn't call them.

CHAPTER 15

Angus laid a warm hand on Sophie's shoulder, surprised to feel its coolness beneath her thin cotton dress. Sophie didn't respond, continued to face forward.

He said, "Laura, where would your sister go? Did you tell her we had this meeting planned ?"

"Yes, Angus. I'll call her again. So far, no answer. If she doesn't pick up this time, I'm going over to her apartment. Unless someone has a better idea?"

"I could go instead of you."

"No, Angus. I'll go. There's this guy in her building that knows her. I'll try to check with him too."

"Him?" Sophie frowned. "Him who?"

"Don't panic Mama, just a friend that lives there."

"I hope this isn't starting all over again."

"Mama, don't upset yourself. Mandy Rose is a grown woman, though she doesn't always act like one."

Cassandra touched her tongue to her top lip but offered nothing to the conversation. At these times her outsider status caused her great discomfort. She tried to stay engaged and at the same time was afraid to say anything that overstepped her bounds. She squirmed in her seat.

"Cassy, take a ride with me. Unless you want to stay here and pig out on all this delicious food." Laura looked at her mother. "You and Angus will be here for Arriona… right?"

"Yes, of course. Call us when you know something, please."

Cassy was already hoisting her shoulder bag and pushing her bare feet into her fuchsia slides. Walking toward the car, she said, "This feels familiar."

"I know, right?" Laura put her arm around her good friend. They parted to get into the little MG Roadster; Cassy forced to fold her long lean body into the passenger seat.

A spaghetti in a teacup.

The two young "almost cops" roared off to solve a mystery.

Why wasn't Mandy Rose at Mama's? What could keep her away? Laura crunched into her thumb nail, biting only a jagged edge of skin, ignoring the pain and the spot of blood she knew would be there.

Cassy cried out, "Slow down Laura."

Laura calmed herself and tuned in to The Watcher, the oversoul part of herself that she'd been in touch with from as far back as she could remember.

The Watcher was signaling an alert message. This prepared her for whatever was in the hopper now with dear sister, Mandy Rose.

She said, "Sorry Cass, didn't realize I was speeding. I'll slow down."

And she did.

CHAPTER 16

Loaded down with ham and swiss po'boys bulging with lettuce, tomatoes and pickles, smeared with mayonnaise, plus two large bags of Wise potato chips and one family size bag of Cheese Doodles, the two cold six-packs of Coca Cola would have to do for drinks. No alcohol beverages sold.

Clyde had managed to fall asleep again. Mandy was glad for that.

It was dark now. A mixed-race couple could hinder registration at the motel. Mandy knew some places held prejudices; racist signs were often tucked in behind the counter, visible and intimidating while not on the front door, or a billboard on the highway, the way it was common into the 1960s.

Mandy shut the car door gently until it clicked. She hurried into the small office that looked decrepit in the way only old buildings in the deep south could look. Years of blistering heat and humidity left a mixture of peeling paint of non-descript color and a strong mold odor. The motel clerk fit right in.

Holding a twenty-dollar bill in her hand, she asked the slightly balding, cross-eyed man if she could have a room on the end of the cottages as she was a very light sleeper. Mandy wanted to be as far away from the office as possible.

The clerk swiped a hand over his greasy extended forehead and narrowed his strange-looking eyes. "How many are yah?" The gravelly voice spoke of years of nicotine abuse.

Mandy widened her eyes and said, maybe a bit too sugary; "Oh jest me and my new hubby. He's sound asleep; didn't want to wake him; exhausted, poor darlin."

The eyes stayed tight and beady. No answer. Then, "How long yah planning to stay?"

"Oh, jest the one night, then we'll be on our way."

"You sure, just one night?"

"Yes, sir. Right as rain. Just the one night."

The clerk waited half a minute while Mandy broke a sweat.

The non-existent hair line got another swipe, then a bony hand turned into a shiny open palm. "Prefer cash. Got a problem with that?"

"No, sir. Cash it is. How much for the night, sir?"

"Well, sign says twenty, but since it's just the one night, gotta make it thirty. I have to make a living, don't I?"

Mandy didn't answer the rhetorical question, just turned to her side to get another bill from her purse. Shit, no tens. She peeled off another twenty, added it to the first one and handed him the two twenties.

He snatched the two bills. "Ain't got no change this time of night of course, missy."

Mandy managed to say after swallowing a gummy lump, "I understand, sir. I know it's late. Glad to have the room."

She wanted to wake Clyde and have him pummel the little creep. She didn't. She left the office.

Her body jerked back at the sight of Clyde's head poking up in the passenger seat. The hair on the back of her neck stood up with the certainty she was being watched. Sure enough, she turned back to the office's open door and there he stood, glowering. She waved goodbye to him and he shrank back.

She hoped Clyde's ginger-colored hair, highlighted by the neon-lit marquee, would satisfy the little twerp's suspicions. Even though he wasn't sure what he was suspicious about. Probably thought she was sneaking in dogs or kids.

She moved the car to the room on the end, which was now hers and Clyde's for the night. She opened the passenger door and rustled him in, sticking to his side to thwart any prying eyes. Without entering herself, she went back for the groceries.

The spartan room held a pine wood dresser and nightstand. An ugly crooked pole lamp was the only light. The sunken double bed had a faded purple bed spread. When she turned the light on, it scared the cockroaches that headed for parts unknown.

She plopped the bags of food and drink on the dresser and took first dibs on the tiny bathroom. Without asking Clyde if he had to use the toilet, she jumped in the shower. The tiny, wrapped piece of soap was like a miracle. She used it to suds up and wash her hair. The sliver that was left would do for Clyde.

She emerged feeling better and was pleased to see Clyde had set out the sandwiches, Cokes and even napkins, all crowded together on the nightstand.

His voice was strained and lower-pitched than what she was used to. He said simply, "My turn." And went into the bathroom.

She popped open a Coca Cola, took a deep satisfying swallow, then sat on the bed to wait for Clyde.

In less than ten minutes, he was out clothed in the motel towel and looking handsome as hell.

She held an opened Coke out to him.

He took it with her fingers on it and put her whole hand up to his lips and kissed, not once, not twice, but three times.

Both were hungry, exhausted and drained but now showered and clean.

The temptation was too much.

He let the towel fall and reached for her.

<h1 style="text-align:center">CHAPTER 17</h1>

The MG found a parking space in the visitor's lot behind the building where Mandy Rose now resided. There was ample room between the yellow lines for the little car and just as well as both doors flew open simultaneously and two stern-faced women burst out.

"You don't have a key, do you, Laura? 'Cause if she isn't home and we can get inside, we might find a clue about where she is."

"No, but she told me where the hidden key is. Above her door on top of the casing, exactly where any crook would look first. But… Mandy never listens to reason."

"C'mon Laura, you can yell at her after we find her."

The two friends went into the well-appointed building. It appeared recently built with two sets of wrought iron railings around the entire structure, giving each apartment on the second and third floor a small patio. The ground floor windows peeked out at luxurious shrubs, creating a private area for each.

They climbed the marble staircase inside leading to the second floor and Mandy Rose's apartment, knocked with a knuckle-busting rap several times, then waited.

Nothing.

More rapping and more nothing.

Laura, the shorter of the two, stretched up and felt around for the key. Her face was a mixture of emotions; relief in her eyes, but a tilted shake of her head showed angst.

Right in the middle of the casing sat the cool metal key. Inserted and twisted, it worked like a charm.

The apartment felt cool with central air conditioning blasting away. Laura suffered a flashback to her uninvited entry into Clyde's bungalow where she'd encountered a still pile of humanity on Clyde's kitchen floor; the dead body of one Bertie Bergeron. The same Bertie Bergeron that

Clyde Bordeaux was incarcerated for having murdered. And apparently he was now moved to a facility for the criminally insane.

Did Mandy's vanishing act have anything to do with Clyde? Clyde, who was apparently the father of Hannah? Laura pushed these dark thoughts from her mind. Her older sister had proved to be an enigma before though. "Christ."

"What did you say?"

"Nothing Cass, talking to myself."

The apartment was nice but hardly well-kept. The dishwasher was wide open with a mixture of coffee cups and small bowls loaded haphazardly. The utensil slot held white plastic forks and plastic serrated knives. The dinette table had partially consumed food in cartons with more plastic dinnerware poking out of them.

A voice intruded, "Hello."

Laura turned to the half-open door and was surprised to see a mop of honey blond hair poking into the apartment. The blond head was followed by a lanky male body and another shout, "Mandy?"

Cassy watched the scene unfold as the incredibly handsome young man entered.

"Oh! Sorry. I was looking for Mandy Rose."

"Who are you?" Laura already had a good idea who he was.

"My name is Mark Johnson. May I ask who *you* are."

"Sure, I'm Laura Bokum, Mandy Rose's sister. And this is Cassandra Allain, our good friend."

Cassy nodded hello at the newcomer.

Mark returned the nod then went back to Laura. His face was one big question mark.

"Do you know where my sister is, Mark?"

"I was just about to ask you the same question."

"When did you see her last?"

"Earlier today. I asked her if she wanted to do something this evening, dinner or a movie or whatever. When I heard noise over here, I thought she'd changed her plans about going to her family's house tonight."

Laura jumped on that. "She told you she was going to her family's tonight?"

"Yes, she seemed quite certain of it."

"Do you know when she left here today?"

"No, sorry. I was gone myself until about five. Her car was gone when I got back." Mark picked up on the gravity of the situation, though he didn't understand why. He clasped his hands on the back of his head and leaned back as though there might be answers on the ceiling.

Laura and Cassy were well-trained in body language. They both detected a genuine concern in this friend of Mandy's.

"Mark, perhaps you can be of some help, if you're willing."

"Sure, I'm more than willing. I've only known Mandy a short while, but I'm quite fond of her. She frankly has seemed troubled to me. She goes to her classes and aside from me, she keeps to herself." He paused. "What can I do to help?"

"For starters, let's exchange phone numbers; keep communication open. Would that be okay?"

"Absolutely. I'll do whatever you think you need me to do."

"Cassy and I are both police academy students, almost cops, so we have mobile phones. They're called Rovers, and you can call me no matter where I am and I'll answer."

Mark knew a lot more might be going on here, but he was still game to be involved. He said, "Wow… Rovers. That's great. My cousin in Sweden has a mobile phone. She calls it a cell phone and claims soon everyone will have one. That'll be amazing. People will call people, not places."

"It's good of you to want to help. Maybe nothing's wrong. She could've gone to a classmate's home to study, do homework, or went to a movie and lost track of time, forgot we were expecting her tonight."

Of course Laura knew no such thing could possibly be true. She could not have forgotten. Either she was dead or she was in trouble. Laura's eyebrows furrowed. The more likely conclusion.

Trouble.

CHAPTER 18

After more than an hour of passionate lovemaking, Mandy Rose and Clyde stayed glued together; choosing to ignore the coughing noises made by the ancient air conditioner. The motel bed held them entwined in its concave middle, reluctant as they were to free each other.

Finally Clyde spoke, and a soft and tender voice mumbled into Mandy's damp shoulder, "I think I've always loved you, Mandy Rose. You must love me too."

Mandy turned her head and whispered in a tired raspy voice, "I do. Today showed me how deeply I love you."

Clyde ran his hand over Mandy's back, down to the curve of her waist and slid leisurely up the mound of her naked buttocks.

That was all Mandy needed to become aroused all over again. She pressed her hand between their bodies, searched and found his already erect penis.

He rolled over onto her and fitted himself between her legs, loving how her thighs tightened around his body. It was as though the time without each other never existed. They fit perfectly together. Both lost in a world of their own making; one where pleasure was all that mattered. Problems real or imagined had no place here. They rode on a cloud of erotic ecstasy that had no ending.

Their second coming together brought new waves of excitement, the pleasures softened and deepened beyond earthly imaginings. The deepening became a powerful crescendo until they cried out together and reached the conclusion that left them both fulfilled.

The lovers, now sated, drew slightly apart and spoke no more. In seconds their breaths were flowing in and out in unison.

The enervated lovers faced a tough road to travel in the morning.

CHAPTER 19

"Angus, I'm really worried. It's past midnight. Where is she?"

"Sophie honey, try to remember Mandy Rose is a grown-up. That said, I can call in a missing person's report if you want. It's not true the way television portrays it. You don't have to wait twenty-four hours before reporting a person missing. It's okay to do it as soon as you feel concern that a person is missing. I can report Mandy missing right now."

"Oh, could you please, Angus. I'm so worried. She knew we had this meeting planned and might have news about Hannah. That's what scares me. What could be more important than news about her daughter?"

Before Angus answered, the front door was flung open and slammed. The two young women entered with a contagious air of urgency that spoke volumes.

Sophie's face clouded up.

Laura looked pale and drawn, and Cassy's head was shaking in little "nos."

Sophie bolted over to them, not letting them get all the way into the room.

"Mama, don't upset yourself. You're already wheezing a little. It won't help for you to have an asthma attack."

"Don't worry about me. Was Mandy in her apartment? Why didn't she come here? Where is she?"

Laura continued in a soothing voice. "Let's all sit down and we'll tell you what we know."

Angus cleared his throat and said, "Yes, that's a good idea." He held Sophie's arm and walked her over to the sofa.

She bristled but let herself be seated.

"Okay, here's what we found out. Mandy was home in the early morning, had coffee with a neighbor; left some time before five p.m. That's what we know. She had plenty of time to get here, even if she

47

waited till just before five p.m. when this same neighbor saw her car gone."

Laura stopped reporting and glanced at Cassy who continued. "We met the neighbor Mandy Rose mentioned. The young man showed up. He seemed to know her pretty well. That's how we found out about the time frame. He lives on the same floor as Mandy Rose."

Laura raised a palm, signaling Cassy to let her continue the narrative. "Now, this young man saw nothing to alarm him before her disappearance. He said he cared for Mandy Rose and perceived that she was troubled, although he hadn't a clue why. He took our Rover phone numbers and gave us his number. He seems more than willing to help with all this." Laura blinked and pursed her lips. "Whatever *all this* is."

Angus, perched on the armrest of the tapestry-covered sofa next to Sophie, said in a clear voice, "I think it's time to call the station and report Mandy Rose missing."

Laura said, "Let me call her one more time."

Angus nodded and said, "Good idea."

Laura bypassed her Rover, which was probably dead; its thirty minutes of airtime used up. It needed to be charged.

She dialed her sister's number using the fancy gold phone at the bottom of the staircase and stood there, hip jutted out as she listened. She listened long enough to be completely convinced Mandy wasn't answering.

"Okay, I'm calling it in. There's enough here to start a report. I'll make sure they get right on it." Now Angus was on the gold phone. "Hello, this is officer Angus Clark. Please put me through to whoever is in charge right now." Angus tapped his foot while he waited.

The three women watched. They also waited.

"Hello, yeah, this is Angus. What're you doing there so late Rick?"

Angus was on a first name basis with the captain, Detective Richard Sloane, since the capture of the trafficking ring responsible for the kidnapping of Hannah and the other children.

"Whaddya mean, all hell's broke loose? Wait, never mind that for now. We have a family situation. Could be nothing. Could be serious. As you know, I'm living at my fiancée, Sophie Bokum's, now. This call is about her older daughter, Mandy Rose."

Angus listened while looking up the long staircase. He answered, "Yes, the one whose daughter, Hannah, was taken. "Well, she hasn't come…" Angus didn't get the whole sentence out of his mouth, instead his mouth dropped open.

All three women moved in a huddle closer to the stricken police officer, not willing to miss a single word.

Angus's voice cracked. "Shit. Are you sure?"

After he got that answer, he said, "No, she was supposed to come here tonight. That would've been seven or eight hours ago." Another pause while he listened. "No, not a word. Her sister and their friend went to her apartment. No sign of her or her car."

Angus leaned into the newel, his forehead beading with perspiration. "When did he escape?"

At the word "escape" Laura and Cassy jumped and stared at each other. Sophie stood open-mouthed, making wheezy crackle sounds as she breathed.

"Why didn't they know earlier he was gone?" Angus questioned.

Morning cell-check was the answer.

Angus spoke clearly. "Captain, please say the patient's name distinctly while I hold the phone out for Mandy Rose's mother and sister to hear." Angus stretched his arm out and aimed the handset at the wide-eyed faces of Sophie and Laura.

They strained their ears to hear the name, terrified of what they might learn.

The voice sounded tinny, like it came from an underground tunnel. Detective Richard Sloane enunciated each syllable as clearly as ice cubes clinking together in a crystal goblet.

"Clyde Boudreaux."

CHAPTER 20

The police department jumped into action to get to the bottom of it.

After the coincidence of Mandy Rose Bokum's disappearance occurring at the same time Clyde Boudreaux, accused murderer, was discovered to be missing from the facility for the criminally insane, it was imperative that answers were forthcoming. Was the young woman involved? Was she in danger?

They asked for and got as much information as was available. Not a lot. Not enough to make sense of it.

Apparently Mr. Boudreaux's cell door was wide open, yet the lock was still intact. The authorities were baffled. No one had ever escaped from what was called "the back building" of the mental institution before.

Or if they did, Bingham Mental Institute never reported it.

This promised to be a stinking big kettle of fish.

CHAPTER 21

Dr. William P. Romero freshly returned from vacation felt no sense of responsibility for the disturbing matter of Clyde Boudreaux.

But he had every intention of getting to the bottom of it. His retirement was scheduled, with full compensation, effective in less than six months, and he didn't intend to have some back-building looney tune ruin his perfect employment record. He expected a full pension and was willing to do whatever it took to guarantee there would be no glitches. He'd seen it happen. It would not happen to him.

This Clyde character would be brought back and kept in four-point restraints until the end of his natural born days.

He chuckled when he recalled how pissed he was when Mabel called to tell him what she knew. He almost bit her head off. He wasn't stupid. He knew she'd been in love with him for years. A good ally to have.

He'd get to the facility early in the morning and speak with that dimwit, Rocelyn. Christ, she was practically born in that back building.

She called herself Rosie. Story was she always slipped her bonds and ran free in the hallways back there. He was upset when he'd first heard it happened, but the aides convinced him she was harmless. He suspected Sam and Blade preferred her to be loose. For their own purposes. He never wanted to know more.

Christ, what a mess.

Six more months.

CHAPTER 22

Mandy Rose and Clyde slept until nine a.m. in spite of sunlight screaming through the motel's threadbare drapes.

Mandy got up, wearing only her black briefs, and padded over to the window. She tried to pull the dusty drapes together to close the gap. Not happening.

Next she went into the bathroom, which looked all the grimier in daylight. She was glad the shower worked. As she closed the door, she heard Clyde yawning and yelled, "I'll be quick, then you and let's get out of here."

Clyde didn't answer, just sat on the edge of the bed and rubbed the sleep particles out of the corners of his eyes. He glanced at the closed bathroom door, then came wide awake. He jumped up and began packing the food into the paper sacks. Maybe he'd skip the shower. They needed to make tracks.

He laid out Mandy's clothes on the unmade bed, noting the foul odor that rose to his nostrils, then climbed into his own duds, eschewing a shower. He wanted to get on the road.

He couldn't be seen in the hospital garb he wore. A stretched-out tee shirt and blue pajama bottoms with no tie to help hold them up over his slim hips. Suicide precautions. The paper slippers, already ratty, were now dirty from the courtyard and ripped underneath. Getting him normal clothes must be high on the "to do" list.

Mandy said, "Oh?" when she saw him back in his pajama ensemble.

Clyde answered, "Your clothes are on the bed. Let's just clear out of here."

She nodded, and letting the towel drop to the floor, stepped on it to get to the bed, refusing to put her feet on the beige carpet spotted with white and brown markings of unknown origin.

Clyde watched her mincing steps and smiled as she climbed into her

52

black briefs again, her shirt and gray pedal pushers stained the color of mud on the behind.

He marveled that she did all this for him. "Mandy, we have to get some clothes for me. Let's go into town, look for a used clothing store. I want to stay away from places that might have cameras or shoplifter spotters."

Mandy appraised Clyde, fully seeing him for the first time in his ridiculous outfit. She laughed out loud.

Clyde looked down at his saggy drawers and paper shoes and let out a howl worthy of an amusement park laughing clown.

Moe Benoit, the owner/operator of the Lazy Tim Motel left his office at nine-thirty a.m. to check on his guests, most specifically the little lady who had checked in late last night with the "new" husband. She'd said one night only and checkout was eleven a.m. sharp. If they were still there then, he'd collect another thirty dollars.

The morning was heating up, gonna be another scorcher. He really ought to sell this dump, retire and move north. Sick to death of this heat. Yes, he was. Finished ruminating, he looked toward the end of the row of motel rooms. The last one had no automobile parked in its allotted space. The door appeared to be partly open. Strange.

He quickened his pace and though the ring of keys jangled from his fist, he had no need for it. Moe pushed the door open, spotted the food wrappers on the end table and smelled his signature cheap soap from the bathroom.

He didn't know why, but he went into the bathroom. The shower still dripped and there were long brown hairs sticking to the wet shower wall. And even stranger, there were several ginger colored curls that must have circled the drain but never made it down the rusty strainer basket.

He was glad his neon sign had brightened up the license number on that white Thunderbird. He should've followed his dream and become a cop. He congratulated himself on jotting down that plate number.

Moe had a real ear for the gibberish that came over his Bearcat police scanner. He interpreted it right down the line. He fantasized about "breaking a big case," making his bones. It kept him going… that scanner.

No time to listen now, but later he'd tune in. Maybe hear about a stolen white Thunderbird.

CHAPTER 23

The sleek black Lincoln Mark VI glided into its reserved parking space. Plenty of room on both sides, befitting the status of the chief of psychiatry. The metal name sign was enameled white with black letters.

William P. Romero MD

When humidity tainted it with the least bit of rust, it was replaced from the stash kept for that purpose.

Dr. Romero, long legged with a small round pot belly and a steel gray monk's fringe on his head, jumped out of the shiny car and strode into the front building of Bingham Central Institute.

Mabel Casner waited on pins and needles for his arrival. She felt responsible for anything that went wrong at Bingham. She was there for the name change from Bingham Asylum to the more acceptable Bingham Central. People still called it Bingham Mental Institute. Or Bingham Asylum too. "Good-morning, Doctor Romero."

"Yes, yes, good morning." He looked anything but good. Truth be told, he looked grayer than usual and haggard. Looked older than he had before he went on vacation.

"Doctor, there are two detectives due here in about an hour, about what happened."

"Yes, yes, of course. Get those two aides from the back building up here. I want to talk to them before the officers get here. Do it now please, Miss Casner."

"Yes, sir. Right away, Doctor."

She pressed some buttons on the *loaded-with-buttons* phone on her desk. Snap… snap.

"It's Mabel, Chrissy. Please send Edward or one of the guys down to the back building and have him escort Blade and Sam to the front office. Doctor Romero wants to see them right away. Tell them no dilly dallying. Right away." Pause. "Thank you, Chrissy."

"Channel them right into my office the second they get here," Romero's said, his head poking out of his office doorway.

"I certainly will, Doctor."

Not for the first time, Mabel considered retiring. She'd always been frugal, had a nice savings account, enough to live on and then some.

She knew Romero was almost out the door. There'd be no reason to keep working here after he was gone. Make a move?

She smiled at her typewriter. It didn't smile back.

Never did.

CHAPTER 24

"Mandy, Woah. Stop." Clyde's head swiveled and he pointed out the car window. "There's a Salvation Army. Pull into the back of the store. I can change in the car. Get me a size medium shirt, size thirty-two pants and a nine or nine and a half shoes. Oh, and get some sunglasses and a hat of some sort. That should do it for now."

Mandy expertly took a quick right and passed through the front parking lot to the back, which looked less groomed. She carefully avoided the broken beer and Coca Cola bottles, then took the time to back in and under a tree. The back seat was in shade.

"Keep down Clyde. I'll be right back."

"I'm not going anywhere."

Mandy shocked herself when she answered under her breath, "Good, that's how I like it."

Inside the Salvation Army store, Mandy found herself among close to two dozen shoppers. All were women except for one old man in coveralls and a teenage boy pushing an old woman in a wheelchair.

"All blue tickets… half off," came a voice from a faulty loudspeaker that pulsed throughout the store.

The pants rack had lots of size thirty-twos that were being avoided. The women were all picking through the trousers on the other end of the rack. They pushed the hangers rudely to get to what they wanted, then another woman would shove them back. *Zing, zing.*

The crush of buyers fascinated Mandy Rose. These women were buying pants for their sons or husbands… or boyfriends.

Mandy Rose coveted the feeling. She hung two pairs of thirty-twos over her forearm, then went to the shirts to look for mediums.

"Excuse me, miss, would you like a shopping cart?"

Mandy turned to face a middle-aged colored woman; her hair hidden under a loden green turban and flashing the most expressive brown eyes she'd ever seen.

56

"Oh yes, thank you, ma'am. Where can I get a cart?"

"Let me grab one for you. You should've gotten one on your way in."

Mandy watched while the turban bobbed over to the row of carts all stuck together. She'd completely missed them on her way in. With one yank, a cart was freed and delivered to Mandy by the helpful lady.

"Thank you so much, ma'am."

The lady nodded and went on with her store duties.

Mandy realized she probably looked needy in her spoiled clothing.

Again, the mediums were ignored and plentiful.

Three almost new short-sleeved cotton shirts were added to the cart. As an afterthought she dropped in a powder-blue long-sleeved shirt. It had a blue ticket.

Now, shoes. She'd forgot to ask Clyde what kind he wanted. She'd guess.

There was a wide variety, lots of nines, fewer nine and a halfs.

She chose a pair of canvas shoes that were named "Air Jordan," size nine, and another pair same size marked "Converse." Two pairs were enough.

She peered all around the store looking for hats and sunglasses when Green Turban approached her again.

"Can I help you find something, miss?"

"Yes, please. I'm trying to find hats and sunglasses."

"Over here, not a lot of sunglasses, they seem to disappear on their own."

Mandy looked confused.

"I shouldn't have said that. Sorry." The woman looked over to a counter where a man was busy with a computer.

Mandy got it then.

"Oh ma'am, I intend to pay for everything I get."

"I'm sure you do. I didn't doubt that for one minute."

By now, they were standing in front of a cover-free eyeglass case. Mandy took all eight pairs and dropped them into her carriage. Hats were close by. She chose four of these, different styles.

Checking out was handled by a young white woman with an unfortunate case of acne. At least Mandy Rose *hoped* it was acne.

Loaded down with her bundles, she kicked the passenger door where Clyde now leaned, mouth slack and eyes closed.

Roused now, he jerked and twisted, closed his mouth and frowned, ready to do battle. That frown melted in a jiffy and his fists uncurled.

"Open the door."

"Okay, okay. What'd you do, buy out the whole damn store?"

"Never mind, just get out of those clothes and put some of this stuff on."

It was like Christmas. One like he'd never had before.

He pulled out the Air Jordans and his face lit up.

Mandy knew she'd done good. "C'mon Clyde, don't take all day. Get changed."

"Getting kinda bossy, aren't yah?"

They both chuckled, feeling like Bonnie and Clyde.

He folded his body this way and that as he wiggled out of the pajamas and into the pants. When they were all the way up and zipped, his ankles were naked.

"What length did you get?"

"How do I know? I just got thirty-twos like you said."

"Christ Mandy, that's the waist. I'm over six feet tall. Didn't you notice how long the pants were?"

"No Clyde, I did not." She scowled at him.

"Never mind. The Air Jordans make up for the high-waters. Can't imagine why anyone would give up practically new Air Jordans."

Mandy had no clue what he was talking about.

Putting the rest of the booty in the back seat, Clyde laughed at all the sunglasses and said, "Didn't you get yourself some new duds?"

Mandy remembered her stained backside and knitted her brows. She shoved the answer to that away. She'd been shoving that answer away all her life.

They pulled out of the back lot and soon were back on the road. She jacked the air conditioning up to the maximum; the buzzing sound blanketing the car's interior, making conversation impossible.

She needed to think.

In minutes, Clyde was sound asleep, his new to him Air Jordans toes up on the passenger's fire engine red floor mat.

Mandy wiggled her toes in her mud-savaged sandals.

Kept her eyes on the road.

<h1 style="text-align:center">CHAPTER 25</h1>

The two worried men were made to go first into Mabel Casner's office. Their eyes darted all over the room, and both held out-of-shape hats in front of their crotches. Bringing up the rear was a spanking new young man as clean and wholesome as the two that preceded him were dirty and contaminated.

"Here they are, ma'am." The young man held his crisp clean cap under his arm and half bowed to Mable Casner.

"Thank you. I don't know your name."

"It's Jim, ma'am. Jim Stone."

"You may address me as Miss Casner. You can leave now."

Jim looked at the two unsavory aides and made a dubious face.

"It's okay. I'll be fine. You can go."

"All right, ma'am, uh, I mean, Miss Casner, if you're sure then."

"I am, you can go Jim."

With one quick loaded look at Blade and Sam, he did a quarter turn and went out the door.

"Don't sit down. Doctor Romero will see you in his office."

She used her phone buttons and announced the arrival of the aides. "Go right through that door. He's ready for you."

Like Siamese twins, they clung together and moved toward the door.

Bang! It swung open.

Their eyes bugged as they crushed their hats into their groins.

"Get in here."

They moved.

Mabel pulled out the newly created file and gave it a name. In her fastidious style, she took a brand-new sharpie and wrote "Clyde Bordeaux." She'd have it all typed for Romero before she went home. The assignment was: Find out everything about this guy. Parents, birthplace, siblings, kids, race, employment… *that's probably a joke. Doubt Mr. Boudreaux ever worked an honest day in his life. Too damn good-looking. Women go for that type. The handsome bad boys.*

Mabel had kept a poker face, pulled out several pens to show her willingness to complete the assignment with due diligence. It meant lots of phone calls. Personal computers were coming, but not here yet. She had an Apple computer at home and was learning to use it.

She took heart in the knowledge that many of the agencies she'd contact would use their technology to give her the information she wanted. They kept data bases up to date.

Her cream-colored Macintosh was her passion, along with her cat, Trudy, who loved to sit with her while she tapped away on the keyboard.

Trudy also joined her for dinner. Tonight filet-o-fish from McDonald's.

Tonight would be glorious. Trudy would come running to her as soon as she walked through the front door. And not just for the Micky Dee's treat. She'd master her computer. Like a dog with a bone, she never gave up on anything. Not even the good Dr. Romeo.

This Clyde Boudreaux thing might prove helpful there.

CHAPTER 26

"Clyde, wake up."

"Huh?"

"Time to eat."

"Oh Mandy, you sweet thing. Kentucky Fried. I want everything. I'm starving."

"Yeah, me too." She set the emergency brake on the T-Bird nestled under a bit of shade provided by the KFC billboard.

She'd ordered everything in large quantities, wanted leftovers so they could get more travel time in today, wanted to make it well into the great state of Texas before nightfall.

Of course the red-headed freckled dork behind the counter had flirted with her. "Hungry, aren't you, honey?"

"What? Oh, it's not all for me."

"Didn't think so, not and keep that figure."

She'd flashed a sour smile, then closed her mouth, not responding.

Apparently there was a conveyer belt back there, turning out buckets of chicken, mashed potatoes, gravy and biscuits, 'cause it didn't take long.

He spun around to gather the order and packed it all into a huge red and white bucket and then into a big bag. A real talented guy.

Mandy was surprised to notice that as skinny as his pipe-stem arms and scrawny upper body were, he sported a very wide derriere. Tapping into her school studies, she conjectured… genetics, yeah. He inherited that bell shape. This made her sad to think of the classes she might miss. She loved school.

Big buttocks dropped the two bags on the counter in front of her. He was finished trying to be amusing; just said, "Drinks?"

"No, thank you. How much is it, please?"

She knew they still had Cokes, warm by now, but she didn't want to carry so much she might drop it.

"Okay, ma'am, that'll kill most of a twenty."

She handed him a Jackson and gathered up the food that was hot enough to be uncomfortable on her arms and hands.

"Wait, you have change."

"That's all right. Keep it."

At the car Clyde was scootched down but popped up and opened the door when he felt Mandy tapping her knee against it.

They were both ravenous, dug right in. The car reeked of chicken and grease.

Mandy said, "Save the bag for trash."

The calorie laden meal relaxed them. Still the spectrum of needing definite plans hovered over their heads; a low black cloud.

Mandy started in, "Once we're in South Texas, I'm going to help you head into Mexico."

Clyde stopped chewing the last of his biscuit, swallowed in a noisy gulp and said, "You mean *us,* don't you?"

"No, Clyde, I mean you. There's no way anyone, except maybe Rosie from that place, knows I'm involved in your escape from Bingham. I doubt her word would hold much credibility. They wouldn't have her in all those restraints if she was a reliable adult human being. What kind of a plausible witness would she make?"

"I can't believe this, Mandy. After all we've been through together you're just gonna dump me? I thought you loved me?"

"Love has nothing to do with this decision. I do love you."

"Don't do this, Mandy. I need you."

His crestfallen face tugged at her heartstrings, but her mind was made up. "Clyde, you'll be better off by yourself."

Now his face took on a stony look, his handsome features locked into a mask of disappointment that morphed into one of barely contained rage. His jaw locked and his green eyes blazed. "So what, we're through?"

"I didn't say that. Just listen. Here's what I propose. First of all, you don't need a passport to enter Mexico. Second of all, with your light brown skin color, you'll blend right in. I'll give you plenty of money, which will help a lot. You can bribe officials down there if you get into a sticky situation. Living is cheap. You won't have to work for a while. I'm going to give you a pile of cash."

"What about you? What're you going to do?" There was an edge to this questioning that would do a prosecutor proud.

"Well, you know I'm going to school to get my degree in social work. I plan to help Laura and her friend, Cassandra, track down those bastards that took our baby. I never expected to become a felon. I only planned on seeing you and assuring you that I'd get you a good lawyer. It all changed when those creeps said they were going to murder you the next morning."

Clyde's face softened and he reached out for Mandy's hand. He rubbed her knuckles with his thumb and said almost in a churchy whisper, "I know this is a bad scene, and I owe you for what you did and are still doing to help me." He bowed his head.

She pulled her hand out from under his and stroked the back of his head as she murmured, "It'll all work out somehow. We'll drive today and tomorrow, and I'll let you out near one of the migrant entry places. You could probably go through the official border, but it's safer to have fewer people see you and maybe remember you. I have a bad feeling about that motel clerk."

"Really, Mandy? Why?"

"I can't put my finger on it. My sister Laura has this kind of intuitive feeling of knowing things. She calls it The Watcher. It's as though she sees things and knows things from an overview, an expanded perspective and understanding of things not physical."

Clyde had a dreamy expression as he said, "That's a sixth sense and beyond the three-dimensional worlds. I'm very familiar with it. If we ever get our daughter back, I'll teach her all about my Voodoo beliefs and the powers that can be tapped into. You saw it, Mandy. You saw it firsthand when that cell door opened."

Even though Mandy Rose had "seen it," she was still skeptical. She kept this thought to herself, not entirely sure why she had the intuitive belief the gris-gris would help free him. "Clyde, I'm kind of tired. Do you think it's okay for you to do some driving and I'll take over later?"

"Sure, I don't see why not. Hand me one of those hats you bought and those Aviators."

"What do you want?" Her forehead wrinkled.

"A hat, Mandy and sunglasses."

She bent over the seat to rummage in the bags in back, and Clyde ran his hand down her rump. She shivered with desire.

He rode his palms all the way down between her cheeks, stiffening his fingers enough to push through where he stopped between her thighs.

She slid down the seat, reached over to where the pants she bought him were already full in front. She unzipped the size thirty-twos and tunneled inside to where he was still without underwear. She loved the silky hard feel of his member in her fist and began to stroke him. He responded by pulling her pedal pushers down to her knees and slipped his eager fingers into her warm familiar femaleness. He moved his thumb to include her clitoris. They didn't last long. They both moaned low and exploded together in shared ecstasy.

It was going to be very hard to drop Clyde off.

Very hard.

CHAPTER 27

Laura's Rover was ringing. This was seldom the case as she only gave the number to family, including Cassy and now of course, Mandy's friend Mark. The sound was grating. Someday they'd improve that.

"Hello?"

"Hi Laura, it's me, Mark. Did you find your sister yet?"

Laura had mixed feelings about this guy. Why was he so eager to help? He'd only known Mandy for a matter of weeks. The Watcher was giving some red flag signs. This caused a queasy mixture of dizziness and nausea, but she needed the help and decided to put The Watcher's warning signals on a back burner.

After a pause, she answered, "No, have you come up with any ideas to locate her?"

"The thought occurs to me that perhaps there's a man involved. I don't have any proof of this, just hate to say it, but it's often the case."

Laura swallowed at his uncannily accurate perception. She debated about how much to tell him. Kicked that aside. Too soon to tell him too much. She'd have Angus see if he had a sheet. *Was she becoming a suspicious cop already?* "Listen Mark, for now please stay close to the apartment and call me or Cassandra if anything comes up."

Disappointed, he said, "Okay, will do."

They hung up.

"Laura, why're you home so early? Did you go to your classes?"

"Yeah, Ma, just didn't stay all day. Is Cassy home yet?"

Sophie laughed and said, "I know she's just getting used to driving and having her own car, so she drives like an old lady."

"Yeah, like you, Ma."

Two minutes after Cassy pushed through the front door and dropped her books on a chair, the door burst open again, followed by a young and jubilant voice.

"Mama, you're home."

"C'mere sweetie, give me a big hug." Cassy bent down and enclosed Arriona in a mama bear clutch that made the little girl all but disappear behind the light cotton cape Cassy wore.

Laura and Sophie watched this demonstration of love with misty eyes.

Both were happy to have Cassy and Arriona living with them.

Cassy looked over to them, a question mark defining her face.

"We've heard nothing, although that Mark called wanting to help."

Cassy furrowed her brows, just enough to convince Laura she also had some misgivings about Mark's over-eagerness to help find Mandy Rose.

Laura opened the discussion. "All right, now we know Clyde has escaped from the mental institute. It's a long-shot, but we should check his house, see if he's there or been there."

Angus joined the crew, opening the door with determination. He looked tired. He walked straight over to Sophie and planted a rather unchaste kiss on her lips as his arm went around her.

Sophie, still unaccustomed to all this ardor, went bright red.

He pulled on Sophie to steer her into where the table and chairs were and the air conditioner was particularly efficient. He thought the cool air would make his next conversation easier to take. "Okay, I'm going to let you know what I know. See if Almadine can bring in some lemonade. This is going to be difficult to relate."

Everyone sat down. Arriona sat between Sophie and Angus. She patted Sophie's knee.

Angus began. "There are some strange facts. Bizarre things. Things that cannot be explained. I hesitate to use this word, but dare I say… possibly… supernatural."

Laura sat ramrod straight, listening not just with her outer ears but with her inner ears. She was no stranger to the supernatural.

CHAPTER 28

The office door clicked shut, entombing Dr. Romero, Sam and Blade in a room charged with fear and anger.

A hollow voice on Mabel's desk phone announced three words. "Don't disturb me."

She opened her mouth to acquiesce but was speaking to dead air. The good doctor snapped the button off so hard it felt like an ice pick in her ear. She sat back, but not for long. In less than a minute, she crept over to the door that was ready to offer up secrets, secrets she wanted privy to.

She took her pearl earring off and placed her ear pancake flat on the smooth wood. Not for the first time.

For someone who wanted privacy, old Bill Romero hadn't mastered the art of speaking at a low volume. Sounded like he had a bullhorn in his pudgy hand. "Don't sit down, either of you."

Two mumbles. "Yes, sir. Okay, sir."

"Now, tell me everything you can remember about how this Clyde fellow escaped from a locked cell and a heavy metal security-locked door. Leave nothing out."

Blade coughed a strangely dainty little cough, then began. "Well, you see, Doctor, we always lock that back door. No way anyone could get out, or matter of fact, get in, after we leave. No, sir. No way. We lock it up good and tight. The security-lock kicks in and then it only opens the next morning. Yep, only the next morning." Blade's eyes were as round as shot glasses to impress a façade of honesty on his ramblings.

"Shut up, you moron. You make no sense. No one can go through a door that's locked. It's Goddamned obvious that door was left open. What've you got to say, Sam?"

Sam hitched his pants up with his elbows, causing his misshapen hat to ride up and down his belly; the hat slipped from his grasp and dropped. He looked down, crestfallen.

"Leave it there and answer me."

Sam still eyed his fallen hat. He felt naked without it. He forced himself to make eye contact with his interrogator for one second, then looked at the gargantuan desk. Not a single pen or piece of paper marred the pristine surface. The desk was barren, save for a black desk phone that sat close to the edge.

"Uh, Doctor, um, I guess we locked the door when we left on Saturday night, 'cause we always lock the door, uh, so I guess we did."

Sam took a deep breath and hoped the questioning was over.

He jumped when Dr. Romero screamed, "What do you mean, you guess?" Either you did or you didn't."

Silence.

"Answer me."

Blade was flinging poison darts from both eyes at the hapless Sam.

Sam was caught like a quivering rabbit between a fox and a coyote.

"Listen to me, you ninny. I need answers. You tell the truth right now, or you're fired. That goes for you too, Blade."

Sam finally found his voice. He looked at his hat again; wished he could reach down and get it. He uttered one anguished syllable. "Uh."

"Talk right now, or you leave and never come back here."

"Uh, well, uh, I'm not sure if we locked it up. I think maybe we did. But I didn't check to make sure it was locked. Maybe Blade checked."

Blade's face went white with fury.

"Okay, you're fired. Out! Right now. Leave the hat."

"Wait, wait a minute, please. No, I think maybe we didn't lock it. No. That's right, we didn't."

"Why? Why the hell would you leave it unlocked?"

Sam brightened and said almost excitedly, "'Cause the cells was all locked, so we didn't need to worry."

"Jesus, you're as dumb as a bag of hammers. Shut up now. Blade, what've you got to say?"

Blade, the scholar of the two, also the more wily, stated, "I went out first, figured Sam would lock the door."

The doctor cocked his head and stared at the two men. This wasn't getting anywhere, so he tried a different tack.

"Was Rocelyn awake when you two left the building?"

Sam and Blade stared at each other, searching for an answer that wasn't coming.

"Oh, 'scuse me. Rosie. I guess you call her Rosie."

Now they both shook. This could go real bad.

Blade spoke first. "Rosie was in her cell in restraints. I know she gets 'em loose sometimes; breaks out, but far as I know, she was tightened down."

Dr. Romero narrowed his eyes at the stricken aides. "Seems like you boys give Rosie a little fun sometimes? Is that right?"

"Don't know what you mean, sir."

"Me neither," Sam joined in.

Dr. Romero's eyes glinted lasciviously as he imagined the two boys and Rosie in the back building having a little "fun."

"All right. You're not fired for now. Go back to your jobs. I'll talk to Rosie. It better jive with what you two just said. Now, get out of here."

Sam bent over and grabbed his hat like a drowning man for a life preserver. He reveled in its soft worn synthetic folds; actually held it to his nose while still in the doctor's office.

Mabel heard the strident, "Now get out of here," and scurried back to her desk, busied herself moving papers around, watched the two degenerates beeline for the exit.

Once out the door, Blade banged it brutally into place with a back hand. It clicked. A nice strong click.

Mable wondered about that kind of manly strength and that poor little Rosie creature, way back there in that back building.

And two of them.

And one of her.

CHAPTER 29

Mandy wasn't happy to be missing school. She was determined to hook up with Laura and Cassy, use her social work degree and help with law enforcement endeavors. They'd be superheroes.

Such were the lofty imaginings circulating in Mandy's brain as she tilted her head back against the passenger seat of her T-Bird and slept.

Clyde was making good time, staying within the speed limit as was his habit of many years. His mind ventured back to that horrible trip to the river with Bertie's slowly stiffening corpse in the trunk of his Saab.

Where was his Saab?

He'd known not to ask rational questions when he was supposedly "psychotic." He didn't ask about his car, his house or even Mandy Rose. He knew her family would take care of her.

Plus, during her visits to him while he was at Bingham Medical after that fucker Felix shot him in the chest; she seemed good. He'd tempered his behavior, feigning sleep much of the time. The doctors were easily fooled. There was no test for mental illness that showed in the blood or on an X-ray.

He didn't know if he'd see Mandy Rose again after she plunked him down near the Mexican border. Mexico, not bad. Plenty of cash, also not bad. He could see himself disappearing, starting a new life. He was sick of Louisiana, well not sick of it exactly. Maybe he needed a new start. He owed Mandy Rose big time.

There'd be droves of Mexican beauties. His groin awakened, and he reached down to reward the growing bulge. He rubbed some more. Soon he knew what it was like to have a full-on eruption doing sixty miles an hour on the open road.

After, he snuck a peek at Mandy. She slept obliviously content. Unaware of the solitary session he'd had.

He did care a great deal about Mandy. And, of course, there was the specter of Hannah. Little Hannah. Not a baby anymore, but a little girl. His little girl.

All of a sudden, several miles ahead, there were red blinking lights approaching a crossroad. A roadblock. "Holy shit!"

His eyes shifted left and right, searching for another possible path to avoid it. Nothing. His stomach dropped down into his bowels. He kept driving, put his right signal on and passed into the slower lane.

Should he wake Mandy?

No.

Laboriously he let the T-Bird slide into place. He couldn't avoid being questioned. He had to sit there and wait as he broke out in a sweat. Was it his imagination or were vans being held longer than passenger vehicles?

He crept closer to the red lights and badges. Two more cars in front of him. Now, his turn.

Mandy Rose slumbered.

"Stop right there, mister."

"Yes, sir."

"What's the reason for your journey?"

Clyde spoke clearly and in perfect English. "I'm madam's driver; taking her to visit relatives in Lubbock, her cousins… sir."

The border control agent bent down to the driver's window in the low-slung sports car. He tipped his cap back a bit and looked inside at Mandy Rose's peaceful countenance, also eyeballed the back seat and seemed placated until another agent came charging over, hand held out in a stop signal.

"Just a minute, sir. Don't move."

Clyde froze.

The new agent looked like a Mexican Santa Claus and was drenched in sweat. Huge wet underarm circles threatened to overtake and meet in the middle of his ample chest.

Out of breath, he huffed, "You can let these people go, Jack. We've got a Chevy van full of blankets and supplies. The guy in the shotgun seat is the coyote we've been looking for."

"Go on your way, mister. Drive safely and honor our Texas laws."

Clyde let the breath out he'd been holding and bleated, "Yes sir, thank you, sir." He hated to grovel but knew when a good grovel was necessary. They left, obeying the speed-limit.

A lesson well-learnt as Texans liked being Texans and didn't much like the other states.

At this precise minute, Mandy Rose woke up and rubbed her eyes.

"How's it going, Clyde?"

"Going good, Mandy. Going good."

She noticed the wet spot on the front of Clyde's pants, chuckled and said, "I see that."

CHAPTER 30

Laura and Cassy were itching to be out on their own; shiny new badges in their breast pockets and trails to blaze.

Angus was old school. He believed in shoe leather, worn down. No stone unturned, including rocks hiding vermin, the kind that walked upright.

As for Felix Guidry, he was tucked away without funds. Prison held little hope for him. The massive fortune he'd squirreled away had been confiscated and sat in a civil forfeiture fund pending approval for absorption of proceeds either/or to the state's budget or the general budget. The lobbying tended toward use for "child abductions and trafficking."

Felix gave some thought to maybe getting privileges for himself if he gave up some names. He'd been tried and found guilty in record time. He knew the state didn't give a shit about him. The state-appointed attorney was a joke. Barely out of law school.

Laura and Cassy still thought Felix could provide some answers.

The NAACP was active and vociferous in bringing about quick justice for all the participants in this trafficking ring. The ring involved not only kidnapping, but manslaughter, as in the death of little Cee Cee, and criminal intent in the deaths of other children named on the list earmarked for organ removal resulting in the child's death.

In many cases, including but not exclusive to, removal of the myocardium, commonly referred to as the human heart, the child died.

Due to the ongoing investigation following the trail of an indeterminant number of children, one Felix Guidry would likely be facing new charges, to be added to the charges, for which he was already incarcerated. The judge had the discretion to sentence him to additional time, stacked onto the time served, delaying a release date.

Felix Guidry would never see a day of freedom again.

Harold Bokum was a broken man. His position as Chief of Staff at Bingham Memorial Hospital and his wealth and standing in the community didn't serve him well while being locked in a six-foot by eight-foot cell.

But unlike Felix, Harry had a larger portion of brain cells. And unbeknownst to him, the woman still his wife was planning to visit.

CHAPTER 31

Angus cleared his throat and hoped he wouldn't sound dictatorial. He needed to get some things clear. He also knew how rookies were overconfident and underexperienced. He'd tread lightly.

"Laura and Cassy, we have a complex situation."

Sophie blinked and yanked on her pink A-line dress. How could she think about the ten pounds she'd gained when her daughter was missing and her granddaughter hadn't been found. She was so sick of worrying and so tired of pain. She nodded at Angus, and he took a neat quick breath and continued.

"I have to concentrate on my leading role in the investigation into the abductions. I'll share everything I find out about Clyde Boudreaux's disappearance, including how or *if* it relates to Mandy Rose's missing status." He tried to keep the language clinical to avoid the emotional turmoil he knew Sophie was suffering. He was proud of her, though she hated it when he said that.

She was handling all this like a Southern Gloria Steinem or maybe a Margaret Thatcher. He pushed those thoughts aside and concentrated his gaze on Laura. "You and Cassy have to play by the rules. You don't want to jeopardize your graduation with behavior that constitutes 'impersonating an officer.'"

His stomach, which had lost a few inches of girth, relaxed and fell. He'd been holding it aloft unconsciously. He frowned as he viewed Laura and Cassy exchange a conspiratorial look that could only mean trouble.

"Okay Angus, we hear you. We understand. Right, Cassy?"

"Yes, absolutely. Don't worry, we'll behave. Everything by the book."

Portia brought in a platter piled high with already constructed po'boys and a tall pitcher of lemonade. She said simply, "You have to eat."

Several thank yous knocked together as they all reached for the tasty sandwiches and pale yellow drinks already poured into frosty glasses. Eating took less than half an hour.

"Sophie, I'll call you later. I'm heading back to the precinct."

Sophie smiled, nodded and thought of the small bottle of gin she'd purchased earlier that day.

CHAPTER 32

"Portia sure makes good po'boys."

"Yeah, yeah, get in the car. We're gonna pick up Blondie from his apartment; take him with us to that mental hospital before they close for visitors.

"Got your badge, Laura?"

"Very funny. We won't need badges, although Angus had a point."

"Does Mark know we're coming?"

"Yeah, called him earlier."

Pedal to the metal now, Laura asked Cassy to call Mark again, make sure he was ready to roll when they arrived. She didn't even have to kill the engine. Mark was waiting outside the building and strode over on sight of the two women in the MG.

Cassy's head swiveled from one blonde to the other, got out to pull her seat forward so Mark could accordion-fold himself into the miniscule back seat.

No complaints from him.

Laura roared off, explaining to Mark about Clyde Boudreaux's possible involvement in Mandy Rose's disappearance. She caught an expression on Mark's face in the rearview mirror that puzzled her. *Was he concerned? Or was that fear?*

Almost dusk now, they pulled into Bingham Central Institute and climbed out of the vehicle. There was still a light on in the building.

They trooped in, Laura and Cassy abreast and Mark lagging behind.

Mabel Casner frowned at the trio. *Now what?* "Yes, what can I do for you? You should know, visiting hours are over."

"We're here about Clyde Boudreaux."

Mabel's shoulders jerked.

"What about Clyde Boudreaux? Are you from the police department?"

Laura let that question hang, just answered plaintively, "I'm not positive, but I think my sister may have visited him. She and Clyde Boudreaux have a daughter together."

Mabel's jaw dropped. Except for the hair coloring, she could see the resemblance between this blonde woman and the petite brunette who'd been in this office a few days earlier inquiring about Clyde Boudreaux. Mable passed the palm of her hand over her cheek, waited for more.

"Did my sister visit Clyde?"

"Not to my knowledge."

"Was she here?"

"Yes, she was. She was concerned about him. I had to tell her that he was confined in the back building."

"Was she able to visit him in this back building? Wait a minute, is that a bad place to be?"

"What is your name, miss?"

"I'm Laura Bokum. My sister is Mandy Rose Bokum."

Mabel went pale and her eyes rounded as she heard the surname Bokum being repeated. Aware of what everyone knew about the Bokums, she flushed and beads of sweat appeared on her finely wrinkled forehead. She gathered herself and placed her hands on her desk to steady her nerves. "I see."

"I'm sorry to upset you ma'am, but my sister is missing. I have to ask again, could she visit him in that back building?"

After a shaky deep breath, Ms. Casner answered, "A person would need approval from a resident's doctor to obtain permission for a visit to someone living in the back building. When your sister was here, I advised her to call Clyde Boudreaux's physician."

"Who is the doctor, please?"

"The doctor is William P. Romero. He's also the head psychiatrist of this hospital and top administrator."

"Is he here now? Can we see him?"

"It's highly irregular. He only sees people on appointment."

Laura insisted. "I'm sure that's true, but this is a very irregular situation."

Mabel considered, then said, "I'll check. Take a seat, please."

Ms. Casner pushed a button on her desk phone and pressed the handset to her ear.

"Oh yes, Doctor, you're still here. I have some people anxious to see you." Pause. "Yes, I told them they needed to make an appointment, but I'm convinced you might want to see this woman." Pause. "Doctor, it's concerning Clyde Boudreaux, the man who escaped—" She never got the rest of the sentence out.

Then she said in response, "Yes, she's here right now in my office with another woman and a gentleman." Left holding the phone in mid-air, Mabel swirled when the door to Dr. Romero's office was flung open and the psychiatrist filled the empty doorway without apology.

"Come right in, please. I'm eager to hear what you might know to help us track down Mr. Boudreaux."

The three trekked in single file.

The doctor went back to his seat and said, "Please sit down."

Laura and Cassy fell into the two available chairs, and Mark stood against the wall, hands deep in his pockets.

"I'm Doctor Romero and you are?" He looked at Cassandra; assumed she was the connection to Clyde.

"My name's Cassandra. Who you want to talk to is Laura."

The doctor squinted at Cassy, then turned to Laura, even more perplexed.

Laura thought, What an ass!

She said, "I'm Laura Bokum, my sister, Mandy Rose Bokum, apparently came here. Though she was unable to, she wanted to visit Clyde Boudreaux. They're parents to a child named Hannah who was abducted several years ago."

Dr. Romero still looked confused. He scratched his balding head, said nothing.

Laura continued. "Now it's possible there's a connection with Clyde's disappearance, since my sister has been missing for going on three days.

The doctor composed his features and said, almost in a whisper, "Did you say your last name is Bokum? *The* Bokums, as in Dr. Harold Bokum?"

Laura's lips twisted a bit as she reaffirmed her opinion of the doctor. "Yes, Harold Bokum is my father and also my sister's father. Again her name is Mandy Rose Bokum." She tried a new tack with this bozo. "I'm worried about my sister. What can you tell me about Clyde's disappearance?"

Dr. Romero was having a conniption. *Christ, the Bokums were mixed up with that colored man. This was bad. How much worse would it get?*

Then he managed an answer. "We have reason to believe the back door to the sleeping quarters was faulty. It's normally locked and working properly. We're looking into that. We think that's how Mr. Boudreaux was able to leave the facility."

Laura stood, feeling as though there was little to be accomplished here. This guy was only worried about covering his ass. She took control. "I'll leave you my telephone number. Call me if you find anything out. Give me your number too." She added, "Please."

The exchange accomplished, the three strolled out the door.

They thanked the receptionist, who seemed out of breath.

Strange. From just sitting? Her chair was still rocking when they exited Romero's office. *Just dropped into?*

Laura's Watcher kicked in.

Mabel Casner was more than she appeared to be.

<h1 style="text-align:center">CHAPTER 33</h1>

The siesta gave Mandy a welcome power surge. Alert now, she wanted to take the wheel.

"Clyde, pull over. I want to drive."

Unknown to Clyde, she'd listened to every word at the border stop. Noted the surroundings and ascertained what made for good entry points into Mexico. The agents had provided useful information for where to drop Clyde off. She calculated the next fifty miles or so would be perfect.

Clyde didn't want to relinquish control of the car. "You sure you want to drive?"

"I'm sure. Get all your clothes into one bag, so you can grab it quickly and jump out. Now, pull over."

Clyde did as he was instructed.

Mandy exited quickly and ran around the front of the car to take over the driver's seat while Clyde just lifted himself and plunked into the passenger seat.

Mandy took off and licked her lips that had gone bone dry. *Was she doing the right thing?* "Clyde, go in my pocketbook and take all the cash in the zippered leather case. Put some in different pockets and some in your shoes."

"Christ, you sound like a professional moll."

"Very funny, Clyde. Just do it."

Clyde reached over and stroked Mandy's head.

She batted his hand away.

Clyde's face took on a sad expression. She meant this. He packed his stuff.

The plastic bag was full. Two hats, an extra pair of sunglasses, another pair of pants, another shirt. He opted to leave the other pair of sneakers behind and wear the Jordans. It made sense to travel light, but he wanted to be prepared for whatever he might have to endure.

Next he opened Mandy's pocketbook and found the zippered case. It was indeed stuffed with cash. Hundreds and fifties and twenties. He pushed small slices of it into his pants pockets, then said, "Mandy, you should keep some of this. You have a long drive back."

"It's all yours. And put some in your shoes."

"If you use credit cards, they can trace us… I mean you."

"Clyde, we need to talk about bigger issues."

Mandy took out a one-inch square slip of paper and handed it to Clyde. "Take this."

"What is it?"

"It's my sister's Rover phone number."

"I'll put it in my shoes too."

"No, Clyde. Memorize it. Right now."

He studied the tiny, neat numbers for a full minute, then announced, "Memorized. When will I see you again, Mandy?"

"We have to play this by ear."

"What, what are we playing by ear?" Clyde had a troubled teenager look on his face, only the pimples were missing.

Mandy said simply, "Get used to living in Mexico. You may be there a while."

The near-perfect get-off place came up all too soon.

"Clyde, this is it. Get your stuff and get ready to move fast. There's no traffic, no time to dicker around."

Clyde grabbed his bag with one hand and pushed his sunglasses up on his forehead. He wanted to see Mandy for what might be the last time in natural light.

They leaned together and kissed, a chaste little kiss that would have to endure. For what? Months? Years? Life?

Mandy poked Clyde with her pointy elbow and he yelped.

"Now Clyde, get out. Go."

She slowed a bit as he shoved out the door and sprinted across the road, crouched down, and headed into the underbrush that had a decidedly worn look, proof that others had passed that way.

Then he stood, tall and handsome and turned his head to her. His eyes were wet. He raised his fingers to his beautiful plump lips, kissed the tips and blew the kiss to her.

She caught it. Pursed her own lips and made a kissing sound. A car was approaching.

He grabbed her kiss with one hand and stooped down in one motion. Then he disappeared into the bushes, his pant legs finally covering his ankles as he scrunched his lanky body into a military crouch.

Mandy Rose checked for oncoming traffic, then did a U-turn and began trucking back. The T-Bird stayed within the speed limit; not eager to take its owner to an unknown drama likely unfolding at home.

God, she missed him.

On the other hand, she probably wasn't too far behind on schoolwork. She could catch up. Craning her neck to view her back seat, she spied the red cover of her textbook *Abnormal Psychology*. There was a pair of Converse sneakers, size nine also bouncing around back there.

She could donate the sneakers back to some thrift store, but tonight she'd get busy reading her homework at the motel.

She was tired.

CHAPTER 34

Mark was fascinated; bewitched.

Laura was like no other woman he'd ever met before. Beautiful with nerves of steel.

Hard to believe she and Mandy Rose were sisters.

The Bokums! Christ! Those people had more money than God.

After being dropped off, Mark hurried into his apartment and rang up Jake. He could count on Jake to know whatever there was to know about anybody. The phone only rang twice. *Breeeeng… breeeeng*, before Mark heard Jake's slurry voice. "Yeah, who is it and whaddya want?"

Mark laughed noisily into the receiver. A forced sound. He hoped he didn't sound nervous.

Jake barked, "Who the hell is this?"

"Don't have a cow, Jake. It's me."

"I'm hanging up if you don't identify yourself right now."

"Christ, Jake. It's Mark. Your neighbor, Mark."

"Ah, sorry, didn't recognize your voice. My head's like those Wham-O plastic bubbles the kids blow up, only mine is filled with regrets and pain, or more to the point, lost memories."

Mark held the phone away from his face and scowled at it. "Okay Jake, can you talk or do you have to go back to bed?"

"Mark, my buddy, for you… yes. I can talk. What's up?"

Mark launched right in; no preamble.

"You know that bitchin' brunette on the second floor?"

Jake interrupted. "Oh yeah, I could definitely eat crackers in bed with her." A low throaty chuckle.

"Jake, shut up and listen."

Jake said, "Zip."

"Now, I'm trying to find out more about her because she may be involved with that colored guy who escaped from the booby hatch."

"Holy shit—I mean—zip."

"It's true what we wondered about. She's a Bokum, as in tons of coin, Bokum. Really frickin' wealthy, as in mansions wealthy. That T-Bird is the tip of the iceberg. She's missing, Jake. Can you do your detective thing and find out more about her? Like if she's married. And Jake, this is important. When was the last time you saw her?"

"Can I talk now, Mark?"

"Yes, asshole, talk."

"Okay, that's easy. I heard her bomb off in that T-Bird late Saturday morning. That engine has a distinctive low rumble, enough to make you shoot your load."

"Jesus Jake, this is serious. Did you actually see her leave?"

"Yeah, cross my heart and hope to die. I looked out the window 'cause I was already up, 'cause I had to hit the head."

"Thanks, Jake. I owe yah one."

"How about a fix-up with the little doll when she's found again?"

"Goodbye, Jake." *Click.*

<h1 style="text-align:center">CHAPTER 35</h1>

Mandy Rose was weary; bone tired.

She needed a good meal, a long shower and time to herself. She could smell herself. She stunk. The thought of putting these disgusting clothes back on her body after a nice hot sudsy shower made her recoil, but she didn't want to go to the mall stores to buy an outfit.

She wanted to throw everything she had on out. She tilted her head with the memory of her and Clyde's lovemaking and all the fluids produced still sticking to her clothes.

God, she had to get clean clothes before she found a motel and could shower. She exited the highway and rolled into town. Everything was still open. The Golden Arches was tempting. She could almost taste the salty fries.

No, she couldn't enter a public place. Her dirt-smeared pants, sticky shirt and muddy shoes were bad enough, but she smelled like a mixture of barnyard animals and human BO.

A brick building came into view. The royal blue awning over the door had a half face logo and the word Goodwill in upper and lower-case letters. A small oval sign read "Donate Here."

She grabbed the Converses to drop in the "Donate Here" bin.

This shopping trip was all about her. She found a parking spot next to an old black chevy with rusty fenders and no bumper. A silver crucifix hung from the rearview mirror by gray string.

A peek inside revealed a sleeping baby with its thumb firmly surrounded by rosebud lips that moved in a gentle sucking motion. The child had blankets rolled up and tucked around it, enclosing it in a cozy bunker. Mandy thought of Hannah. The bundle of blankets was bubble-gum pink.

She shook her head and pulled on the handle of one of the Goodwill doors. A bell jangled over the entrance. She knew what was expected of her now. Not her first rodeo.

She saw a carriage sitting alone in one of the aisles and headed to it. A hand came out to claim the shopping cart before she reached it. The hand belonged to a young woman with red hair, black roots in the part on the top of her rather small head.

"Oh," Mandy exclaimed.

The woman who now had both hands on the cart took in Mandy Rose's sad and smelly wardrobe and said, "You can have this one. I'll get another."

Mandy was tongue-tied.

The woman smiled broadly and walked away.

Mandy called after her, "Thank you, ma'am."

Then she went straight to the pants rack as her most necessary replacement. To her surprise she found two pairs she liked in her size and a skirt that looked fabulous as she placed it against herself. She winged them into the pilfered carriage.

Shirts were even better. A beige all-cotton pullover, two blue camp shirts and three black jerseys, two of which were her favorite style, V-necks.

She was amazed to see that she could try the shoes on. No one gave her any icy stares. She picked a pair of multi-colored Keds and black flats that looked barely worn and then she couldn't resist a pair of red canvas cork wedges, a little high; but she liked feeling tall.

She also found a blue and white scarf to tie her hair back. She could swear it was one hundred percent silk.

The total amount the cash register rang up was mind-blowing. She didn't even have to use a credit card. Under ten dollars for all of this loot.

When she left the store, the Chevy with the sleeping angel was nowhere to be seen. Gone.

Anxious now to shower and eat, she chose to stay in town; find a hotel that advertised dining.

She was getting discouraged as she headed away from town without luck, but her spirits soared when she saw the familiar Holiday Inn sign. She pulled one of the black jerseys over her head before she went in to register. The clerk might not notice the rest of her and might not have a good sense of smell.

The hotel clerk didn't look old enough to vote, but the chubby blonde knew her job well. Mandy was checked in and jumping in the shower within half an hour.

Clean and smelling like carnations, she padded over to her bags of clothes barefoot and naked. She laid the pants and beige top on the bed and rummaged for the shoes. The shoes had been forgotten. She saw three bags where there should be four. "Probably still in the car," she lamented to herself.

She was repulsed at the thought of putting clean feet in those gross shoes so was beyond thrilled when she discovered paper guest slippers. Reminded her of Clyde. She pushed the thought away.

No bra and no panties, not an issue, but she craved those red wedges.

Talking to herself again, she said, "Okay, back to the car." Her stomach growled as Clyde's face again filled her inner screen. *Was he hungry?*

Nothing she could do for him.

In her new duds, she traipsed down the flight of stairs and exited to where her car was parked. She keyed the door open and kneeled on the driver's seat. Yes, there was the missing bag. It was in her grasp when a sparkle of light intruded. *Had she accidentally pushed the car's interior light?*

She pressed the bag to her chest to allow a better view. What could possibly be making that light?

The parking lot had pole lights that shone into the car. But no, that wasn't it. Something in the car was glowing. Hungry as she was, it couldn't be ignored.

A closer surveillance uncovered the general location of the shimmer. The footwell on the passenger side of the car had a spot in the corner that radiated a beam of light. She leaned in over the bag of shoes and gasped.

Her mouth fell open. Her skin shrank. Her heart pumped so hard she stopped hearing, not even the crinkling of the bags as she shook.

Dear God in Heaven.

There. On the floor lay Clyde's gris-gris, pouring out its powerful light.

Mandy's mind rebelled.

Clyde was without his gris-gris. Without his shield. He was not protected. His power gone.

What had she done?

He never would've forgotten it if she hadn't been rushing him.

She could still hear herself. "Clyde, this is it. Get ready to move fast. No time to dicker."

He'd trusted her.

But no, she told herself, she had to stop feeling responsible for everybody else.

He could've said no. He got along without her help most of his life. She hadn't held a gun to his head. And she gave him tons of money. American money. Worth more in Mexico. He'd be fine. Plus he had Laura's Rover phone number. Said he'd memorized it.

Mandy knew he wouldn't open that can of worms until he absolutely had to.

Still, he had the number. He was a big boy.

She decided to put the shoes on before going back into the hotel, only now she wasn't in the mood for the red wedges. She reached into the bag and pulled out the Keds. The clerk had tied them together by the laces. She needed the interior light to see to separate the double bow the girl had put them in.

There were pieces of gravel stuck to the bottoms of the hotel's paper slippers. After getting those sticky things off her feet, she hazarded a peek at herself in the car's mirror. Tears had streaked her newly scrubbed face.

Done untying the sneakers, her hand was free to swipe the salty water away. Shoes on and tied, fit perfectly, just like in the store. She chanced a smile. It felt good.

Mandy Rose left the bag with the red shoes in the car and hurried across the parking lot and into the hotel. The dining room was on the first floor. As she entered, she noted the holiday atmosphere, the scent of good food, the tinkling sounds of glassware and cutlery and diners chatting. It was like a symphony.

Seating was immediate. The hostess was a svelte brunette with an engaging smile. When the waiter came to her table, she pushed his proffered menu away and chirped, "Young man, I'll have a large steak, medium rare and whatever goes with it that you think is good." Another chirp, "And a carafe of your best red."

"Very good, miss."

Mandy surveyed the dining room and sat back to wait for her meal.

She tucked the Keds under her chair and wished she'd worn the red wedges.

CHAPTER 36

"I don't understand why you think visiting him will help."

"Angus, I don't know if it will help, but I have to try."

"Why, Sophie?"

"Harry had at least knowledge of Clyde Boudreaux. Mandy knew Clyde. No, more than knew him. Hannah's father. According to Mandy Rose, Felix Guidry invited this Clyde fellow to engage in the sordid goings on at the Leprosarium. This included the selling of children for adoption and the trafficking for…" Sophie hesitated and swallowed, but her eyes remained dry… for, um, sexual purposes." A dry cough escaped her. "And worse, for organ removal."

Her blue eyes filled with liquid that dripped slowly down her soft pink cheeks. She swiped at them with the hanky she held. "Try to understand, Angus, Harry might tell me things he hasn't divulged to the police. In spite of every despicable act he's guilty of, I have to believe he cares about his daughters."

"I'm not so sure about that, Sophie honey. On a different note, he might see a self-serving benefit to a liaison with you."

"I agree. I'm going to make a deposit in his commissary account. Most of his assets, as you know, are frozen. This is reason enough for him to want to keep me in his camp."

"At least let me take you there and wait in the car."

"No. I want you to find Mandy first, before anything else. And then find out where my granddaughter is. And the other children too. Some of these children's lives may be saved if you uncover what these craven beasts did with them."

Angus sighed; knew he wasn't going to win this and she had a good point.

"Okay, Sophie. Mandy Rose has a good head on her shoulders, and I believe she's motivated to get her human services degree. I don't think she makes the best decisions about men. And there may be a man involved in this."

"I know, Angus. I'm still worried about her and won't feel good until I know she's okay."

Angus put his arms around Sophie and kissed her tenderly on the forehead. "I'm leaving for the station to check on progress."

"Okay, see you later, sweetie."

Angus headed to headquarters and made it in record time. He applied the emergency break to his truck and slapped his forehead when he recognized Laura's MG in the parking lot. "Oh, geez."

He hurried into the building and stopped at the front desk. "Sarge, can you tell me where Laura Bokum is?"

"Sure, Angus. She and another woman are in with Sloane." Trudy pointed her thumb in the direction of Detective Sloane's office.

Angus strode over to the Chief of Detective's door, which was closed. He knocked twice on the frosted glass and waited as he heard the desk Sergeant's phone buzz and knew he was being announced.

A deep resonant voice called out, "C'mon in Angus."

He pushed the door in, scanned the three faces.

"Pull up a chair, Angus. I was just about to call you."

Neither of the girls spoke.

Laura's foot was pulsing up and down as it dangled from a crossed leg. Cassy sat forward, leaning her elbows on her knees as her long legs stretched out in front of her.

Detective Richard Sloane said three words.

"We have news."

CHAPTER 37

Sophie Bokum had planned to visit the prison the following morning, but with Mandy Rose still missing, she changed her mind.

She and Harry had created two smart and beautiful young women. Sophie believed their father would have enough decency left in him, or enough fatherly love, that he would be agreeable to helping her if it would aid in the search for their daughter. This she thought, even though Harry had sexually abused Mandy Rose. Maybe guilt would be the motivator?

Sophie looked in the mirror and adjusted her blonde curls to be flattering on both sides. The nervous flush on her face created a palette of pink that set off her clear blue eyes. She hoisted her gray leather purse, perfectly matched to her pale gray dress and shoes, completing a very attractive and stylish look.

She did one more neurotic check in the purse's zippered compartment. Yep, the cash for Harry's commissary account was there. She drove mindfully to the prison.

The expansive building looked foreboding. She could hear her footsteps tapping as she went up the cement stairs and entered through double doors into a dingy room with murky yellow lighting and low ceilings.

The desk clerk was a woman about her age with purple lipstick. *A new fashion?*

The blue uniform she wore told Sophie she was a cop.

"Yes, ma'am, can I help you?"

"Yes, please. I'm here to visit my husband and leave some money for him in his account for, um I think, it's called a canteen?"

"Okay, visiting hours are almost over. Do you want to come back tomorrow earlier?"

Sophie knew she had to see him now. "Right now. Please."

"You're not allowed to bring a purse into the visiting area. There's a locker over there. I'll give you a key."

"Okay, thank you, ma'am."

She was corrected. "It's Officer. Officer Cohen."

Sophie felt chastised and stupid. She smiled at the woman and offered her hand.

Officer Cohen accepted the proffered hand and broke into a smile also. "Here's the slip to fill out for depositing money in your husband's account. What's his name, first and last. I'll have him paged."

"Harold… Harold Bokum."

Officer Cohen rounded her eyes at the name and said, "And you are?"

"Sophie Bokum."

The surprised look didn't fade. "Please put your purse in the locker. Take this key and lock it, then leave the key with me, Mrs. Bokum. We'll do the deposit when you finish your visit."

"Please, call me Sophie."

Sophie had become increasingly uncomfortable with the title Mrs. Bokum.

She locked up her purse and when she turned back, Officer Cohen was pressing a button to let her into the visiting area. A gray metal door creaked open.

Sophie walked through a short hallway, painted a bilious green, then through an open door that led into a huge well-lit visiting room.

Before she was allowed to sit, she was searched. The female member of the two officers patted her gray suit all over and glanced at the gray pumps. After she passed muster, the woman waved her over to a long row of tables.

Sophie was shocked to see so many prisoners and visitors. The inmates, mostly colored men of all ages, sat talking to their visitors across the table.

She took an empty metal chair on the visitor side and waited. Movement on the other side of the huge room caught her eye. A door opened. A man standing there in a khaki uniform held it open while an older gentleman slid through.

Sophie blinked, blinked again, then rubbed her eyes.

He was shrunken, grayer and balder. His prison clothes hung on his body. His wizened face was one big question mark.

Harry swept his gaze along the table, stopped cold when he saw her. His eyes puddled. He didn't notice.

He quickened his step and got to her in seconds. He pulled out a metal chair and fell into it and stared. Eyes bulging. "Sophie!"

"Hello, Harry."

"Sophie… you're here."

"Yes, I'm here. How are you?"

"I guess I'm okay. Doing better than I thought."

"Really Harry?"

"Yeah, I think so."

"Harry, I'm here for two reasons."

Harry leaned forward, reached for Sophie's folded hand. She pulled back part way, allowed his fingertips to stay connected to her knuckles. Then sat up straighter, leaving her hands on the table, suppressing an urge to grimace. "I want you to tell me what you know about the people in charge of the kidnappings at that Leprosarium."

"Sophie, those are very bad men, well mostly men. There were some women also but not in charge. They made a lot of money working there, but none were running the operation."

Sophie was repulsed by Harry's use of the word "operation." She had to get through this, couldn't alienate him. "I know Felix Guidry is in jail. I also know, pending the outcome of the ongoing investigation, there'll be more charges brought, maybe some for you too."

Harry's mouth twisted and a gurgle sound bubbled up from his chest.

"I want to know about Clyde Boudreaux. As you know, he's Hannah's biological father."

"Yes, I know that."

"Was Clyde involved with taking those children?"

"I don't know everything that went on between Felix and him. I do know I never saw any proof Clyde was involved with all that happened at the Leprosarium."

Sophie peered into Harry's eyes. She thought she saw a spark of something decent. *Was it honesty?* "I'm not sure how much news you get here under lock and key." She paused. "Clyde was charged with murdering Bertie Bergeron, who worked at the Leprosarium and was known to the kids as Bertie Hurtie. After he was brought in, he had a nervous breakdown and considered mentally ill so was subsequently confined to Bingham Central Institute."

Harry furrowed his brows.

"Now Clyde has broken out and is not to be found."

Harry pinched the bridge of his nose, said only, "Broken out? Is that possible?"

"Apparently it is. Here's the part that concerns me… concerns you too."

Harry's eyes popped.

"Mandy Rose has also disappeared. Missing the same amount of time that Clyde has been missing."

"Christ Sophie, you think there's a connection?"

"Yes. I'm afraid I do. Either that or something worse has happened to our daughter."

Harry's head dropped. He pulled his hands off the table and let them fall to his sides. He hated what he did to Mandy Rose when she was a little girl. Sweet and innocent little girl. *Was he to blame for all that she suffered now? Clyde? Hannah?* He should be punished.

"Harry, stop blanking out. I need your help. This is no time for self-pity."

Harry lifted his head. "You're right. What do you want to know?"

"Names. I want names, places, people involved. People higher up in that organization."

"A lot of that information was kept secret. There were codes used to protect the men at the top from being identified. I do remember the initials L.B. Yeah L.B."

"That's good. Is that all you can come up with?"

"Um, I also heard B.C., short for Big Carl." Harry pressed his hand to his forehead; tried to jump start his brain. "I think L.B. was higher in the pecking order. I know there're other facilities in the cartel." Harry scrunched his forehead as he strained to recall more.

He opened his mouth, then pinched his chin as though the memories surfacing were too painful to verbalize. He knew the words "sex trafficking" conjured horrors, too depraved to envision. More reprehensible was the specter of "children" being slaughtered for their organs. He'd lied to himself about all of it. Selling babies was how he got involved originally. He'd told himself Hannah would be better off somewhere else. Then the cartels took over, sex trafficking, organ trafficking and the Leprosarium was overrun with kids being "processed."

He suspected Bertie Bergeron was intimately entangled with the evil activities that went on. No, he knew she was. A truly despicable woman.

He didn't want to know more details about why the kids called her Bertie Hurtie. Why would he? He was guilty as sin.

Harry felt like he was waking up from a nightmare that had lasted for years. His hands were moist. He rubbed them on his thighs to dry them. He so wanted to touch Sophie again.

"Visiting hours are over in five minutes. Say your goodbyes now." The intercom was scratchy but specific.

"Is that all you can tell me, Harry?"

Harry was close to swooning at how beautiful Sophie was. Pink and blonde and tender.

"I'll think more, see if I can remember anything else." He paused. "Will you come back?"

Sophie evaded the plea and said, "I'm leaving you money in your account. It's cash, so it'll be available immediately."

The insistent intercom blasted, "Visiting hours are now over. Leave by the aisle behind your chair. Do not linger. Visiting hours are over."

Harry put one hand palm up on the table. It lay there alone.

Sophie twisted her knees to one side and stood. She waved goodbye with the tiny soft hand Harry yearned to touch once more.

CHAPTER 38

Mandy Rose awakened disorientated.

She smoothed the clean sweet-smelling sheets she lay on.

Yes, of course, she was in the Holiday Inn. Last night was a bit hazy. After her steak, she'd ordered a second carafe of red wine. The finest.

It did the trick.

Without pajamas or underwear, she'd slept au naturel. She stretched arms and legs in all directions, enjoying the silky sound her limbs made as they slid across the high-quality linens.

Then she stopped. Thoughts silently screamed.

Clyde.

Mandy Rose now knew Clyde practiced a very powerful form of Voodoo. She was fascinated. She recalled that heavy metal cell door puff open with a whispered hiss. Clyde wasn't amazed, not even surprised. He'd expected that cell door to open.

She wasn't even sure why she'd brought the gris-gris with her. Just knew it belonged to Clyde, he'd revered it, and she'd more than once sensed an energy from it when she held it in her hand. Even thought she'd heard a slight humming sound that made her heart tingle.

She was now a believer. The amulet that did it was in her purse. She felt afraid of it but strangely attracted.

Guiltily she thought not in Clyde's pocket where it ought to be. Clyde who'd kept it close to his body for most of his life. He'd told her it was gifted to him from his granddaddy. His granddaddy was lynched. Clyde had watched. If it wasn't for a gentle-minded white woman, he would have been strung up beside his grandfather on the same tree. She'd saved his life. That was when it registered in his brain, that all white people weren't bad.

He'd told her, she was the only person ever to hear this story.

She spoke to her hands. "It's my fault. I rushed him."

She tortured herself some more with her hasty words. "Clyde, this is it. Get ready to move fast. No time to dicker."

And Clyde did. Jumped right out with his plastic bag of clothes and bolted, then stopped across the street. Kissing her goodbye… for Christ sake… kissing her goodbye…

His executioner.

Did he stop and turn and try to signal her? Did he realize he was naked? Unprotected.

She had roared off; truth be known, eager to be rid of him.

What kind of a monster was she?

She'd allowed her daughter to be taken. Who knew if the spoken promise of a good home, being adopted by a loving family who wanted her was even true.

Was she in a family now? Being loved and appreciated? Or was she a victim of sex trafficking? Was she being used? Abused? Treated as a thing?

Mandy Rose knew little about those horrid cartels and what tortures befell its young victims.

She had to stop doing this to herself. Time to go home. Not much to pack. She stuffed her filthy clothes and shoes into two different hotel pails, put some toilet paper on top. Who knew why she had to cover them, but she did. If she got a quick bite and left this morning, she could drive straight through and be back by evening.

The dining room featured a short order cook dealing up bacon and eggs, any way you wanted, plus toast and coffee.

She approached the cook, with only an older man in front of her, ordered two eggs over easy, four bacon strips and buttered rye toast and a nice mug of coffee, lots of cream and sugar the way she liked it.

Soon, well-fortified, she was on the road home.

Chapter 39

Angus said goodbye to the desk sergeant. "Thanks, Trudy."

He tilted his head. "Any time, Angus."

Laura and Cassy were alongside Angus as they exited the precinct.

Once through the door, Angus proposed coffee and a sit-down. "Let's go to that coffee shop up the street near the laundromat. You can get something to eat there too. I want to discuss all this before I tell Sophie what we know. Glad as I am about the leads, nothing is exactly definite as in facts. Don't want to get her hopes up prematurely."

"'Kay, meet you there."

Soon all three were seated in a high-back red vinyl booth; the last one available in the popular coffee shop.

The waitress looked tired, black under-eye circles and favoring one foot, but she flashed a very acceptable smile as she took their orders. Her little pink cap was at a strange angle. She must've felt it because she gave it a little practiced shove; not bad, more centered.

"What'll it be folks?"

"Do you have any of those pastries called bear claws?"

"Yep, our specialty, how many?"

Angus looked to the girls for approval and got it. "Yeah, three coffees and three bear claws."

"Comin' right up."

Angus folded his hands on the table, a silent message; wait until she brings our order before we discuss anything.

Must've all been hungry, or in need of a sugar fix; they all dug in the second the three monster-sized pastries were placed in front of them.

A few minutes later, Cassy began. "Angus, how much of what Detective Sloane said is gospel?"

"He wouldn't mislead us. Rick felt the information was accurate enough for us to go to work on it. The C.I.s, that is confidential informants, are paid and make damn sure what they pass on to us is good. Give us bad info and you lose your status as a C.I. The guy called Big Carl is likely not the kingpin or a major decision maker, but he is higher up the food chain than say Harold or Bertie. "So, we have two names. That's a start. And initials keep the names hidden, even from the people involved in the scheme."

"So, we also have L.B. No clue yet what those letters stand for, not even if it's a man or a woman. I think we have to face that we won't catch all of them."

Angus's head went from one girl to the other and he said, "When do you two graduate?"

In unison: "In days." They both laughed.

"Great. You can do more after you have the badges. I want you now, if you're willing…" Laura and Cassy nodded enthusiastically… he repeated, "if you're willing… to visit some of the homes where the rescued kids are and just make friends with them, especially the girls. It'll be easier to interview them if they are already comfortable with you."

"Yeah, we understand. We can start right away, after school."

"Unfortunately, there was no news about Mandy Rose." He looked solemnly at Laura. "Sorry Laura."

"I know. I think she'll turn up soon on her own."

"Right, we'll talk to Sophie tonight. She said she planned to see Harry tomorrow."

Laura laughingly said, "Knowing Mom, don't be surprised if she didn't tool right on over to that jailhouse after we left."

Angus nodded and rubbed his jaw. He needed a shave. "All right ladies, enough for now. Tomorrow's another day.

Laura was beginning to appreciate Angus. He was calm and genuine. She liked that.

CHAPTER 40

The two women tucked into Laura's MG, looked into each other's eyes.

"Are you thinking what I'm thinking?"

"You bet, Laura. I have the address with me where a lot of the girls are staying."

As they watched Angus pull away, headed back to the precinct, Cassy said, "Let's go back in and buy a pile of those bear claw things to take with us."

Laura already had the door open and exclaimed, "Great minds think alike."

After a short drive, loaded with three big bags of scrumptious smelling pastries, they pulled into the driveway of a two-story wooden house with black shutters and all the shades drawn on the windows. There was a "Beware of Dog" sign in red block letters next to the front door.

They rapped hard on the entrance door as the music coming from within was very loud.

A shout. "Who is it?"

"Officer Angus Clark sent us. We're Laura Bokum and Cassy Allain." Not entirely true, but not really a lie.

"Okay, hang on."

The door swung out and went wide when the bulging bags with the coffee shop logo on them were observed.

Jessica smiled broadly. "Uh oh, I know those bags. Bear claws, right?"

"You got it. And plenty of 'em too."

Jessy held her rounded tummy that shook when she laughed, full out acknowledging her love affair with bear claws. She said, "They're like a bad man who's a good lover. You know he's gonna hurt you in the long run, but you let 'im in anyway."

Laura thought of Clyde and her sister. *Was Mandy Rose devouring bear claws right now?*

Once in the house, they were immediately surrounded by young girls. Different sizes and different skin colors.

Jessy took over the scene. "Come into the kitchen, we can all fit at the table in there." She waved her hand to the archway that led to a huge eat-in kitchen, suitable for a wedding reception. No chairs, just long benches around two doors that served as a long table. The girls piled onto the benches as Jessy placed white buffalo china platters in the middle of the table and a pile of napkins in several places for easy reach.

Pitchers of milk soon joined the feast. Paper cups were plopped down.

Laura whispered to Cassy, "Wow, these kids seem to be doing great here."

Cassy responded, "I think it helps that Jessy is colored and also full of love and fun."

Jessy's head bobbed up. She'd overheard this exchange beneath all the chatter. Not in the least offended, she nodded in agreement.

"Miss Jessy, can we have two each?"

Jessy smoothed the forehead of a cocoa-hued girl, maybe four or five years old, whose hair was still long but tied into two ponytails, one on each side of her pixie face. "We'll all have one and a glass of milk. After that, we'll see."

The youthful voices were infectious and heart-warming. Soon all the little mouths were busy chewing and drinking milk.

Cassy led with, "Is it okay if we talk a bit about the place where you were living before you came here?"

Some jaws stopped, mid-chew; others chewed more slowly. The bravest few, two to be exact, said through mouthfuls of sweet dough, "Okay." And, "Yeah, guess so."

Now Laura said softly, "I don't want any of you to be upset. You don't have to say anything unless you feel comfortable."

Some girls, eyes downcast, studied their sugary treats.

Cassy said, "I'm Cassy and that's Laura. We want to catch the bad guys who took you and put you in that building where you were living before you came here."

Laura wondered if Cassy was moving too fast. She qualified, "You can think about this and talk to us another time when we visit."

A chubby little darling whose bangs needed trimming, ventured, "Will you bring more bear claws?"

That broke the tension.

Cassy said, "Of course we will."

Laura said, "When we visit, bear claws come with us.

These kids had been fed on gruel and beans for so long, they were starved for anything sweet.

Laura noted they were filling out a bit from their previous skeletal forms. Little sunken faces were getting cheeks.

Cassy tried again. "How about if we all do one thing to start. See if you can remember any names you heard. Could be the bad people talking or could be other kids that told you their name."

Several girls grimaced and said in a chorus, "Bertie, Bertie Hurtie." Others chimed in. "We called her Hurtie Bertie too. She was awful. She was mean and got happy when she hurt you."

"She liked to hurt you," another tiny colored girl added.

Jessy's face darkened with sadness and her brown eyes filled with water.

Cassy persisted. "Okay, that's good. Bertie Hurtie." Now listen up, I have something to tell you."

Laura wasn't sure it was appropriate but didn't interfere.

All the faces turned toward Cassandra. "The lady, whose real name was Bertie Bergeron, that you all called 'Bertie Hurtie' is gone. She's not here anymore."

"Is she in jail?"

Cassy had to make this clearer. Laura still wondered if it was too much information.

"No, not in jail. Bertie Hurtie died."

"She's dead?" This from double ponytails.

"Yes, she's no longer alive. She'll never hurt any children again."

The silence was thick as mud.

"Will she still go to Heaven?" from a dark-skinned beauty who hadn't spoken yet.

"I don't know, sweetie. I guess God forgives bad people after they die and they're not hurting anyone anymore."

She spoke again, beautiful ruby lips pursed first, then she uttered almost imperceptibly, "I don't understand."

Laura was going to let Cassy get out of this one with no help from her. Not like she had the answer.

Cassy said, "God's ways are a mystery to us. Kind of like we don't understand why there are bad people."

A very pale little girl with reddish blonde hair said, "I'm glad she's dead."

There were a number of little heads that nodded in agreement.

A paper-thin light skinned cherub offered, "I remember a bad guy too. I know his name. It was Harry."

Laura's heart was clamped in a powerful icy vice. Her breath halted.

Cassy answered, "That bad man is in jail."

The little strawberry blonde said with a deliberate tone, "I wish Harry was dead too."

Laura felt sick.

"Are there any other names you can remember?"

Another new contributor spoke up. "Mostly they called us numbers. There was the twins, they got called names. Jodi and Judi."

Emboldened now, another girl said, "Yeah, but sometimes we talked to each other at night, if we didn't swallow the pill they gave us to make us sleep."

Ponytails said, "When some new kid came, they remembered stuff about their family. Sometimes they said their names. Lotsa times it was just babies and they went someplace else. I don't know where."

Laura and Cassy were encouraged with all this input, hard as it was to hear.

Some of the girls still hadn't spoken; just picked at their big doughnuts; still bone-thin. Paper dolls with hair.

This would indeed be a challenge.

"Wait a minute, I remember another name. I heard it more than once 'cause that bad man Harry said it."

"Can you tell us what the name was?"

"I can, yes I can." Ponytails said, her eyes shining with pride.

"What was the name, honey?"

"It was Hannah."

CHAPTER 41

Laura and Cassy stayed and shared an early dinner with the girls at the safe house. It was a simple affair of hot dogs, beans and mashed potatoes. Some of the children continued to chatter through the meal while others ate little and said less.

With school in the morning, they decided to head straight home.

Both were lost in their own thoughts when the MG pulled into the mansion's circular driveway.

Laura took note of the fact that her mother's car was parked all the way to the left, unlike where it was when they'd left earlier in the day. *Jesus, did she go to that prison alone?*

A melody filled the great room, the speakers playing to an invisible audience.

Laura shouted, "Ma, where are you?"

"In here, dear."

"Did you eat dinner yet, Ma?"

"No, I just got back a short while ago. I expect Angus soon. We'll eat together and share any news."

Laura was still burping the hot dogs and was fine with eating something else cooked by Portia or Almadine.

"Okay, Ma"

Cassy slipped her shoes off as she dropped into the sofa in the great room. She lay her head back and soaked up the soothing notes of a Brahms' symphony, one of the few composers she recognized. Arriona was a fan also and wanted to learn more about classical music.

"Good idea, Cassy. Let's eat in here," Sophie said as she entered.

A pitcher of lemonade, along with a carafe of white wine, were placed on the capacious coffee table. Almadine, happy to have everyone home, said, "Arriona ate earlier and is asleep already."

Cassy, no longer self-conscious, poured herself a glass of lemonade.

Sophie slanted the carafe of white wine into a slender wine goblet, filled it and admired the way it caught the light of the huge crystal chandelier. Then she took a long draught.

Laura noticed, opened her mouth to comment, then said not a peep. She poured herself a full glass of the clear white wine also.

Angus trudged through the front door, went straight to Sophie and kissed her still-glistening lips. He poured his own wine, raised it for half a second, said, "Cheers" then drank.

Cassy chortled. "I'm trading my lemonade for some of what you all are having."

A pleasant moment of gentle laughter eased the tension that all, except Almadine, felt.

Cassy excused herself to visit Arriona's bedside and kiss her daughter goodnight.

Soon all were seated, poking at the food Almadine had prepared. Only Angus ate with gusto.

"No need to finish here, let's talk." Angus relayed what he and Laura and Cassy had learned from Detective Sloane. "The names we got were Big Carl and also the initials L.B. They're being investigated. Some of the pieces are starting to come together."

He looked at Laura pointedly and said, "I got a call from Jessica at the children's safe house; told me you two were there tonight. What were you able to learn from the kids?"

Cassy sat straight up and spilled as much as she could remember. They'd decided ahead of time not to take notes, so it didn't seem so "official." That might've intimidated the children.

"More than one of the kids remembered Bertie Hurtie. That's, of course, Bertie Bergeron, the woman Clyde Boudreaux is accused of poisoning. And," Cassy darted her eyes to Sophie, "they'd also heard the name Harry."

Sophie and Angus were on the edge of their seats.

Laura's face twisted in pain as she gazed at her mother. She added to Cassy's story. "They also remembered hearing the name Hannah."

Sophie lurched forward and cried, "Hannah. What else did they say about Hannah?"

"That's all we got for now, Mama. Some of the girls were eager to talk, so we will get more. We have to be patient."

Sophie tucked both lips into a thin line, then bit down on her lower lip, willing them not to quiver.

Laura continued to study her mother's face. "Mama, your lip is bleeding. Stop biting it. You hate it when Mandy Rose abuses herself like that."

Sophie took a deep breath and licked her wounded lip, then it was her turn to speak. "I went to the prison today."

"What?" asked Angus.

"Yes, Angus, I did. And I saw Harry."

Angus's face contorted with pain. *Would this woman ever let him love and protect her?*

Laura, ever the voice of reason, said, "And."

"And he looks awful. Skinny and pale. He seems contrite."

Laura rolled her eyes.

Sophie went on. "He gave me information, much the same as your detective related to you, Angus. Are you ready for this? The same names, with a bit more detail."

Nods all around.

"Harry said one of the big bosses of the cartel is called by his initials… L.B. and another, probably lower on the totem pole is a guy whose nickname is Big Carl. He told me he'll try to remember more. I left him money in his canteen. That might jog his memory. He seems a broken man."

Angus wasn't too happy to see Sophie having so much compassion for the man who was legally still her husband. He knew Sophie had a tender heart.

He observed Laura's face. She knew her mother's tender side also.

Angus said to Sophie, "Yes dear, this information *was* acknowledged by the department. It's accurate. You don't have to visit Harry again."

Sophie's mouth tightened at the seeming dictate from Angus, but she said nothing.

Cassy had fallen asleep. Smart girl.

It was late, they were all exhausted. Tomorrow was another day.

Everyone hoped Mandy Rose would be home by tomorrow.

CHAPTER 42

Bright and early at the precinct, Angus was notified of a meeting concerning the abducted children.

If a case that involved victims, promised to be of long duration, the police often gave it a name. The name given to the case involving Hannah and the other missing children was "Cartel of Tears." Someone suggested, "Hannah's Horrors," but Angus struck that down immediately. Too personal and in poor taste, though often the names given to the worst and most vile of crimes were in poor taste. Kind of black humor.

The memo said, "C of T 8 a.m. – interrogation room # 3."

Some law enforcement agencies have a group of detectives dedicated to major crimes such as homicide. In smaller departments, such as Angus's precinct, detectives work on all manner of cases. These "line" detectives are proficient in interviewing victims, witnesses and suspects, as well as photographing and processing evidence at a crime scene. They may also testify in court.

Angus Clark had the temperament needed for a homicide detective. His close relationship with the Bokums made him a leading contributor in the "Cartel of Tears" case.

He had strong problem-solving and communication skills and the ability to work under pressure in high-stress situations. Not to be forgotten, Angus had a passion for helping the community. Not a job for the faint of heart, but some heart was necessary.

Angus instinctively knew Laura and Cassy would make good cops. As long as they practiced a healthy degree of fear and could tone down their Maverick tendencies.

He grabbed a paper cup and filled it to the brim with black coffee from the pot on the green laminate counter. It resembled prune juice and he knew from past experiences it would taste like unsweetened cocoa.

Richard Sloane sat down at the head of the scarred table. He made scraping noises with his metal chair as he pulled in closer. His hand held a sheath of papers; the top sheet covered with handwritten printing Angus recognized as the detective's own.

"This case is big. This case is Goddamn huge. As you know by now, other states are involved. It's a poison that has spread throughout our country. We have some leads. We also have some names.

"When we dismiss here, I want you, Angus, and two others to get on the street and find out what you can about someone called Big Carl and also anything you can find about someone with the initials L.B. We know both of these individuals are male. Be discreet. Go to your C.I.s. Take some cash from the kitty to use for encouragement. No tough stuff. We may have to tap these same sources over again as this case develops. We're dealing with dangerous people. These lowlifes have little regard for the lives of children and will kill to protect their treacherous operation. If you get too close to the underbelly of their livelihood, they could empty out their holding places where children are hidden and relocate. We don't want that. Talk to each other and spread out. We have to stop these bastards.

"Okay, Go. Good luck."

Angus stood and said, "Wait just a minute."

Eight men froze halfway up from their chairs. The scraping noises halted as they dropped back down in their seats. They stared at Angus and waited.

"My fiancée, Sophie Bokum, visited her still-husband, Harold Bokum yesterday in prison. This tidbit needs to be added to what Detective Sloane just shared. She asked him for any names he could provide to help this investigation. You may recall his granddaughter is one of the victims. His objective in cooperating may be a lighter sentence. That said, he gave the same names. This tells me two things. One, that those IDs are accurate, and two, there are bigger bosses yet to be discovered. So, I know you guys know this, but bring in any information you get, no matter how unimportant it may seem. I'm not try'na tell you your job, but this is a heartbreaking case and the sooner we crack it, the more young lives we save."

A few mumbled, "We know" and "Okay, Angus" or "Right."

The room cleared out rapidly. All were eager to find these sons-a-bitches. Several of the men had been there at the Leprosarium when the big bust was made. They saw the children, the little girls, drugged and marching like Zombies. Some of these guys were dads.

CHAPTER 43

Officers Billy Jensen and Cartwright Spencer headed for Needle-town, which wasn't actually a town. One quick glimpse exposed how it got its name.

Winters were easy in Louisiana.

Staying warm was only an occasional misery for the hordes of homeless. Each year the number increased as visitors went to Mardi Gras and couldn't find their way back home. It wasn't illegal to be homeless or to sleep out in the open.

Government subsidized food was plentiful and dropped off at or near Needle-town.

Some of these homeless, more often men, added to their living comfort by keeping their ear to the ground; collecting information useful to the cops, who would pay money for it. The official name for these people was a C.I. or confidential informant. They were often referred to as "snitches" by others. When it went awry and they ended up dead in an alley, they were called "rats."

Billy and Cartwright had pockets full of ones and fives. They made their way into Needle-town.

They wore old army surplus duds and full-brimmed caps. Cartwright, over six feet tall and the more identifiable of the two, sported round-shaped sunglasses pressed close to his big square face and had shaved his scruffy beard.

They approached a three-sided cardboard box that had a holey pair of socks hanging over one edge. Laundry day. Two naked feet poked out of the opening from ratty gray curtains, the lopsided drapery hooks still attached.

"Yo, Weasel… you 'wake, man?"

"Watcha want? Can't yah see I'm sleeping?"

"We're here on official business. Get up."

Billy kicked the dirt-encrusted bottom of Weasel's foot, then inanely wiped his shoe on the calf of his pants.

From the depths of the carton came, "Come into my office."

"We ain't going in there. Get up."

Billy added, "Get out here. We ain't shitting you."

"Patience Billy, he's a fucking goldmine."

A hand came out and grabbed the socks as Weasel wiggled forward. The filthy feet apparently had to pass a smell test because first one then the other got drawn up and sniffed before the less than pristine socks were yanked on.

Billy, observing Weasel's flexible limbs, raised his eyebrows; once again vowed to scale down his ever-burgeoning pot belly.

Soon Weasel sat in front of them, in an almost perfect Yoga pose. He finger-combed his mass of curly brown hair. His morning toilette finished, he gave the two officers his full attention.

Billy thought miserably, Christ, no bald genes in Weasel's family.

Cartwright, the more experienced of the two, took over.

"Weasel, we're looking for some people."

The man on the ground cleared his throat importantly and said, "Is this about those missing kiddies?"

"Yep, can you help us here."

"We was talkin' 'bout that last night. Maureen started blubbering, said her boy was took. She ain't never been the same. Said she was gonna listen for any rumblings. Said she heard one thing, might be sumpthin'."

"Can you tell us what that one thing was?"

"Sure can."

"Can you tell us now?"

Weasel hesitated. He knew the drill.

Cartwright pulled a fiver out of his pocket, held it out to Weasel.

It was snatched and crammed into his back pocket in seconds. "'Kay, what Maureen said was… she was downtown and… she can still look okay when she smooths her skirt down and spit shines her black flats… and… well…"

"C'mon Weasel, out with it."

"Uh, sorry, I kinda like Maureen… she's…"

"Enough. Tell us what she said she heard."

"She ain't gonna get in no trouble, is she?"

"Weasel, she's fine. Remember this is about the little kids, like her kid that was snatched."

Blowing air out of pursed lips, Weasel continued. "She saw a white limo in front of the Ritz Hotel. When it pulled into the curb, the colored driver got out and ran around to open the passenger door. A big fat white guy in a light blue suit got out, huffing and puffing, and said to someone else in the back seat, "Take those kids to Georgia.

"Maureen said, 'Didn't sound like no father I ever heard. Said it mean-like.'"

"Then what, anything else?"

"One thing didn't make no sense."

"What, Weasel? What else?"

"Maureen said she heard the person inside the stretch say, 'Right away, Carol.'"

"Now, this guy didn't look like no Carol."

Billy picked up on this right away. "Could the person in the limo have said Carl?"

"Nope, leastwise, I don't think so. That ain't what Maureen said."

"So, it was the Ritz Hotel?"

"Yep, the Ritz."

"Did Maureen see the fat guy go into the hotel?"

"She didn't say nothing 'bout that."

"Okay Weasel, you done good. Is Maureen around today?"

"No, she don't always stay here; wish she would. I kinda like her."

"We know you do. Where else does she hang?"

"Sometimes over on Whitey Place. You know where that is?"

"Yeah, we do. Under the bridge, right?"

"Yeah, but she might be back here later today."

"Thanks, Weasel. Keep your eyes and ears open."

As an afterthought, Billy said, "You smoke?"

"Sure do," said Weasel, smiling and displaying two missing bottom teeth."

Billy dug in his pocket for the half-empty pack of cigarettes and dropped them in Weasel's lap.

"Kools? Is that all yah got?"

Cartwright shot Billy a look that stated clearly, "Don't be an easy touch, they'll take advantage."

Billy said, "See yah, Weasel."

As they walked away, they heard Weasel ruminating, "Yeah, I kinda like her."

When back in the squad car, Billy asked, "What's next?"

"We have to get someone in plain clothes registered at the Ritz."

"Yeah… you think that's Big Carl?"

"I do, Billy. I do."

CHAPTER 44

Mandy Rose wasn't mentally prepared to face anyone in her family yet. She regretted that they were probably worried about her. Could people have made a connection between her absence and what was probably all over the news about Clyde's escape from Bingham.

A tug at her heart for Clyde was relieved somewhat when she reminded herself she'd given him plenty of money. That would make the transition in Mexico easier. *But without his gris-gris?*

The tug grabbed again, this time included difficulty breathing, a whoosh of held breath. She panicked when this ushered in a bout of hyperventilation. Her head spun and the air around her sparkled with tiny black dots.

She pulled off the road and parked in a convenient highway rest area, slid her seat back as far as it would go. Her head dipped beneath the steering wheel, bumping her knees, and in a minute, the buzzing sound retreated. She held fast to her shins and waited.

When her equilibrium balanced, she opened her car window for some air. Bad move, now she smelled cheap food and grease and visions of the diner she waitressed at in Santa Ana threatened to plunge her back into the panic attack. "No!" She heard her own voice proclaim. "Get a grip.

"McDonald's. Of course. I need to eat something."

She opened the car door and swung her legs out into the sweltering humid air. Another wave of dizziness clamped down on her. She used her thumbs to press down on her temples and remained very still.

"Are you okay, miss?"

"Huh? Oh, sure. Fine."

A slender thirtyish man was leaning over in front of her. A look of concern made the dark eyes behind black-framed glasses appear like monster olives that threatened to come alive.

A small voice said, "Is she gonna die, Daddy?" The child poked Mandy's knee with a tiny pudgy finger.

The man blanched, then passed his palm over his forehead before he gave his explanation for the unusual question from his daughter. "I'm so sorry. Her aunt passed away unexpectedly a little over a week ago. She's become more than a little obsessed with death."

Mandy was touched. She looked into the little girl's cherubic face and recalled why she was called to the social sciences. "No honey, I'm not gonna die. I'm just hungry. A cheeseburger and fries will make me all better."

The child frowned, not entirely convinced. "You better get *two* cheeseburgers. That'll fix you up."

"Thank you, dear. You're very helpful."

"I know, that's what Daddy always says."

"My name's Mandy, what's yours?"

Mandy Rose's heart stopped cold when the child patted her knee, looked her straight in the eye and said, "Hannah."

The father laughed and said, "Her name is Ava, she changes it every few weeks. Right now, it's Hannah."

Mandy climbed out of her car and locked the door, then she bent over to bring her face close to the small girl. The father watched.

Mandy said, "So long, Hannah, nice to meet you."

"Bye, Mandy."

Father and daughter, holding hands, headed off to their car.

Mandy Rose went into McDonald's, got two cheeseburgers, fries and coffee with extra sugar and lots of cream. The food worked its magic as she enjoyed it inside in the air conditioning among the other travelers. She crammed her refuse in a trash receptacle that was so full it threatened to regurgitate.

On the road again, feeling better, she calculated how long it would take until she could get back to her apartment. She would not be heading to the mansion.

Would Mark be home?

<h1 style="text-align:center">CHAPTER 45</h1>

Mandy Rose was glad when her apartment building came into view. She parked and gathered her "new to her" clothing and trotted through the front entrance; took the elevator one flight up to her floor. She never understood why driving long distances was so tiring. *You're just sitting there.* Yet, she felt enervated; only mundane thoughts in her head.

She keyed into her apartment. It was icy cool. Didn't she turn the A/C off before she left? She swung her glance to the air conditioner controls. The little door was open. She never forgot to close that.

More things were *off.*

She plopped down her purse and packages as the feelings of being intruded upon grew. The used cups were still on the table. Nothing was trashed. She felt like Goldilocks. Someone had been in her apartment.

Her eyes ping-ponged back and forth, looking for more clues. A chair at a different angle. Her tiredness left. On impulse she bolted out her door and trudged over to Mark's apartment.

Three knuckle raps produced a welcome male response. "Yeah, hang on. I'm coming."

"It's me, Mark. It's Mandy. Open up."

"Mandy." He shot to the door, undid the useless lock and yanked the door open.

Mark put both hands on Mandy's shoulders and pulled her in so abruptly, she lost her footing and fell into him.

Both of his lean muscular arms went around to steady her.

They remained entwined that way, long enough for both of them to become self-conscious. When disentangled, neither mentioned the overly long embrace.

"Where the hell've you been?"

Mandy hadn't concocted a feasible reason for her absence. Then again, why would Mark have a right to expect one?

Things were closing in on her. Another panic attack threatened. She wouldn't let her churning emotions about when to trust and when to balk take over. Feeling powerless, she practiced her breathing ritual. She breathed in through her nose, counted to seven, held her breath for four, then released through pursed lips to the count of eight. A soothing whooshing sound was created and welcomed. She repeated this relaxation technique again. And several more times. Her body responded. Her mind cleared.

Mark watched, fascinated.

Mandy's gray clay color returned to a rosy pink.

Without speaking yet, she took a clearer, less emotional look at the facts. Of course the mental hospital would've reported Clyde's escape. Of course when she didn't show up for the agreed upon meeting to discuss Hannah's disappearance, everyone would've become concerned… or alarmed.

Shit, having a cop in the family brought a whole new meaning to everything.

Plus Mama, oh yes, Mama would've been crazy with worry. *But would anyone have connected her not coming home to Clyde Boudreaux?*

Mandy realized her shoulders were shaking, though her breathing was even now. She twisted to look at Mark, who was standing there in his raggedy cutoffs and a wife-beater tee shirt.

Her hearing reasserted itself as her oxygen replenished.

"Mandy, Mandy, Earth to Mandy Rose."

She pushed his hand off her shoulder, being sure not to do it roughly. "I hear you, Mark. The spell is broken."

Mark hunkered down, still barefoot, in front of her. "Mandy, you should know, the authorities have been notified of your disappearance and more importantly, they are considering a link between your missing status and the successful escape from Bingham Central by one Clyde Boudreaux." Mark added, "This man is apparently intimately connected to you."

Mandy had to think fast. "Are you telling me Clyde got out of the hospital he was being held in?"

"Yes, that's the story. Haven't you seen the papers?"

"No, but I rarely read newspapers, or listen to, or watch the news."

Mark studied Mandy Rose. She was a real enigma to him. Still hunkered down, he ventured a question; aware it might be construed as being too intrusive. "So, where were you?"

"I felt like the walls were closing in on me. No matter where I looked, it felt like a danger zone." Mandy wondered how much Mark knew about her. Did he know about Hannah? He apparently knew about her connection to Clyde, so he probably did. "What exactly do you know about me or my life?"

Mark stood as his legs were seizing up from his squat position. He rubbed behind his knees, then pulled a kitchen chair over to be close to her and said, "Sit down, Mandy."

She did.

"Are you ready to hear all this?"

"Yeah. I have to hear it."

"Okay." He paused. "Well, when your sister came here with her friend…"

"Laura was here?" That explained the changes at the apartment.

"Yes, her and her friend, Cassy. I went over to your place and they were there; very concerned as it was late and no one knew where you were." Mark took a deep breath and let it out. "I called your sister later, to see if I could do anything to help find you."

"Wait, did she give you her Rover telephone number?"

"Yes because at that point, we knew this Clyde character had escaped and might be involved."

Another deep breath. "We went to Bingham and met with Boudreaux's psychiatrist, a Dr. Romano, who was also quite distressed about the disappearance of a locked-up patient. He's looking into finding out how the cell door and the outside hospital door could've been opened when they should've been locked. Apparently there were two aides or guards stationed there that day."

Mandy kept her features neutral, not letting any emotions surface.

"So that's all I know. Have you been home yet, or called anyone to tell them you're okay?"

"No, I haven't."

"They're worried about you."

"I understand that. Listen Mark, I don't want you to call Laura. It's my family and my place. I have to sleep. I'll drive over there. You stay out of it, please."

"If that's what you want?"

"It's what I need."

"Will you keep me informed?"

"Yeah, sure."

Mandy gave Mark a one-armed hug. She resented his unsolicited role in her personal life, but what was done was done.

Back in her frigid apartment, she climbed in bed fully clothed in her Goodwill duds, unfolded the perfume smelling puffy quilt and pulled it up over herself. Exhausted, she slept.

Chapter 46

Sleep worked wonders, according to Mandy Rose's reflection in her bathroom mirror. The ornate white frame added to the picturesque scene that featured flawless pink skin and shiny chestnut locks that drifted to her shoulders.

She made the somewhat quirky decision to continue wearing her Goodwill outfit. She smoothed the skirt out and checked herself in her full-length mirror. She pursed her lips and said to her reflection, "Not bad for five bucks and change." Her opinion was it was rather on the cutesy side, but she guessed that's how her mother saw her.

To keep the image working she added a little rose-colored gloss to her lips.

She retrieved the softly glowing gris-gris from her purse and gently placed it in her underwear drawer beneath her panties. Satisfied, she barreled down the stairs, jumped in her car and took off, wanted to get there maybe before everyone was home.

The circular drive at the mansion showed her mother's jag. The sun, low in the sky, made a sparkle party on the always clean and waxed Jaguar. She glanced away from the blinding glare and pushed out of her T-Bird. The slam of the door reminded her of Clyde's exit not so very long ago. The door crashing shut felt final. A chapter in life, done and gone.

To herself, she said, "Stop it, knock it off."

Inside the mansion was cool and aloof. It was also silent. Arriona would be home from school soon. Wouldn't she? And where was Mama?

A tinkling sound caught her ear. It had a familiar ring to it. "Mama?"

Mandy Rose tracked the sound to the kitchen. Arriona and Sophie sat at a well-turned-out table, apparently enjoying a tea party.

Her mother tilted her head, like a bird dog, listening for more noises.

Arriona saw Mandy Rose first. The child bounded from her seat and cried, "It's Aunt Mandy. She's home."

The little girl hurtled herself into Mandy Rose's mid-section, knocking the air out of the object of her affection.

"Oof." Mandy recovered quickly and enveloped Arriona to her body. Arriona's arm went around Mandy's waist.

Sophie was now fully alert and laboriously getting to her feet. In doing so she knocked over her "tea" cup. She watched the colorless liquid spread over the lavender tablecloth, turning it a darker shade of purple.

The penitent look on her mother's face broke Mandy's heart. Most of all, she felt overpowering guilt. *I can't believe I'm hurting this woman again.*

She verbalized none of this.

"Hi, Mama."

"Mandy Rose, we've been worried sick about you. Where've you been?"

"I needed time to myself, things I had to figure out for me and my life."

Sophie's voice broke as she pleaded, "But Mandy, the police are searching for you."

"I'm sorry, Mama." Mandy was sick herself. Sick of all the damn drama. She turned her attention to the little girl whose eyes were big brown saucers, going from one woman to the other.

Mandy felt more guilt. "Arriona, can I have a cup of the tea you've made?"

"Okay, Aunt Mandy. Do you want my flavor or Gramma Sophie's flavor?"

"I'll take a cup of yours."

The child picked up the vintage ceramic teapot that was circled with happy little hand-painted rosebuds and poured. The pale amber liquid went neatly into a cup of the same happy design. She did this with poise and grace, her little face tight with concentration, her tongue pointed a bit gingerly, lest the tea "get" spilled.

Mandy lifted the cup, pinky aloft and sipped. It was very sweet. "Delicious tea, Miss Arriona. Is this Earl Gray?"

An angry voice burst into the festive chatter. "Mandy, I want to know where you've been. You made all of us sick with worry. What is the matter with you?"

"I understand, Mama. I'm not ready to be interrogated. Just trust me."

Sophie made it over to her daughter, wrapped her arms around her and pulled her to her bosom. In a weepy voice, she said, "I'm glad you're home."

"Me too, Mama."

Arriona was already bolting toward the door when it crashed open. Acute seven-year-old hearing detected any and all arriving vehicles.

Laura came flying through the great room into the kitchen, looking like she was out for blood. Her eyes blazed fire and brimstone.

Cassy also entered at the front door, stooped and hugged her daughter fiercely.

Arriona squealed, "Mama, too tight."

Mandy put her arms up in a defensive pose when Laura came hurtling toward her, stopping only a foot away.

"Where the hell have you been?" Spittle flew out of the younger sister's angry mouth as she shouted loud enough to wake the devil.

The mother of these two women watched with a mixture of shock and pride. She was rooted to the spot she stood in. Would Mandy Rose answer Laura?

But nope, Mandy Rose still was not talking.

"You have some explaining to do big sister. I'm calling the precinct right now, let them know you're back. Not missing anymore!" Laura went to the house phone, called the station and informed them to abort the search for her sister.

She was told that Angus was on his way home.

Right on cue the door opened again, almost bumped into Cassy and Arriona, who hadn't moved yet, preferring the relative peace in their little world.

Angus, ever the plain-speaking cop, said, "What's going on here?"

"Hi Angus, I'm back. I apologize for leaving without notifying everyone I'd be gone for a few days. But let me remind you all, I'm an adult and a free agent. But," somewhat contrite, "I'm sorry for causing people to worry."

Angus took a deep raspy breath and strolled over to Mandy. His calm demeanor was always a welcome diversion from the family histrionics. "I'm glad you're back. Your mother was very concerned, and you're right, you are an adult and don't have to explain to everyone if you go away for a few days."

"Thanks, Angus." She gave him the very first hug, a quick one to be sure, but definitely a hug.

Sophie beamed.

"Now, that said, the only fly in this particular ointment is the seemingly coincidental escape of one Clyde Boudreaux from Bingham Institute. This young man hasn't been spotted to date, nor do we have any clues as to his location."

He directed his gaze to Mandy. "Can you shed any light on this subject, Mandy?"

She locked eyes with Angus and stated in a clear voice, "No, I don't know anything about that."

Laura's head snapped to eyeball her sister. "Nothing, Mandy? Nothing?"

"As I told Mama, I just needed time to myself. As for Clyde, I thought he suffered a complete mental break down and was locked up in a secure facility?"

Laura twisted her mouth but kept her eyes on Mandy.

Cassy and Arriona came into the kitchen.

Everyone knew it was time to stop badgering Mandy Rose. The truth would come out eventually. But not this minute.

Laura and Angus exchanged a look, both raised their eyebrows. Both knew Mandy Rose was lying.

Sophie sat down at the table and wished she had another cup of "tea."

<h1 style="text-align:center">CHAPTER 47</h1>

Mark was kicking around his apartment doing some heavy thinking. First he paced, then he sat and rested his chin in his hands, elbows on his kitchen table.

Bounding up again, he almost knocked over his bright red stool he favored for kitchen dining. He grabbed it before it hit the floor or knocked into the twin stool he'd painted royal blue. The snow-white table made a decidedly patriotic statement. Today he wasn't impressed.

On days like this, he missed his younger sister, Junie. Only two years apart, she'd perished along with their parents in a horrible three car pileup on highway I-49.

That was the longest night in his life. He would've been in that car too if he was a better son. They'd wanted him on that trip to visit his grandparents in that nursing home.

June placated their parents. He could still hear her. "Ma, let Mark skip this one. He's got a job interview on Monday. He needs to prepare."

"He didn't."

His parents relented; wanted Mark to get his life on track.

Junie had winked at him as she trailed her mother and father out to the waiting Lincoln Continental Town Car, destined to be turned into scrap metal.

She was wearing a white cotton blouse and a below-the-knee black watch plaid skirt, in honor of the conservative grandparents' ideas on proper dress for a respectable young lady.

God, he loved her.

He suffered a familiar stab of guilt for all the damn money that became his as the last Johnson standing. The cash cow gave more milk after the grandparents went to their glory. He was loaded. He'd never get his life "on track."

He was embarrassed over his bloated bank account. He'd never earned a penny of it. Could the Bokums fill that empty burned out hole in his gut? He was hell-bent on being of assistance, whatever it took.

He nodded his head with a jerky motion and sat down again. He copied down the Rover phone number from the piece of paper Laura'd given him into his little phone number book. He used black ink.

CHAPTER 48

Clyde wasn't scared. Not exactly scared. Not piss your pants scared.

It'd all happened so fast. He felt abandoned; like when his granddaddy got lynched that dusty sun-scorched day.

His grandaddy kept his high-ankle shoes, though the white bastards stripped him naked, using a knife to cut his raggedy clothes off his poor old shrunken black body. They did him the best favor. He hated the whitish raised flesh on his ankles; looked like oversized maggots coiled around his skin and bone ankles. His grandaddy winked at him. Their little secret.

Those shoes were gonna walk him through the pearly gates, so he said.

Clyde was mostly on his own after that. Mostly on his own all his life.

The Air Jordans were clumping along, but he watched the edges of the miracle sneakers get fuzzy in his vision. He was weeping. "Christ, no time for this."

He wiped his eyes with the back of his hand as he noticed a barrier fence coming into view. It was made of wooden stakes with black metal wire crisscrossed between the posts.

He could see broken places. He could wiggle easily through those holes.

Beyond the fence was open land. He wasn't alone.

Heading toward him was a man and a woman. There was a small child riding atop the shoulders of the man. The child leaned his head to rest on the man's hatless head. The boy had longish black hair that draped over the adult's ear. All looked coated with a pale dust.

As the distance lessened, the two men sized each other up.

The woman cried, "Mira! Mira!" Using a slightly crooked bony brown finger, she pointed at Clyde.

Clyde lifted his hands over his head to show he was no threat.

The man, understanding, did the same.

The woman opened her mouth to say more but changed her mind, just looked at the man, probably her husband and the child's father.

It was a very short encounter. The men shook hands and smiled. The child woke up and stared at Clyde, possibly the first black man he'd ever seen.

Clyde knew only a smattering of Spanish. He managed a, "Buena suerta."

The woman found her voice, sang out, "No hay mal que por bien no venga."

"There is no bad that does not bring good."

The men nodded; the boy gaped.

They each continued on their journey.

Clyde felt better for the exchange. He went over his meager repertoire of Spanish phrases, vowed to get a book for gringos as soon as he got into Mexico.

The open land was once again barricaded with a wood and wire fence. Large cactus plants could be seen in the distance. After making it past the second fence, there were bushes that looked more lethal than the wire fences. Loaded with prickers, these could dig a bloody path in any exposed skin. He was glad for the long-sleeve shirt and pants, but he feared for his vulnerable ankles.

He wished he'd paid more attention to the stories he'd heard bandied around about immigrants coming into the States, but even more about Americans being snatched and held for ransom.

He knew there was a bus that went to Reynosa, a big city. He was also aware of the dangers in attempting to take a bus. Plus, he had a lot of American money, a red flag for all kinds of disaster. Kidnapped, robbed, beaten, or worse, killed.

Houses were coming into view now. He recalled they were called ranchos. Many of them had huge porches with big chairs filled with women in long colorful skirts and men who wore short sleeved shirts, jeans with big belt buckles and strangest of all, Mexican boots with long pointy toes.

The men all wore cowboy hats and sat up abruptly as Clyde was spied in their path of vision.

The country was wild. Scrambling across the open dusty land were farm animals, loose and kicking up fine billows of dust. Chickens clucking and going in all directions, pigs pushing their snouts into loose soil, looking for who know what to eat. Seems like they should know better. Poisonous spiders lurked in the soil? And, of course, dogs. The dogs all seemed to have some terrier in their lineage.

He needed to seek help. He was hungry and painfully aware he had a long road ahead of him. He had to avoid the buses, as attractive as sitting down sounded to him.

Clyde went up to a rancho that had red shingles and was made of wood, not clay as some of the others were. A man in farmer's clothing came out the door as he approached. The green pickup truck parked on the side of the house had wooden seats inside and looked as though it might be a vehicle for farm hands to travel to day jobs, picking crops.

Clyde lengthened his stride as a dark thought snaked its way across his brain. Christ, bounty hunters. Could they be looking for him? He was a fugitive from America. Hell, was it still legal to bounty hunt?"

Too late. Then he remembered. Rattlesnakes.

Christ Mandy Rose. What did you do to me?

It was so damn hot, even the ice baths at Bingham sounded good. He kept walking. What else could he do?

As he came closer, he extended his hand to the man who stood with legs apart and hands firmly clamped on his hips. The man turned his head to one side and spit a lunger that traveled like a bullet.

Clyde kept his face open and friendly and tried a little more Spanish. "Hola. I want work. Trabajo, por favor."

The man kept silent.

Clyde attempted more communication. "Mi familia en Mexico… mi primos." Clyde placed his dark hand over his heart on the dusty Salvation Army shirt.

The man's features softened. He said. "Why you no fly."

Clyde answered, "No dinero."

The farmer let his arms drop to his sides and took the last few steps toward the Negro Americano. A smile lit up Pedro's sweaty face, and his knobby arthritic hand pushed out to welcome Clyde's youthful brown one.

Clyde's face brightened as he recalled how to say he was hungry. "Tengo hambre. Tengo mucho hambre."

The farmer chuckled out loud and stepped aside to make room for Clyde to enter his casa.

The smells inside the house were inviting. A combination of spices and tobacco. His nose tingled in anticipation.

Three children played a game on the floor, which was polished to a high sheen. Two girls and one boy, all appeared under the age of nine.

They stopped the game, which consisted of dominoes being moved around on smooth tiles. The girls had long dresses and their jet-black hair reached to their waists and gleamed as shiny as the floor. The boy, the youngest, tried to appear brave, but his sisters had him outmatched. They stood and chorused, "Hola."

Clyde answered with the same greeting.

A big-breasted woman wearing a bright orange and red dress came out from another room into the large kitchen. She was nonplussed also. "Hola, señor."

Pedro said, "Mi espousa, Maria." He gazed fondly at the buxom woman.

Clyde joined in, said, "Mi nombre es Clyde."

Pedro continued. "Clyde necesito la comeda."

Maria smiled broadly, always happy to feed people. She pulled a wooden chair out from the table and waved her hand toward it.

Clyde didn't need to be asked twice.

She bustled over to a vintage refrigerator and pulled out a sack. It was lumpy. Clyde's mouth watered as he realized he was going to have some "huevos."

She put a pot on the back of the black stove and lit a fire under it. The beans smelled like a miracle food, spicy and rich.

Into a yellow bowl she expertly cracked four eggs and added some unknown spice before she whipped it to a pale yellow. She held the bowl high and waterfalled it into the frying pan, which was already heated and ready. The sizzling sound and the rich aroma made Clyde's mouth water in anticipation.

The older daughter pulled open an aqua painted drawer that held tortillas.

Clyde was beside himself to be getting treated so good by strangers. He pinched his nose with his thumb and forefinger to stifle the happy drip that threatened and might precede watery eyes.

When the feast was placed in front of him, all except the farmer wanted to watch him eat.

Maria loved to see people eat her cooking, especially hombres. The children were also in the audience until Pedro clapped his hands twice, and the girls and the boy went back to sitting on the floor with their dominoes.

Maria and Pedro sat with Clyde at the table as he shoveled in the creamy yellow eggs and dark brown beans, which, to Maria's delight, he wiped up with the tortillas.

She poured him some hot black coffee. He drank it with a, "Mmmmmm, bueno."

Pedro said simply to the tired American, "You sleep aqui… here."

"Mañana en camion." He tried again. "Mañana en carro."

Clyde chewed and swallowed and said, "Si, mañana en carro."

"Mañana trabajando," he and Pedro said at the same time and laughed.

Clyde added, "Gracias, mi amigo, muchas gracias."

"De nada, mi amigo."

CHAPTER 49

Laura was livid. *Would this sister of hers ever grow up?*

Laura was aware of the sexual molestations their father subjected Mandy Rose to and gave her sister lots of slack because of that abuse. Mandy'd had counseling and was now being educated as a social worker. Psyche 101 states that people often became fixated at the age the sexual abuse starts. Nothing was helping Mandy Rose. The damage was permanent.

This same maturity fixation was also true of alcoholism. Not applicable, but now Mama was hitting the bottle again; sneaking gin into every liquid; not drinking openly to excess, but surreptitiously leaving for trips to the bathroom while others were having a glass or two of wine together.

"Christ… this family." Laura wanted answers.

She sidled over to her sister, put her arms around her, leaned in and whispered in her ear, "Mandy, let's get outta here."

Mandy twisted out of Laura's full nelson and spat, "What for?"

Laura knew she had to put the kid gloves on and temper her approach… baby steps.

"'Cause I think we need to talk privately, just you and me."

Cassy watched this exchange as she played with Arriona's pigtails, smoothing each one with her long slender fingers.

Mandy knew she had to have Laura's trust. Laura'd never failed her before. She needed Laura.

"Laura, let's go to the Crab Shack." Spoken clearly for everyone's ears. "We'll bring back some goodies for everyone."

Angus looked hard at the two girls but bit his tongue.

Sophie took another sip of her "tea."

Arriona became animated, waved her arms about. "Oh yay, bring back Cajun French fries. They're my favorite"

131

Cassy knew her role. Always, like Angus, the voice of reason. "Bring me some of those fries too and crab cakes."

Angus hoped this liaison would shed some light on what was going on with Mandy and if they were lucky, Clyde Boudreaux.

Angus chimed in, "Bring us all crab cakes and Cajun fries."

Mandy cried, "Let's go!"

Outside, headed for the MG, Laura tilted her head back to get a full shot of her sister and exclaimed, "Where the hell did those clothes come from?"

Mandy giggled and answered, "Why? You want to borrow them?"

Laura shook her head and folded into the little car.

Mandy considered trusting Laura one hundred percent but wavered; Laura was almost a cop. Would she trust Angus, who *was* a cop?

The scant conversation dried up altogether as they pulled into the Crab Shack's parking lot.

Laura jumped out. Mandy took her time, putting her legs out one by one, stalling.

Once inside, the infectious sight of people having fun, the smells of savory clams and spicy side dishes worked to lift their moods. Even the sounds of laughter amid the inevitable know-it-alls, already in their cups, was inviting.

Laura's VIP spot was ready, so was Babette, who whirled over to them as they settled into the red leather booths.

Laura eyeballed Mandy. "Sazeracs or brews?"

Mandy answered by tilting her chin toward the waitress. "Babette, I'll have a bottle of Coors and some of those fries I smell."

Laura snorted, just said, "Same for me, please."

Babette hoped they'd order more, thinking only of her tip.

Laura started, still chafing from the ordering rebuff. "So Mandy, where were you?'

"Here and there."

"C'mon Mandy, stop playing games. You can fool Mama, but don't give me a fucking snow job." Laura dropped the kid gloves.

"Who's giving you a snow job? Say what you really want to know, Laura."

The beers were plopped down on top of clean Crab Shack coasters; brown bottles, cold and dripping. The two stout beer mugs sported pasted on Clam Shack Logos and were frosted to perfection.

"Fries coming right up."

The sisters waited to continue their talk.

Laura recalled a while ago when they were here and discovered they were both Clyde Boudreaux's lovers. Mandy had taken refuge in the ladies' room, had a total freaking meltdown, ended up on the floor near the damn toilets. Laura blew out a breath to clear that memory.

Two brightly colored boats of crispy fries arrived and joined the beer party.

Mandy became aware she was hungry. She snatched two long orange tinted fries and popped them in her mouth as a pair.

Laura gaped at her sister.

Mandy ate more with her fingers and felt herself relax as the food and alcohol worked their magic.

Laura followed suit, using the long wooden prongs that came with the pile of succulent fries, stabbing them one or two at a time.

Unspoken pact to eat and drink first.

Laura bided her time but tapped her foot, no relation to the beat of the music that pounded from the juke box. AC/DC and Judas Priest getting lots of quarters and most of the airtime.

Frazzled nerves calmer now, Mandy Rose spoke. "Before I tell you anything, I need your solemn promise it goes no further." She paused. "That includes Cassy."

"Ouch. Now you're scaring me."

"C'mon Laura, we're sisters." Mandy knew stating that fact would extract the promise she needed. *Emotional blackmail?* So what.

Laura wiped her fingers that were already clean on her napkin, placed it folded next to the almost empty fries boat and said in a somber voice, low enough not to travel, "Okay, Mandy."

"Okay, what?"

"Okay, I won't breathe a word of what you tell me to anyone."

"Not even Cassy?"

"Not even Cassy." Laura put her hands beneath the table, folded them, almost in prayer, and leaned forward.

Mandy said smoothly, "I took Clyde to Mexico."

"What?" Almost a shout.

"Well, not all the way of course, but he's on his way there."

Laura's mouth dropped open and her eyes rounded. "Holy shit, Mandy. How did he escape? How did you hook up with him? Don't tell me you helped him es…"

Mandy broke in. "Yes, Laura. I helped him escape."

"Why?"

"I just wanted to see him."

"And?"

"I overheard two guards planning to murder him early the next day. So… you see, I had to."

"I still don't understand. He was locked up."

"Well the guards left the door open to where the cells were in the front of the building, so they could get in the next morning when it should've been locked. I beat them to it."

"Christ, Mandy. The whole fucking state is looking for him, calling him a dangerous murderer."

"You and I know that's not true."

Laura got still as she recalled a person, not moving, on the floor of Clyde's house when she broke in to visit him. That was never fully explained. What she said was, "How did he get out of the cell? That must've been locked?"

"It was. That's the one thing I cannot totally understand. I know what I saw. I know it happened."

"What Mandy? What happened?"

"The gris-gris."

"What are you talking about?"

"I had Clyde's gris-gris. That's Clyde's Voodoo amulet. It protects the wearer from evil and gives them good luck."

"Keep talking."

"I had it in my pocket when I went to visit him."

"Yeah?"

"Clyde knew its power. I only suspected it. I slid the gris-gris into the slot on his cell door."

"C'mon Mandy, then what?"

"The door opened."

"That's crazy."

"I know what it sounds like, but I was there. I saw it. I watched that locked cell door open."

Laura tried to get her breath. Half a minute passed while she digested this unholy story. "Okay, so now Clyde is free. Then what did you do?"

"Well, we got in my car and left. We stayed at a motel, bought some clothes in a Salvation Army store for him, then drove till I got to the let-off place for him to continue into Mexico and I let him off."

Laura said, "Salvation Army? Is that where you got the clothes you're wearing?"

"Nope, mine are from the Goodwill store."

"Wow, you'll have to take me to your new fashion find," Laura panned.

The new subject felt easier to discuss than escapes from mental hospitals, murderers on the loose, locked doors that magically opened and trips to Mexico for fugitives.

Babette had slipped in at their table, a questioning look on her lovely brown face.

"Yes, two more Coors and later we'll put in a large order for fries and crabs to go."

Babette grinned and slid away.

"Now what's going to happen to Clyde down in Mexico. *If* he makes it to Mexico?"

"I gave him plenty of money."

"That'll help, if he doesn't get mugged. How's he going to contact you if he needs more help or wants to return. He might not like living in Mexico."

Mandy hesitated, then went on. "Okay, here's the part you're not going to like."

"I don't like any of it. Just tell me what else there is."

Mandy bowed her chin slightly, then lifted it. Her forehead shone as she tilted her head back and said, "Laura, he's memorized your Rover phone number."

Two more icy Coors arrived.

The two sisters stared over the tops of the brown bottles into each other's eyes.

Mandy put her hand on the table. Laura covered it with hers. Both hands were cool.

The pact was made.

CHAPTER 50

"Sophie honey, Mandy's home. You can relax."

Sophie looked at Angus, her eyelashes still full of tiny rhinestone-like tears. Her mouth smiled, but it didn't reach her eyes.

"Yes, Angus, I'm fine. Are you going back to the precinct?"

He surrounded her with both arms and pulled her into his chest. "I'd like to but only if you're okay."

She mumbled into his now-sweaty shoulder, "I'm okay. Go. We need to find out about Hannah and the other children." She repeated, "Go."

"All right, I'm gonna change my shirt and leave. I won't be too late. We have to set up an undercover operation for the hotel before that guy leaves."

"You mean Big Carl?"

"Yes."

While Angus went to change into a fresh shirt, Sophie planned to continue having her own special "tea" party. He'd be gone for at least two hours, maybe three. She felt her stomach to see in any more flab had accumulated. She pinched the bulge over her belly button. "Not bad."

She gave herself permission to add some salty snacks to her beverage.

After another hug and kiss, Angus left. Sophie heard the masculine rumble of his Ford pickup as it pulled out of the circular drive. She saw no reason to switch from Arriona's teacup. She reminded herself Cassy and the child were still in the house. Gone were the days of total isolation.

She scratched her head, mounding her blonde upsweep into a strange rooster-like comb.

Cassy found her sitting with her teacup drink, snacks and weird hairdo in her favorite chair. "Arriona's asleep. Where's everyone?"

"Angus went back to the precinct. Laura and Mandy are still out, not sure when they'll get back. Don't know why they went."

136

Cassy shifted her jaw to the side and said, "I'm afraid we won't find out why either. I'm going to bed to study for exams."

"G'night, Cassy"

Cassy looked at the way Sophie held the teacup at an angle. A clear liquid threatened to empty into the seated woman's lap.

"Good night, Sophie."

Chapter 51

Developments were moving at warp speed at the precinct.

Every available officer wanted to help bring down this ring of sex traffickers and organ traffickers. Tough cops had a tender center when kids were involved. Tootsie Pops, all of them. They confessed to hugging their own children a bit tighter and longer at bedtime.

The war room's whiteboard screamed with broad black marks, naming known offenders and possible suspects. A second board held, in red marker, the names of children tracked down to several different locations.

Angus was surprised to discover a sting was scheduled for that night. And he had a leading role.

Middle of the night sting.

Sloane wasted no time. "Angus, tonight. You're going in with Jensen, Hugo and Spencer. The kids are holed up in an abandoned winery and almost certainly those on the *dispensables* list. We had to give some clemency to the Chatty Canary we grabbed the night of the Leprosarium bust. He gave definite info on two of these children."

Angus nodded. He was aware of this intel, but a sting tonight was news. These kids were marked for organ removal. That meant harvesting young healthy kidneys, livers, lungs and hearts. Often from the same small body. These children were destined to lose their lives before they'd even begun. Young innocents slaughtered to satisfy the voracious greed of cold-blooded men and heartless women; yes, there were women.

Sloane stood, legs apart, hand resting on his sidearm as he barked, "Angus, why weren't you here earlier?"

Angus felt torn. This was never an issue when he lived with his mother. Pearl always knew his job came first. "Sorry, Captain. Give me the orders." He knew he wouldn't be getting home early. Sophie'd have to understand.

"Okay, you four are going into the winery. Assume the people in charge are armed and dangerous. There'll be additional manpower waiting outside, hidden from view."

Angus coughed and held his hand to his mouth. "What about the kids? Do we know how many there are? Do we have a location in the winery where they're being held?"

"Don't have all the details. We know there's a back entrance with a loading dock. It's a one floor brick building with a cellar. There are offices and a huge open room where the wine barrels are located. That's what we know. The rest is up to you and your crew."

"Got it. When do we leave?"

Sounds of scuffed feet announced Jensen, Hugo and Spencer, dressed in tactical gear.

Sloane dictated, "Suit up Clark, that includes armor."

Angus complied. He never argued when bulletproof vests were called for. His nice clean blue shirt would be covered with a standard issue vest that could save his life, then a dark long sleeve shirt.

The men, all Caucasians, smeared black make-up on their faces, being sure to cover the backs of their hands. They couldn't risk discovery. Every camouflage must be used. Lives were at stake.

Sloane, a believer in battle cry, bellowed, "Go. Go. Go."

Angus Clark jutted his jaw and led his hyped-up trio out the door to where the "unmarked" waited. They piled in.

Spencer rang out the directions to the old winery that now held not wine for celebrating but children for slaughtering.

Angus drove purposefully and cleared his mind of everything except their mission. He could see the black van in the rearview mirror that was their back-up. There was no cop chatter as they drove to the winery.

The building looked dark and foreboding. There were three cars parked close to the front entrance.

Angus expertly followed the partially grown over with weeds driveway that led to the loading dock in the rear of the ancient building. He reached up and snapped the switch shut that eliminated the interior light on the unmarked police car's roof.

He snugged up close to the shoulder-height dock. Massive overhead doors for deliveries appeared to be in locked position with vertical handles. No entry-point here.

A side door for humans with three steps leading to it had a rusty padlock hanging from it. No problem for these cops.

Spencer said in a stage whisper, "Let Billy… he's a natural."

Jensen stepped to the door, took a hard look at the set-up and whispered, "Piece of cake."

Sliding smoothly from his pocket came a long metal device he introduced effortlessly into the lock, did a calculated twist movement and *bam*. The lock fell open and Billy pulled on the cold iron handle. The big door groaned once and floated outward.

They were in.

It was dark, and as they bumped into each other, they became aware of a splinter of light at the end of the corridor they now occupied.

"Show me the schematic."

Cartwright pulled it out of his pocket along with a pen light, unfolded it and illuminated it for Angus's perusal.

First time Angus laid eyes on it, but he was attuned to maps, loved them. It took thirty seconds for him to get his bearings. "We're going down this hallway and through the double doors on the right. Offices should be right there."

Billy looked sorrowful. "Yeah, but where are the kids?"

"Probably in the barrel room." Angus continued with authority. "We'll incapacitate whoever we find. Try not to shoot to kill. We could learn from them."

Three answers. "Got it." "Yup." "Okay."

As they approached the double doors, they heard male voices. Maybe three or four; hard to tell.

The doors were of the swinging variety.

Billy whispered, "Thank you, God."

"On my count. One. Two. Three."

They slammed into the doors that didn't disappoint. They flew inward and three surprised mugs dropped as though they'd seen a ghost.

"Don't move."

"You move, we shoot."

Four black Glock 22s aimed menacingly.

The three men in the room froze.

One wise-cracked, "What the fuck?"

"Shut up and tell us where the kids are."

Billy yelled, "Now"

Angus said, "Cuff 'em and tie their legs. Double knots. No one leaves unless it's in a body bag."

Billy's young face was contorted with pure hatred. He went right to work, cuffing and tying. He used his almost-new shiny cuffs first, then Hugo's and Spencer's.

The clatter the cuffs made was music to the enforcement officer's ears. "Get on the horn to let the others in. These assholes need to be watched. Tell our guys to go around back, the welcome mat is out.

The youngest of the traffickers seemed most eager to be of assistance. His ruddy face was soaked with perspiration. His blond hair stuck to his high forehead. He was obviously a good-looking chap. The blue eyes still held a youthful hopefulness; a sky without clouds. He offered, "Go through the doors and keep going until you see another big door. Go in that door. It's the winery. The kids are in the barrels."

Then he added, "Grab some water from the jugs on the floor. Some of the kids might be very thirsty."

Might be?

The hardened cops each cringed in their own fashion.

Angus twitched his jaw down and swung it side to side, not keen on what he was about to view.

Billy licked his lips.

The doors they'd just come through made a creaking sound.

Angus, thinking it was cops, said, "You got here fast."

Two round black holes pushed through between the double doors. One hole exploded. Chest high for anyone unlucky enough to be standing in its path.

Angus, less than an arm's length away, squatted and gave an upper cut, open palmed, to the two barrels that poked through.

Billy, who'd been kneeling, tightening knots on the floored men looked up in time to see Victor take the blast square between his shoulder blades.

A direct hit.

A mortal hit.

Spencer dove into the swinging doors, knocking the intruder and his shotgun to the ground.

One second later, Angus leapt onto the shooter's chest and Cartwright twisted the long gun out of the butcher's hands.

Victor only had time for one second's surprised look before he crumbled down to the floor, grabbing his chest.

Angus and Cartwright dragged the unexpected attacker into the room by his feet.

"Tie this fucking bastard up, Billy."

Billy's face was ashen. "Okay, Angus," he said in a tiny voice.

Cartwright balled his fist and slammed it into the man's reddened face. His head lolled to one side, nose crushed and bloody. The shotgun lay abandoned on the floor; smells of burnt charcoal and sulphur made nostrils water.

Angus knelt by Victor Hugo. The man's fingers were painted red. The astonished look had vanished, replaced by the open-eyed death stare. His eyes were pale gray tomb stone twins.

Now there were four bound men on the floor. And one dead man. One of their own.

Why didn't he put that vest on? Angus was a nest of feelings. Guilt for not checking vest compliance. Sorrow for the loss of a good man. But mostly, anger.

Anger at the way things were in this world.

He wiped both eyes with his forearm and steadied himself for the next part of this unholy mission.

The winery.

And the barrels.

CHAPTER 52

The winery was milling with cops.

An ambulance had been called for Victor Hugo.

A second call was put in. "Dispatch, send two squads for removal of four perps at Wingate Winery. Yep, all cuffed and incapacitated. Address, 66 Wingate Road, Lawlor." He paused. "Yes, officers at location. Investigation concerning possible kidnapped children... Recovery of same in "Cartel of Tears" case."

Angus plodded along the dark and dreary corridor until he came to the described door. It was a massive oak door with a wooden sign carved over it, no longer legible, but appeared to have once proclaimed to the world, "Louisiana's Finest Wine." All that was left was a capital F, a lower case I and N, a capital W and another lower case I and N. It said Fin Win.

The door opened easily, allowing the stench to assault the senses of whomever ventured into the inner sanctum.

Angus was no longer alone. There were five of them now. Sirens approached; more good guys on the way.

Angus turned on his little black pen light and saw the milk jugs on the floor, four that he could see, filled with dubious looking water, stuff floating on top of the murky liquid.

Barrels lined both sides of a well-trodden path.

The top quarter of each lid on the side was sawed out. Empty except for wooden splinters that jutted out from the edges. The top quarter was a hole, dark inside with porcupine needles all around

To keep little hands from exploring for escape?

The barrels lay on their sides, much the way they had when fermenting Louisiana wine.

Angus felt sick to his stomach and called out, "Can anyone hear me?"

No answer.

Angus wondered if all the kids were already gone. He called out louder, "Hello."

A slight scuffling sound came from a barrel halfway down the left row.

Angus tried again. "I am a police officer. I'm here to help. We want to take you to safety. No one can hurt you anymore." Angus didn't want to frighten what he now felt certain were children encased in wine barrels.

Unbeknownst to them waiting to be ripped open for their organs.

"Dear God in Heaven." Billy motioned toward a barrel where a tiny hand waved up and down. The maw of the stained and dirty barrel was black. The little pale fingers hesitated, still unsure. They hung in mid-air, not moving now.

Angus took a step forward, closer to the barrel.

Billy arrived next to Angus. He said, "Let me." Billy went over to that particular barrel and put his hand, palm up, through the opening. He crooned gently, "You're safe now. We'll take you all away from here. We're police officers."

Something in his young ingenuous voice broke through the fear and reached into the little heart that was still beating.

A tiny voice said, "Help us. Please help us."

Then another, "Please take us out of here."

Two voices from one barrel. "We're thirsty." "Do you have water?"

One of the officers entering the wine barrel room found a light switch and flipped it on. It was a dreary yellow light, but visibility improved.

Barrels were coming alive with little fingers motioning and begging voices crying for water.

Two rows of cut-out barrels. Small hands in many shades of white and brown. More waving.

And the voices, some cracking, but all jubilant, even if subdued.

A crescendo… a chorus of, "Help us. Please help us."

Angus contemplated whether these children had any inkling of the destiny planned for them in the hands of these fiends.

"Cartwright get child welfare right away. Prepare them for new admissions. Tell them we need water, blankets and immediate transportation to Bingham Memorial. These kids are all dehydrated and possibly much worse." He pointed back to the entrance door and said,

"Don't give them a drop of that disgusting jug water. It's contaminated; could be fatal if it's drank."

The officers were peeking into the barrels, making contact and soothing the children's fears. They worked to convince them their torturous existence would soon be over.

Billy reached his palm in and was rewarded with a bony, paper-thin hand that gingerly clung to two of Billy's fingers.

Everybody was trying to help.

"What've you got there, officer?"

"I think it's called a hack saw."

"Can you open these barrels bigger?"

"It looks like this is what they used to open the tops of the lids."

"Look."

"Oh sweet Jesus."

"Oh my God, they can fit through the openings."

"These kids are skin and bones."

Billy put his big hands into the barrel and grasped the captive child under her armpits. He laboriously extracted the little girl from its fetid recess. The girl was little more than a paper doll, probably weighed less than thirty pounds. Her short pink nightie was caked with feces, and her pipe-stem arms and legs were blanketed with sores, some healed, some open and wet.

She grabbed Billy around the neck and held on like a little koala bear; amazing him with the power of her grip.

Great salty tears streamed down the young cop's cheeks.

Over in a darkened corner, a young rookie bent over and regurgitated. He tried to be invisible by putting his elbow in front of his chin but lost the battle when a late lunch of fish stew came bumbling out of him and pooled on the dirt floor.

Billy started toward the door, not sure where to bring his delicate cargo. The tears dripped off his chin.

Other children were extracted from their loathsome barrel homes.

More help arrived.

Cases of bottled water were carried in along with boxes of fresh pastries.

The children were all starving, their eyes bugged disturbingly from their little faces. Distended bellies resembling late-stage pregnancy was the plight of each and every child.

Those bastards never even fed them.

Somebody was on top of their game because medical personnel streamed in and more ambulances were careening into the back entrance.

Each child was handed over with the utmost care as the delicacy of their condition could produce bone fracture. They were "that" emaciated.

Angus yelled to Cartwright, who'd just placed a teeny colored boy with a great fluff of curly hair into a green blanket held by a ponytailed nurse. "Spencer, gather all the files and paperwork you can get your hands on." He continued. "This could be the break we've been waiting for."

Angus knew that could be construed as cold-hearted in light of what was happening here right now. He also knew without facts, including names, these despicable scumbags would not be stopped.

The tickling in the back of his mind came from thoughts of Sophie and her granddaughter.

Hannah would be older than these kids appeared to be.

He wondered to himself, Why is it always Sophie and Hannah I think of and not Mandy Rose and Hannah?

He didn't know the answer to that one.

CHAPTER 53

Exhausted, Angus left the winery at three-thirty a.m., eyes drooped and bleary; breathing shallow. His mouth hung open to capture needed oxygen. He was drained.

The pictures in his head tortured him. Each child extracted from those fetid barrels looked worse than the last. Maybe his ability to process such horrific abuse was taxed so repeatedly that he'd been left depleted and emptied; fortitude plucked clean.

Pure anguish.

The sound of the ambulance sirens soothed his frazzled nerves. He dipped his head and visualized the twin boys logged in together, one of them already cold while the other curled into himself to garner any warmth left in his own thin frail body.

His twin was dead.

There was one black body bag filled to capacity. Victor Hugo was a large man. Angus knew Victor felt the Kevlar vests constricted his movements. There was on some cleric's desk a work order pending approval for some extra-extra-large size vests. It would pass muster now.

Alongside that big black plastic bag were two other bags. These two bags were almost flat; the plastic top sticking to the plastic bottom. Only a tiny mound, less than three feet in length, separated the plastic sheet. These were children.

They'd all ride together to the hospital before the next journey to the morgue.

Angus, totally enervated, hoped more than anything everyone was sound asleep at the Bokum residence. He cut the engine as he rolled into the circular drive. Sophie's Jag was absent, likely in the garage. The girls' cars were parked next to his truck.

He felt the hoods of both. Both were cold. Good.

Inside, he removed his shoes and climbed the stairs in stocking feet.

He needed a shower. Badly. The guest bedroom had a bathroom. He headed there. In the hallway, he crept painstakingly, using tiny quiet steps.

He heard a creaking noise, and the door to his and Sophie's bedroom parted. There was a bedside table lamp on. In the doorway stood Sophie, her long blonde hair down, billowy white nightgown in shadow with the light on behind her.

He went to her.

She could see his face and read his wretchedness. She pulled him into the bedroom and wrapped her arms around him, stroking his back as he sobbed. "My Angus, my poor man."

"Oh Sophie. It was awful."

CHAPTER 54

Pedro awakened Clyde before sunup the following morning.

Farming started early in order to take a small break midday when the sun was high and scorched already weary backs, slowing production.

The truck made two more stops to pick up men, and Clyde found himself one of eight workers heading into the fields this side of town. They were tasked with picking the early corn. The most basic food in the country was tortillas, so corn was the primary crop.

They drove for a few hours over bumpy roads that jostled the men inside the truck and caused the beige and brown dirt to invade the interior where they balanced themselves on wooden benches attached to the sides.

Clyde slept as did most of the other men. Their nostrils were caked with dirt. They rubbed their eyes to clear the dust. Nobody complained.

The truck made a wide turn around a rundown shack and continued farther to come to a dusty screeching halt. Acres of corn stood waving at the men. The burlap sacks were piled high by the squat building.

Pedro used few words. "Let's go. No early breaks."

Clyde felt like his lower back was about to jackknife. A sharp pain shot up his spine. He winced inwardly, said nothing.

He learned a long time ago, "When in Rome, do as the Romans do."

He hopped off the back of Pedro's truck, did one quick rub and push where his pants connected his butt to his back. That was it. No bitching. His gaze reconnoitered the field as he made his get-away plan. The bulk of his journey was over, or so he thought.

He had a hard square of cornbread in his pocket, compliments of Maria.

Clyde kept his head down, carried his corn sacks over one arm and headed into the tall stalks. He figured he'd be in the city before the end of the day. He patted the wads of money that bulged in his pants pockets and wiggled his toes for confirmation the large notes were in there. They were.

He started to feel real good.

CHAPTER 55

Almadine made griddle cakes and sausages and the coffee was rich, hot and plentiful. The whole household was seated.

Angus, mostly recovered from his heartbreaking ordeal, clean and rested now, dug into a pile of flapjacks with gusto.

Sophie, having heard the gruesome stories from the winery, sat somewhat subdued. She was drinking a large mug of coffee and picking at some sausage bits.

Mandy had slept at the mansion, and she and Laura kept exchanging looks that perplexed Sophie and Angus but pissed Cassy off.

Casandra knew when she was being left out of the loop.

Arriona, picking up on the tense undercurrent with the grown-ups, was uncharacteristically whiney. "I don't want sausage, just one pancake. I'm not hungry."

"Okay, honey. Almost time for school anyway," her mother coaxed.

When the table was cleared, Laura and Cassandra took off for what would be the final day of classes. The graduation ceremony would take place the following day.

"Tell me what's going on," Mandy Rose demanded. She stood up and planted her hands on the table, leaning into Angus.

Angus filled her in, making sure she knew there was no way Hannah was one of the abused unfortunate children earmarked for organ removal.

She sank into her chair, shaking her head from side to side. "Those monsters."

"I'll be glad when Laura and Cassy have their badges and can interview the rescued girls again."

"What can I do to help?"

"We have to do things by the book. Soon you'll have your degree and can talk to the girls also. Your social work skills will be helpful."

Not wanting to leave Sophie out, Angus said, "Sophie, you can continue your relationships with the other parents you're already familiar with. Some little thing could be really important."

Sophie sighed heavily and vowed to herself to do just that. She thought of Hannah again, remembering the little girls Angus had helped to rescue last night.

She wanted a drink.

CHAPTER 56

Clyde angled toward the edge of the field, picking corn in his row as he watched for an opportunity to slip away. It came up sooner than he'd expected. Hidden from the other pickers, he dropped the two almost full sacks he carried and bolted for the stretch of open field. He felt vulnerable but smelled exhaust fumes.

"Holy shit, I'm near the city." He patted his shirt pocket and gasped. It was of course the Salvation Army shirt. The pockets were low and floppy from many washings. He grabbed them both with his now free hands.

He knew his pants pockets held the rolls of cash Mandy gave him. "Where the hell is my gris-gris?" Spoken in anguish to nobody. "What's wrong with me? How could I have lost it? Fuck. Fuck. Fuck."

His mind traveled backwards in time, replaying his actions. He knew he'd had it on his lap after he escaped Bingham. Then what? The motel. It was in his pocket.

Salvation Army clothes. He'd changed in the car. Ate at K.F.C. His eyebrows rose as he remembered screwing around with Mandy Rose.

He drove while Mandy slept, passed the border patrol, then the drop-off.

"Holy fucking shit, it must be in Mandy's car."

A shroud of panic took his breath away. He kept walking. He kept sweating. He kept chastising himself.

He was grimy. He was hungry. He was without his gris-gris. The first time since his granddaddy had given it to him that he didn't know where it was.

He felt naked.

He came upon a street. It was only partially cobblestoned. The rest almost bald dirt.

The buildings were all low and made of yellow, orange or cream-colored stucco. None of them were straight; all had a directional lean.

He saw a group of young men. They saw him. His heart stopped. The sweat on him dried to a crisp.

They spoke rapidly in Spanish and sauntered toward him. Their eyes narrowed and telescoped to Clyde, spelling trouble of the worst kind. The mouths of all except one sported sinister smiles.

His bowels turned to water.

They wore demonic pointy boots, stylish and menacing. The tall bearded one removed his belt and wound it around his huge knuckles. They closed the distance between themselves and Clyde.

He heard the shortest one chuckle and say to his pals, "Gringo tienes mucho dinero. Mira el Jordans."

Shit, the fucking Jordans were gonna be his downfall.

The knot of hombres didn't hurry. No reason to. The street was empty except for one old woman in a shawl who frowned, looked at the developing scene and hurried down a narrow street. *Clop, clop, clop.*

Now it was just him and them. They closed the distance fast and surrounded him. Two grabbed him by his arms from behind, yanked his feet out from under him.

He splattered hard to the stony surface, crushing his coccyx bone. Tears sprung to his eyes. He'd never been so scared for his life.

The Jordans were being wrenched off his feet. They pulled him along, scraping his already wounded buttocks.

A war whoop! "Santa mierda."

"Miralo."

"Dinero!"

They were all over him. They tugged off his pants, rifled through his pockets, exclaiming in joyous shouts, "Santa mierda."

And in English, "Holy shit."

With raucous laughter they saw that Clyde wasn't wearing any underwear. "Ja, ja, ja. No ropa interior."

They pummeled him. First with bare knuckles, then the huge buckle was used with force, slamming into the side of the fallen man's head and crushing his temple until blood spurted all over the attacker's face and shirt and drenched Clyde's chest, which was now naked.

He was curled into a fetal position, totally naked on the ground. Pointy cowboy boots found new places to pound.

He tried to cover his head with his arms and discovered that left his testicles unguarded.

The short one, again, took advantage of this with glee and attacked with boots that had four-inch points, topped with silver caps. These boots were lethal weapons.

A second story window from the adjacent building lit up. Although no one called out to stop the slaughter, the band of attacking thieves dispersed rapidly. They knew if the polizia came all the money they'd stolen from Clyde would switch hands and would now be called "evidence."

Soon the street was barren and windows were shuttered. The dark-skinned naked man moaned; a low throaty sound. It only lasted a few seconds. His breath was precious. His testicles throbbed. He saw nothing but blackness as both eyes were swollen shut. He lay there for over an hour before a young woman dared to approach him.

She laid her fingers under his neck to feel for a pulse. Barely there. Thready, but consistent.

She called up to the man in the window she'd come from. "Pablo, come help me with him."

CHAPTER 57

The man whisper shouted through the cracked window, "Are you loca, Monica?"

"Get down here now, Pablo." She was furious he was making her repeat herself. Others might hear.

Pablo's mop of jet-black hair disappeared from the window, and he scurried down the one flight of splintery stairs that leaned to one side. Still mumbling, "Loco," he kept his body scrunched to make his young lanky six-foot plus height less of a target.

She directed, "You take his upper body, I'll grab his legs."

"Christ Monica, he's naked and he's colored."

"Yes, he's also a gringo. Grab under arms and don't let his head fall back; his neck may be broken."

Monica Garcia had taken her nephew Pablo to Mexico after he'd gotten in trouble in El Paso. Lately he was becoming more of a problem, although she loved him dearly. "Pablo, you go in first."

He shoved the building's red-painted door open with his hip as he hefted the unconscious bleeding man into the dark building. They bumped and struggled, wending his body up the narrow windowless staircase. He was dead weight.

Pablo wasn't finished complaining. "Jesus, Monica. Where we gonna put this guy?"

"Shut up and do what I say."

The door to their tiny apartment stood ajar.

"Good thinking, that," Monica said, lifting her head as she noticed Pablo had left the door open for easy entry. She caught his little pleased smile. She smiled too. Still such a baby in a grown man's body.

Pablo jutted his butt out and pushed the door open fully. One small lamp was lit using one of the only two outlets in the place the aunt and nephew called home. No lampshade; more light that way.

"Put him on the mattress."

The grouchy face returned. "What?"

"Do it."

There was no resistance from their burden. They stretched him out on one side of the mattress.

Monica said, "Heat some water and bring me a towel."

He obeyed without remarks.

After Monica washed all the visible bruises and abrasions, she covered him with a large green paisley scarf that went from his navel to above his knee.

He wasn't moving, but he was breathing. The pained look on his handsome features, softened.

"What're we gonna do with him?"

"Right now, I'm not sure. All I know is I couldn't let him die right under our window."

"Did you see all the money he had on him?"

"I saw."

"Maybe he's rich?"

"Maybe. No way to tell much except he was screaming in English and he needed help."

"Maybe he's a crook, a criminal?"

"Are you a 'criminal,' Pablo?"

Pablo shrugged his shoulders and looked down. *Point taken.* He owed Monica big time. "Mira, look, his eyelids moved."

But it was too soon for Clyde to open his eyes and face his new reality. Both lids retreated.

CHAPTER 58

Mandy Rose resumed her studies. She was in an accelerated program to get her human services degree soon with an eye toward future graduate education in psychology. She planned to be involved with Laura and Cassy in finding the missing children. *Maybe Hannah?*

Her face clouded as she thought of her little girl. It was all so long ago.

It was good to be back to her apartment. Tired after a full day in school, lugging books and big yellow legal pads, her favorite choice for writing, she trudged up the stairs.

She was hungry so wasn't altogether unhappy to see Mark coming out of his apartment with two paper bags with grease marks on their bottoms, headed for her door.

"Mark, what're you up to?"

"Dinner Mandy, dinner. A schoolgirl has to eat."

She was too exhausted to argue. If memory served, all her fridge held was a slice of pizza that would not have improved even if she nuked it.

She let him follow her into her apartment after she used her key to enter. He took all the food out of the bags and spread the feast on the kitchen table. From his back pockets he pulled two cold bottles of beer, the coup de gras. They both dug into the Chinese take-out.

Once they felt sated, Mark began the conversation he was there for. "Mandy, I know you and that Clyde guy both disappeared at the same time. Do you trust me enough to tell me what's going on?"

Mandy swallowed what she was chewing and licked her lips. Telling Laura was one thing, but Mark was a whole different story. Yet he already knew so much. She took a short sip of her almost empty beer; wished she had another.

She stalled.

He covered her cupped hand with his and connected with his eyes.

"I want to help. I care about you." He'd gotten over his mild infatuation with her sister, Laura. He did have feelings for Mandy Rose.

She blew air out through puffed lips, then gave in. "Okay, but the more you know, the more you are involved, and that could be dangerous for you."

"I'm willing to take that risk."

Mandy dabbed her mouth with the skimpy little square napkins provided with the Chinese take-out. She threw worries away and jumped into a narrative that included dropping Clyde off near the Mexican border.

Mark slept at Mandy Rose's for the first time.

CHAPTER 59

Mandy Rose opened her eyes, felt a pressure across her chest as she lay flat in her bed.

It was an arm. The arm draped over her was pale and had golden hairs that glistened as the morning sun dripped onto it. A tint of strawberry.

She turned her head to face her bunk mate. The mop of luxurious hair, also strawberry blond. The man's forehead was buried in it.

Oh my, what have I become?

She felt a stir deep in her lower abdomen. The sight of his curly reddish blond chest hair was making it difficult for Mandy to deny her strong sexual attraction to Mark. She reached her hand down, slid past her belly and let her knees drop open. Her own two fingers searched between her thighs, found the slippery liquid that was aching to prepare foolproof entry for male penetration.

Mandy sniffled and ran her hand along the silken hair on the arm that held her captive.

That was all that was needed. Mark shifted and let his arm lazily slide over Mandy's now hard and insistent nipples. With one turn his lips were on her breast and sucking mightily.

She pushed the sheet off both of them and kicked it away for total freedom.

His mouth still devoured her moist nipple; his fingers reached down between her parted thighs and slipped into her.

This caused man and woman to moan with pleasure.

Mandy threw her head back against the lavender pillow as Mark gave her nipple more attention, treating it with little bites that hurt deliciously. Perfect tiny bites. She was wildly excited. She wanted him inside her.

He rubbed the back of his hand over both nipples, back and forth, back and forth. The golden hairs on his knuckles were teasing her, driving her insane with desire, impatience and raw need. She watched him place his hands on either side of her head and rise up until his erect penis stood straight out from his slim hips. A cloud of golden hair surrounded his member.

He eased himself down to her mouth.

She eagerly welcomed him. She grabbed his well-muscled buttocks and pulled him into her mouth until her throat was so full of him, she felt a climax threatening.

But no, she wanted more.

She pushed him over on his side and presented her vagina to him for his enjoyment.

And hers.

His penis throbbed with fullness, craving release.

That was all it took. Both exploded in ecstasy. After the final throes of pleasure, they lay quietly together.

Still her vagina was wanting more.

He began to toy with her opening. First he pressed in one finger, then two, then three. He had to taste her. He licked her, letting his tongue explore up and down her rapidly, keeping one finger inside her.

She had him in her mouth again.

He pulled his penis out of her hungry mouth and flipped her over on her back. And mounted her. This was a slow and easy coupling.

He went in and out very smoothly until they both could hold off no longer.

Mandy Rose felt the explosion between her legs, in her lower belly, her butt cheeks, all the way down her thighs. He came in thunderous waves of pleasure rolling over him, and then rolling again and again.

She moaned, "Oh, Mark."

Mark answered, "Mandy. Oh God, Mandy."

Later, still in bed, she whispered, "Mark, what's happening to us?"

He answered, "Let's not try to find answers yet, let's just enjoy what we have."

That suited her just fine.

CHAPTER 60

The graduation ceremony was almost anti-climactic as Laura and Cassandra already felt like cops.

They ate, breathed and slept it.

Angus and Sophie sat in the front row on the provided metal chairs with Arriona between them. Arriona felt very grown up as she wore a blouse and a skirt, not a dress, and black patent leather shoes with gold-colored buckles.

They cheered equally for both young women. But Arriona stood on her chair, one hand on Angus's shoulder for balance, the other waving wildly as she shouted, "Yay, Mama. Woo hoo."

Sophie's blue eyes watered, and she wiped them with a pink tissue as Angus patted her knee.

He was eager to get going. There were very bad people that needed to be stopped.

Laura and Cassy now had shiny new badges and police issue Glock 22 service pistols.

Back at the house with no stops in between, they laid out their plans. No one mentioned Mandy Rose's absence.

Almadine hugged and congratulated the new cops. She also had the crawfish ready.

She used an old family recipe of garlic, corn, potatoes, sausage and lemon slices. She also favored a nice helping of cayenne pepper. The heat was turned off under the big black pot and the delicious aroma filled the air.

Arriona helped put out yellow bowls and shiny utensils.

Everybody discovered they were famished. All ate heartily, including Almadine, who never had a problem telling you she loved her own cooking.

The only liquid served was iced tea, bristling with tiny round ice cubes.

The group sat while Almadine cleared the table.

Angus jumped in before the last plate disappeared. "I have news." He had their attention.

"We have an undercover cop registered at the hotel where we believe Big Carl is staying. She's good, done undercover before and gets the job done. We've brought the desk clerk into confidence. He's young and enthusiastic, claims he wants to go to the police academy next year. So what're the odds, right?

"The night clerk is also undercover; we have all the bases covered. We want to see if Big Carl gets visitors. We also will have him followed if he leaves the hotel."

Laura and Cassy listened, both with plans of their own.

Sophie announced she was taking Arriona out for ice cream.

Cassy said, "Fine, don't let her overdo it, please."

They were already walking away, but Arriona hurried back to kiss her mother goodbye. "Bye, Mama."

"See you later, sweetheart."

Angus's head dipped as he said, "We can start questioning the kids we have. The ones we discovered last night are all still in the hospital. We can probably talk to them also but not until tomorrow or the next day. Some of these poor kids were barely alive. Apparently those devils didn't think it mattered for organ removal to keep the unwilling donors healthy.

"We'll be following up on any leads we can get. That includes you two."

Cassy eyed Angus, exclaimed, "You know we're ready. What's going on, Angus? What haven't you told us?"

Angus wiggled deeper into his seat and cleared his throat.

The brand-new cops waited.

"We have new intel. There were more lists. Some gave destinations. The individual identities are unclear because though some names are given, most are just numbers. We have a pretty good idea where the kids sold for adoption went and who they are because there are some actual names for these particular kids. Mind you, just first names, and those might be wrong."

Laura and Cassy groaned.

Angus now pulled a piece of paper from his wallet. "You both can begin by finding the parents with children that have these names. These kids have probably been missing for over two years."

Laura and Cassy exchanged a look.

Laura asked, "Why just one list? Can't we split up and cover more ground?"

"No."

"Why?"

"Because these kids are all mixed race or colored. It's better for the trust issues you'll face if you go in together."

Cassy said, "He's right, Laura."

Laura sighed, then nodded. "I guess so."

Chapter 61

Sophie knelt in front of Arriona and said, "Can you keep a secret?"

Arriona's eyes bulged with excitement. She had secrets with her friends, mostly about which boy they were in love with. Herself, she didn't care about boys. They were stupid and messy. She'd made up a boy she "liked" so she could have a "secret" too. She wondered if Gramma Sophie liked a different boy from Grampy Angus. She thought, Poor Grampy Angus.

"Sure, I'm real good at keeping secrets."

"Okay, we're going downtown and having lunch at a hotel."

"But I'm not hungry."

"That's okay, you can have a bowl of ice cream, three different flavors."

"Wow, but ice cream's not a secret." Arriona tilted her head, her little face full of curiosity.

"No, ice cream's not the secret. The secret is the hotel. We can't tell anyone we went to the hotel. Understand?"

Arriona decided adult secrets didn't make any sense, but she nodded happily, thinking only of the ice cream.

Sophie parked the Jag in the hotel's parking garage and led her little companion into the lobby.

Arriona had become more accustomed to opulence but was fascinated with the golden doors on the elevators. She longed to push those buttons. They were red, her new favorite color.

"Stand right here where I can see you, and I'll find out where the restaurant is."

Arriona's eyes were fixated on those gold doors and red buttons. While Sophie leaned forward and listened to the hotel clerk's directions, the child darted over to the elevators. The red button was within her reach and her little hand seemed to have a mind of its own. *Plunk.*

The elevator was already on the ground floor, so the doors swung open wide immediately. A bell sounded. *Ding.*

She looked inside; tiptoed in as if being quiet meant she'd be invisible.

A whole row of buttons with numbers on them. Arriona's lucky number was six and she could reach it. *Plunk.*

The doors closed with a whoosh. Now the little girl was moving up. Her face was shiny and wide-eyed. She held onto the skinny railing in the elevator as it ate up floors.

On the wall near the ceiling of the box she stood in, there was an arrow, moving in a circle. She watched, entranced, as it spun. Three, four, five, six.

The bell rang. The floor rumbled. The box stopped. She gripped the railing and Arriona wondered how she'd get back to Grammy Sophie. "Oh, why did I do this?"

She didn't like elevators. It made her head and belly feel like she had the flu. She walked through the open doors. Everywhere she looked, there were doors. Hallways and doors. Long hallways, lots of doors.

Maybe she should get back in the box, but the bell had rung and the doors were shut tight. She was scared.

One of the doors in the hallway opened. A big fat white man came out, butt first. He had something in his hand. He pushed it into the door and it made a crunchy sound. He wiggled the door's handle and it stayed closed.

He turned and saw her, and Arriona remembered all her mother's warnings. Stay away from strangers. Don't talk to them. Don't let them touch you. Run from them as fast as you can.

Her little shoulders were shaking. His eyes glistened.

The man pocketed his key and pasted on a big smile, but only his mouth grinned, his eyes terrified her. She sensed danger.

The man said in a low syrupy voice, "Hello there. Are you lost, honey?"

Arriona was frozen to the spot.

He went on, "Let me help you find your parents."

Big Carl was perplexed why a colored kid was here in this hotel. He was also seeing dollar signs. She was a real cutie, would fetch some serious buckos. Lotta white guys were partial to young Black pussy. He could take her right into his room and have a taste. Highly motivated, he moved fast.

Her adrenaline kicked in and she spun around and ran. Her legs were young and fast.

His were old and slow.

At the end of the hallway, she saw a gray door with black letters on top that read "STAIRS." She got there well ahead of the fat man and used both hands to push with her whole body on the heavy door. Luck was with her as it swung in and revealed a staircase of cement steps leading down, the direction she wanted to go.

Her Kangaroos were tied in double knots, so she wouldn't trip and helped her fly down the stairs.

The big man was behind her, huffing and puffing. He clomped down the stairs, making a racket as he hit each step. *Pound, pound, pound.*

Arriona kept seeing more stairs and didn't know where she'd be if she went through one of the doors she came to on the flat areas. She saw the number five, then four, then three, but she resisted going through those doors. Should she go through number one? Some tears had dried on her face and left chalky streaks all the way to her little determined jaw.

She stole a glance backward. He was one flight above her. He was breathing heavily, and his smile was gone. His big arms reached out with hands that were giant claws.

She didn't take the door marked one.

He didn't either.

The last door said, "LOBBY." Catching her breath between repetitive hiccups, she had no air left with which to speak. She knew to use both hands to push on the lobby door.

She heard the fat man say bad words.

The commotion she created as she slammed into the lobby was a surprise, a welcome surprise. Arriona spotted her Gramma Sophie. She was moving her arms all over and talking to a policeman. The frightened child ran straight to her gramma and barreled into her.

Sophie's face lit up and her arms opened to wrap the hurtling little girl in a safe cocoon. She smothered the child's head and face with kisses. Then her face morphed into a combination of fear and relief. "Where were you?"

Still breathless, Arriona said, "Wanted to go on the elebator."

"Why were you running?"

"Bad man after me."

The broad-shouldered cop listened, and his walkie-talkie went to his mouth to issue orders. "Lock all doors. Cover all fire-escapes. No one leaves this building. Backup needed. Ritz Hotel. Possible attempted abduction."

Sophie, holding on to Arriona, said, "Officer, can we go?"

"No, ma'am. We have to question the child. This man is probably still in the building, and he's dangerous."

Sophie understood. She said, "You think this is related to the kidnapping case going on now?"

The tall cop looked at her again. He scratched his knuckle as recognition seeped into his memory banks. "Uh, are you who I think you are?"

Sophie opened and closed her mouth, said, "Probably."

The cop said, "The Bokum woman? The grandmother?"

"Yes, that's me." She smoothed her dress down.

Then he uttered, "Angus Clark?"

She had to confess. "He doesn't know I'm here. He'll be upset about what happened today."

The cop let a held breath out and said, "I'm going to have you and this little girl go sit in the office and wait there." Sophie started to leave.

The cop added, "After we ask her a few questions to help identify the man who chased her."

The tall cop squatted to be at Arriona's level. "Honey, can you tell me what the man who was after you looked like?"

Arriona shot a look at Sophie. She'd been taught not to be racial or make fun of people.

"It's okay, sweetie. Tell the policeman exactly what he looked like."

Arriona thought it over. She wanted the bad man to go to jail. He scared her. "He was white and he was very fat." She hesitated.

Sophie said, "You're doing fine."

"Can you tell me what he was wearing?"

"He had on a white shirt on top and um maybe black pants, or dark brown."

"What color was his hair?"

"Brown and floppy, like white people's hair and a little bit bald in the front."

"That's very good."

"Now this is important. Can you remember which floor you were on when you saw him?"

Very distinctly, Arriona said, "Six, the elebator said six."

"Was he in the hallway when you first saw him?"

"Nope, he came out of a door."

The cops face lit up. "Do you know which room, which door?"

"Yep, I can show you, but I don't want to go up there by myself."

The cop patted Arriona on the head. He was beaming. His voice was full of smiles as he said, "You're gonna make a good detective."

It was her turn to beam. She said, "My mama just graduated to be a cop." Then she added, "And, my Aunt Laura."

Sophie took a deep cleansing breath. She knew Angus wouldn't be happy she'd come here. Cassy would be even more upset because she'd put Arriona in danger.

Trying to put a positive spin on it, she thought, Sounds like they have Big Carl by the short hairs.

He wouldn't make it out of this hotel.

Chapter 62

Big Carl slouched in a gray metal chair as his sausage-shaped fingers drummed on the battered wood table. The bright and shiny handcuffs spoke of new issue.

Carl Edwards never made it out of the hotel. Trapped like a rat. He was scared. Not from the police. Nope. The cartel had his bowels in a painful puddle. He eyeballed the tiny red dot near the ceiling in the corner of the room. Voyeurs.

Bam, two men charged into the room, one white and one colored.

The white guy scraped a chair up to the opposite side of the table. When he seated himself, his legs shot out and kicked Carl's crossed ankles. The cop's eyebrows shot up and his mouth twisted in mock apology. "Oh my, I'm so sorry, so very sorry, Carl."

Carl scrunched his feet in.

The colored guy leaned against the wall with one shoulder and folded his beefy arms. His dark eyes shone with pure hatred. "So Carl, what? You can't get a grown-up woman. You like little girls?"

Carl's jaw sunk in.

The cop continued. "Or maybe you prefer young boys?"

"You better talk to us if you ever want to see life outside of steel bars again."

"I want a lawyer."

"Are you sure, Carl? Are you really sure? This is your only chance to help us; maybe get a lighter sentence, if what you tell us helps us get those pricks."

Carl blew air through flattened lips, stopped drumming his pudgy fingers. "What do you mean?"

"What we mean, Carl, is give us some names and addresses, and we'll put in a good word about how cooperative you've been and how much we appreciated it."

Carl looked down. He was caught between a rock and a hard place. "Can you keep my name out of the papers? Do I have to testify in court?"

"For a guy in handcuffs, you've got a lot of questions."

"Here's what I recommend." Now it was the other cop speaking. He placed both hands, fingers splayed on the table, and jammed his face less than a foot from Carl's nose. "For now, your ass is safe from your perverted colleagues. Give us a place to start. Don't wait till someone else starts singing. We won't need you then."

Carl twisted his whole face; swallowed noisily. "Can I have some coffee?"

"Sure, Carl. That gonna help you fuckin' talk?"

Carl knew he was cornered. "I'll talk."

"Don't you fuckin' lie either. Whatever you had in your hotel room is either on its way here or is already here. That includes your little video collection. There'll be a preview tonight. No popcorn. Want a front row seat, Carl?"

The fat man practically wrenched his neck looking over his shoulder, away from his two interrogators.

The sandy-haired cop slapped down a pad of paper and a ballpoint pen and spun it to face Carl, whose face now resembled a sweaty beet.

Carl grasped the pen as though it might jump up and stab him in his carotid artery. Without much of a pause, he started writing.

Scratch, scratch, scratch, the blue pen made marks on the white page. The author looked in the air, furrowed his brows, then penned some more. Fat fingers turned the page. A veritable fountain, spewing feces.

James and Joe exchanged a practiced cop look; their eyes screamed. *The mother lode.*

CHAPTER 63

Carl was yanked up by his elbow, escorted back to his cell; never got his coffee.

James and Joe responded to a call informing them that three videos were about to be shown in the audio-visual room. They tightened their stomachs and entered the small, darkened room. The VCR was lit. Both men had daughters under the age of six. James one and Joe three little girls. They sat down with Officer Angus Clark and Officer Janet Marsh.

Janet pushed the video in, holding the thing like it was a dead rat. She sat back down, crossed her legs.

The light from the video played across the faces of the cops who all looked like they didn't want to be there. First came a blue background. Three words written in red. A child-like scrawl. *Come Play with Me.*

The opening scene is a room, the only furnishing a double bed. The beige walls are streaked in places, possible water damage.

On the bed is a child. Her eyes are pale gray and huge. She's wearing pink lace panties and ballerina slippers, also pink. The little face has well-rouged cheeks and the lips are colored a vibrant hot-pink. She stares past the camera with haunted eyes, frightened beyond belief.

It isn't hard to know she watches her capturer to see what she will be instructed to do.

Fear is a formidable taskmaster.

Her blonde kinky hair in a topknot on her head wobbles when she moves her knees and pulls her only covering, the tiny pink panties, down to the black sheets. She's exposed.

"I've seen enough."

Janet jumped up to obey Angus's outcry. She promptly ejected the disturbing image.

"I'd like to fry those bastards."

Joe said, "That piece of shit Carl gave us names and places. Most of them in abandoned industrial park areas."

Angus said, "Let's move fast. These kids are earmarked for sex trafficking, not to be destroyed for organ removal."

"I want no mistakes. And I don't want them to be warned, so we're hitting more than one at the same time."

Janet queried, "But do we have the manpower?" Janet never minded the term "manpower."

Angus, in command, said, "We need a heavy hitter for each strike and enough firepower to back our attack. They need to know we aren't fucking around. We hit tomorrow night. James, get those addresses typed up and have clerical put directions on the same sheet."

Angus barked, "Bulletproof vests. Tomorrow we strike."

CHAPTER 64

"Monica, you're gonna bring trouble down on us, having this guy here. This morning, getting coffee at the bodego, two of these malos hombres were there, hanging out, bragging about what they did to this dude and all the money they took off him, in the thousands."

Monica's eyes widened. "You don't say?"

"Yeah, they also were yapping about getting a 'ransom.'"

"Oh?"

"Yes, but they're small potatoes, shit for brains. I don't think they're *connected*. I worry they'll come here."

"Pablo, he's well-hidden. I don't think you need to be concerned." Monica didn't want her cousin going off half-cocked, maybe doing something that made those creeps come to her door. She wouldn't admit it to Pablo, but she was also worried.

Thump. Thump. She heard a clomping noise coming up the stairs and hurried into the teeny bano where the tall handsome stranger lay with his knees up in the ancient bathtub. She yanked the aqua shower curtain around the metal ring and sequestered the supine form. It wasn't perfect, but the man had settled right in after she and Pablo lifted him and trudged the few steps from the mattress to the bathroom. He never woke. Monica thought, Sleeping beauty.

Monica bent over to study the features of the man she'd been harboring for over twenty-four hours. Sensing her, he blinked and worked his mouth in movements, suggesting a lack of moisture.

What was she doing? She wanted him to speak. She wanted him to be on his way.

Clyde looked up at her and spoke for the first time since he'd been pummeled nearly to death. "Where am I?"

Before she answered, he added with rounded eyes, "Who are you?" His arms began to pinwheel as he struggled to sit up in the cramped tub. He tried to put his elbows on the edges to lift himself.

"Hmmmm, you're lucky no broken arms, mister."

He stared at her. Then he looked down to see his nakedness and let his head drop back against the tub, followed by his elbows. He opened his mouth and furrowed his brows as memory drifted back to him. "Oh my God, you saved my life, didn't you?"

"Si, probably."

"Why?" He switched to Spanish. "Por que?"

Monica said, "I speak English. I'm from the States."

Clyde sighed. When he took a deep breath, he felt a strong pinch on his side and yelped.

She said, "Broken ribs, maybe more than one… maybe three."

"Why did you help me?" he persisted.

Her eyes misted. "You needed help. I was there."

Pablo listened at the door and spoke through the opening, "Those hombres took a lot of money off you. They want more. If they can find out who your relatives are, they'll ask for ransom."

"For now, they don't know where you are, but they're pretty sure you're alive. Those greedy bastards won't let this rest."

Just then there was a heavy knock at the door. *BAM, BAM, BAM.*

Pablo said, "Holy shit!"

Monica whispered, "Get out there and answer it, follow my lead."

Pablo chimed, "Un minuto."

Taking his time to get there, he opened the door. It was the short fat one. "Si?"

The fat bully stood with legs spread and arms akimbo. A small cuchillo sat in a leather sheath and hung from the belt that encircled him below his bloated belly. The knife glittered, looked razor sharp.

Pablo knew the worst thing was to show fear. He said in Spanish, "What do you want?"

"I want to find a gringo Negro." The porky man shoved his whole body into the small apartment.

Pablo puffed out his chest, stood to his full height and barked, "Nobody like that here."

"What's behind that door?"

"My cousin is on the toilet."

The man strode to the bathroom and hammered the door with meaty fists.

Monica said, "What do you want, Pablo? I got my period, bleeding a lot. Leave me alone."

Porky's face fell. He grimaced with undisguised revulsion and backed away. Not one more word was uttered as he retraced his path and raced out the door.

Once safely in the hallway he stopped and in a low gruff voice said, "You better not be lying to me, boy."

Pablo knew better than to answer.

<h1 style="text-align:center">CHAPTER 65</h1>

"I want her brought here to me. I'm not going back there to that hellhole of a back building."

"Yes, sir." Mabel Casner hastened to have Dr. Romero's order followed. Pressing buttons on her desk phone, she called the wall phone in the back building. She waited, tapped her short, but well-manicured, fingernails on her leather jacketed logbook, took solace in the crisp clacking sound.

After seven rings, Blade answered, "Yeah?"

"Who is this?"

"Uh, this's Blade, ma'am. What can I do for you?"

"What you can do for me is bring that young woman, Rosie, for Doctor Romero."

"Right now?"

"Yes, right now, and the sooner the better."

"Right-o, ma'am."

Mabel hung up, not looking forward to seeing Blade again, but curious as all hell to meet Rosie.

Fifteen minutes later, not Blade, but Sam entered. He held a slight woman in a long gray shapeless dress by her elbow.

She was gawking at everything. She seemed delighted in her unfamiliar surroundings. Her eyes sparkled. The young woman groomed herself with her hands, like manic butterflies flying all over, pressing down her dress and smoothing back her unruly carrot-colored hair. Her eyes shifted left to right and back again, over and over.

Mabel announced their arrival.

When Romano answered on the phone system, Rosie broke from Sam and charged over to it;

to inspect the magical box that talked. Her eyes shone. "Wow." She touched it reverently, to see if it would talk again.

Louder now, Romano ordered, "I said bring her in here."

Rosie jumped back, knocking Sam almost off his balance. He grabbed Rosie's hand, led her into the doctor's office and closed the door behind them. He could still hear Slade's orders, "Don't leave Rosie alone with Romero. I mean it."

"Not you."

Sam tried once, "But Doctor, what if Rosie gets…"

He never finished as Dr. Romero howled, "I said not you. Get out of here."

Sam obeyed, backed all the way out.

Rosie was in a state of ecstasy. She'd been in that back building since she was nine years old, never had a visitor or seen anything else in all of her life that she could remember.

"Sit down, Rosie."

"Where? On the floor?"

"Take that comfy chair right there." He pointed.

She backed into it and plopped down.

"Now, missy…"

"Nope, my name's Rosie."

Dr. Romero folded his hands on his desk and leaned toward her. *She seemed pretty lucid.*

"Um, Rosie, do you know why I've asked you to come here today?"

She crossed her eyes and assumed a scholarly pose, obviously straining to find the correct answer. "Nope, nope, nope. I'm such a dope, dope, dope."

"Okay," he continued. "Do you remember a man, a colored man who lived where you live?"

"Where I do? With me?"

"Yes, but not in your same cell… uh room," he corrected himself.

Her eyes crossed again and she leaned onto one knee, placed her chin in her cupped hand.

Dr. Romero was reminded of Rodin's *The Thinker*. "Rosie, try to remember this man; a colored man."

"Can I have some chocolate if I remember?"

Romero was getting impatient. "Yes, yes, all the chocolate you want."

"With nuts?"

"Yes, yes, nuts too."

That struck a funny note in the doctor's frontal lobe.

Rosie snuggled into the cushiony chair and sang, "Clyde, Clyde, Clyde's inside."

The doctor cocked his head to one side and in a coaxing, almost erotic, voice mimicked, "Clyde, Clyde, where inside?"

Rosie was enchanted. Perked up, she took up the duet. "Clyde, Clyde, let's slide over to Clyde."

Doctor's turn. "Clyde, Clyde, where inside?"

Rosie was jubilant, eyes shiny, lips dripping with drool. "Clyde, Clyde, let's give Clyde a ride."

Romano took up the amended chorus. "Clyde, Clyde, where inside?"

It wasn't lost on him that his professional reputation rode on this insane exchange.

Rosie held her belly and let forth a volley of rapturous zany laughter. Beyond excited now, she bellowed, "Clyde, Clyde, gonna ride."

This left an opening and the good doctor also bellowed, "Clyde, Clyde, gonna ride."

Now Rosie rubbed her forehead and looked for all the world like she just won the lottery. A little softer, she wailed, "Clyde, Clyde, not inside."

He let her relax. Her shoulders drooped and her head hung to her chest.

Almost funereal, she whispered, "Clyde, Clyde, not inside." Then she clammed up. No amount of cajoling or promising of chocolate treats would unlock the caverns of her mind again.

She closed her eyes and tucked her legs up under her buttocks, somehow aware enough to pull her dress down over her knees in modesty.

Dr. Romero never completely satisfied his fascination with the phenomenon called "mental illness." The interrogation was over. He'd try again. He replayed her last ditty. "Clyde, Clyde, not inside."

"What did she see?"

CHAPTER 66

Monica spooned weak tortilla soup into a bowl and carried it into the bathroom where Clyde lay sleeping in the tub.

She knelt and balanced the bowl in one hand while pulsing the slumbering man's shoulder with her free hand.

His eyes shot open; a disoriented stare skimmed the cracked and stained ceiling.

Monica knew his name now and she used it. "Clyde, wake up."

His head turned to look at her astonishingly beautiful face. "Monica," he said in one breath.

"You need nourishment to get your strength back." That's all she told him for now.

"I hope your cousin didn't mind lending me his pants and tee shirt?" he asked. Clyde hated charity.

"He knows you couldn't leave here in your birthday suit." Her mind pictured that birthday suit with a jolt of desire deep in her groin. She flushed brilliantly.

He noticed.

"I can feed myself now." He needed to get his life back. His ribs were still tender, but he felt better every day.

Monica was increasingly attracted to this tall handsome Negro as she got to know him. She handed him the bowl of soup and spoon and left him to deal with it.

The one other room in the apartment tripled as kitchen, bedroom and living room. It left little personal space. No privacy, except for the bathroom. Monica and Pablo had to pull the curtain against Clyde to do their toilet functions.

Pablo, with much bitching and resistance, assisted Clyde in relieving himself.

It was not a pleasant living arrangement.

Monica waited tables in a nearby restaurant. Take-home leftovers were a staple for her and Pablo.

Pablo took odd jobs, though not enough to support himself. He was gone most days; making Clyde wait until he returned to urinate.

Monica, alone in the living room portion, looked at their lamp that was their only source of light. It was crooked, leaned to the left. As she moved to set it straight, she felt a new heft to it.

"What?" she spoke out loud. The bottom of this lamp was hollowed out and normally didn't weigh much. She turned it over and peered inside. Crumpled papers were stuffed up the center of the old lamp.

"Could only be Pablo." She poked her fingers in and grasped the ball of note paper, unraveled it and smoothed it out on her lap to decipher the scratchings.

Numbers, figures, divided by five.

Monica knew Pablo was restless, wanting to break free. He'd stated that he felt safe from the American authorities and craved a life of his own.

"Well, I do too," she thought out loud. She was tired of taking care of a full-grown man as her life passed her by. She could go back to the States if and when she was free of him. She wasn't wanted by the police.

These notes were suspicious. *Was he going to team up with those men who beat Clyde nearly to death?*

The papers in her hands looked like a plan to get money. But how? After mulling it over, she decided she'd take Clyde into her confidence. Time was of the essence.

At that exact moment, Pablo burst into the apartment.

Monica tightened her fingers, squeezed the crumpled papers into her fist. She put both hands in her lap, the empty one folded over the one full of incriminating notes.

"What's wrong with you?"

"Nothing, why?" Monica answered, keeping her voice neutral.

"You look like you just seen a ghost." Pablo strode over to the one closet and pulled out a fancy blue shirt that had embroidery on the front yoke. He threw his dirty tee shirt on Monica's lap. "Wash that, will yah?"

Her heart was thumping in a tightened chest. She had to play it cool, appear her usual helpful self.

"Sure Pablo, no hay problema."

He took stock of himself in the cracked mirror over the small table that held the lamp.

Monica stopped breathing.

Patting his hair down on both sides, satisfied with his appearance, he turned to leave in his clean blue shirt, rolling the sleeves up to his elbows as he walked.

"Will you be home for supper?"

He gave a dirty smile. "No, I may not come home at all, then again, I might."

Monica heaved a sigh of relief when she heard the door slam. She waited five minutes, then went into the bathroom.

Clyde was wide awake, the tortilla soup bowl empty, the spoon in it. "I feel great, Monica. I want to leave."

"Good, that's exactly what I came in here to tell you. We both need to get out of here."

"What?"

"My cousin's planning, with those guys who attacked you, to make money off of you."

Clyde's sharp mind calculated the schemes that might be afoot. He said, "Help me get out of this fucking tub." Then he said, "Do you have any money?"

"I have a paycheck to cash and some tips, not a lot."

"That'll do. Where can we go so I can use a phone?"

"I have a friend, Leticia. Pablo doesn't know her. I never trust him around pretty women. Rape often goes unpunished around here." Her face paled with a sordid memory.

Clyde shuddered. He liked this woman. "Do you have shoes for me?"

"Yes, an old pair of Pablo's boots."

"Good, get them and the money and let's boogie."

She leaned her body close to the recovering man as his large fingers covered her shoulder and pressed down for leverage. She could smell his personal scent.

One long leg straddled the edge of the tub and stopped; Clyde fought a bout of vertigo. The second his vision cleared the other leg came over.

She grabbed both of his shoulders, made him sit on the toilet.

"I'll get the boots. Stay there."

She returned with brown scuffed chukka boots and a handful of coins in a gray sock.

Together they got the boots fitted to his naked feet. He said in response to her concerned look, "Forget the socks. Don't need 'em."

Monica said, "He might not be alone when he gets back here. He knows you're feeling stronger."

"I'll pay you back, Monica."

"Never mind that now. Let's go." She smiled and copied his phrase that she liked. "Let's boogie."

The door slammed a second time.

CHAPTER 67

Sophie was alone in the mansion. The only sounds were the crackling minutiae of the central air conditioning and the newly installed lighting system. She felt left on the shelf.

There was a bottle of cold tonic in the fridge and Monkey Gin in the cupboard. Yes, and even bright green limes, thinly sliced the way she always preferred them. She'd sliced them herself.

Ice cubes? Yep.

"Maybe just one."

She checked her belt to see which notch it was in. The fold where it had been comfortable only two weeks ago stared daggers at her.

"Oh pooh, just one."

She sidled over to the liquor cabinet, reached behind the open bottle of Monkey 47 to the one in back with the handsome cork-like top and pawed it until she grabbed it by the neck.

She headed to the fridge.

She half hummed and half sang an old favorite of hers. "You always hurt the one you love, the one you shouldn't hurt at all. You always take the sweetest rose and crush it… hmmmm, hmmmm." She stopped. She'd heard herself.

She repeated, "Crush it." She hummed those two words. "Hmmm, hmmm, Crush it."

Sophie ran back to the cabinet where the door hung open, accusing her. She shoved the still capped bottle of gin back in, making several other bottles of less enticing brews topple.

"No gin," she told herself.

Into the library she went. She took out an *Encyclopedia Britannica* and a thick pad of lined paper from the massive mahogany desk. She thumbed the pages of the correct volume until she came to "Sex Trafficking in America."

184

To make the research less stressful, she went to the refrigerator and pulled out a nicely chilled bottle of Pino Grigio. She chose a civilized wine glass and toddled back to the over-sized desk. The wine poured and tested, she wet her finger and leafed through the lightweight papers until she had what she wanted.

Maybe I could be of more help finding Hannah if I knew more about what happens to children when they're taken.

As Sophie read and drank and drank and read, she felt herself being ground to a pulp. "Human trafficking in the United States generates billions of dollars for the traffickers. One victim can generate up to $300,000.

"Every thirty seconds someone new is forced into sex trafficking. It's the fastest growing criminal industry in the world. Much of it is underreported.

"Age of females used, averages eleven–thirteen years old. For males, this tends to be younger. Infants, toddlers and young children are subject to rape in the porn industry. This includes boys and girls. Violence has increased and videos continue to depict more and more rape and torture of children.

"Sex trafficking is the most common form of trafficking in the United States. The USA leads the world in pornography production and distribution; one of the leading causes for demand and the purchase of children is for sex.

"Our American children are bought and sold in the commercial sex industry every day."

Sophie's eyes were flooded with salty shame. *It's my fault Hannah was taken. If I wasn't so wrapped up in my own self, my own problems, I would've checked on her earlier. I would've scared the rat away. She'd be with us all now. I hate myself.*

Sophie pushed the leather-bound volume as far away from her as her arm could reach. She scraped the heavy desk chair back and went to the refrigerator once again. She thanked the Pinot Grigio for giving her a good head start as she tucked the bottle of tonic water under her arm and bumbled over to the liquor cabinet.

The gin was right where she'd left it.

<h1 style="text-align:center">CHAPTER 68</h1>

The squad room was abuzz with excitement. Faces were animated in anticipation of a three-part sting. With destinations confirmed, the despicable sex traffickers were to be apprehended and the children they held captive, rescued.

The three videos retrieved from Big Carl's hotel room had been viewed and more than one officer had to look away while they watched children; little girls and boys, with innocent, still-squeaky voices, be exploited and debased. Tiny still-hairless bodies positioned to expose their undeveloped genitals.

The cherubic faces looked lost and alone. The silent screams begged, "Please help me."

Tonight was the night; the first of many. Three dungeons of horror were earmarked for a "Blue Blitzkrieg." They intended to fill the cells.

Secrecy was imperative. The element of surprise was their tactical weapon. Every man and woman listened intently to Angus.

He stood on both feet by a whiteboard and pointed to the three objectives targeted for tonight. His face was haggard from lack of sleep, but his jaw was set in steel and his eyes were hard-boiled. "I don't want to say this more than once. *DO NOT LEAVE HERE WITHOUT YOUR BULLETPROOF VEST.*"

Then he bowed his head and said, "We all miss Officer Hugo. Victor was a good cop, honest and brave and dedicated." He looked up to see each and every cop with bowed heads and clasped hands and continued. "We take three unmarked. We leave in one hour. You all know who you're traveling with, and you should all have memorized the directions.

"I want these stings to happen simultaneously. I want no warning phone calls. Understood?"

A low rumbling of yeses and nodding heads assured Angus the teams were ready.

Captain Sloane entered the room, stopped next to Angus, who stepped back to give him the floor.

"Hang on. I have one thing to say."

Everyone stopped shuffling and talking and gave their attention to the man who held it all together, a man they respected.

Sloane's face was tight with determination. "Bring those bastards down and make sure every one of you returns in one piece. That's it."

The cops dispersed. Most went to their lockers where they stored their Kevlar vests. Some had to procure their bulletproof vest from the supply window. The chatter continued, postulating about the imminent offense operation.

All were eager but knew there could be violence and gunfire as these bastards were confronted. Officer Victor Hugo's murder at the hands of these criminals was also in the back of their minds. The squad room settled into quiet as each group clumped together with the others traveling in the same vehicle.

Angus surveyed the group and was satisfied with what he saw. He waved his hand and announced, "Let's move."

They trundled out to their respective cars and piled in. Doors shut with loud thumps. The three unmarked exited the police station parking lot. Two went right and one left.

The station was located almost in the center of the three destinations.

Angus drove to his quarry, thinking about Sophie. She'd seemed preoccupied lately. As he came to the industrial park area where he was headed, he noted the few streetlights that provided illumination were skimpy and yellow and there were long empty stretches with no lights at all. Obviously the bulbs had been destroyed. Probably shot out.

It was inky dark. The brick buildings looked ominous with only a half moon and a few scattered stars to give them shape. Hard to see any numbers, but coming up on the right was a lot with two vans and two cars parked in front. The building was lit from within. It had to be the place. The other buildings were completely dark.

Angus said, "Ninety-nine percent sure this is it. We go in by the side door, weapons drawn. We move fast. Shoot if necessary."

He cut the engine and coasted to the side of the creepy brick structure. They piled out and went low, bent knees and weapon held in front of them with both hands. Heads swiveled in all directions. No movement other than their own was detected.

The door to the building was dirty and slightly ajar. "Those sons of bitches were so fucking arrogant and cocksure, they assumed they were safe, didn't even close the fucking door."

Angus put the side of his finger to his lips and shushed the pissed off cop.

The four cops slipped into the hallway where crying could be heard, coming from a room to the left.

Straight ahead, down the corridor, voices of men rumbled, one man louder than the others.

Angus opened the door to the room that held children. Again, he put his finger to his lips and said, "Shhhhh." Softly he said, "You're gonna be okay. We're gonna get you out of here."

The kids ranged from a couple of boy toddlers to at least eight girls aged anywhere from four to eleven or twelve. Their eyes were saucers, wet saucers. One of the older girls said, "They'll kill us. They have guns."

"Shhhh, don't talk. You take everyone into the corner there and stay there. No noise please."

Her skinny arms went around the shoulders of the other bigger girls, and she said, "Help me do this."

They listened to her. The children were bundled together and pressed into the dark corner that now looked like Dante's Inferno, a conflagration of named arms and legs; bony limbs sticking out in unusual protuberances.

Angus smiled broadly at the Alpha female. "Great, keep them all right in the corner."

Some of the little ones began to moan. He gave them one more stern, "Shhhh."

Inside the office at the end of the hall, one of the men said, "Do you hear that?"

"No, what?"

"Those brats have stopped whining."

"Well, what did you inject them with?"

"Nothing, I didn't. It's just weird, why they got so fucking quiet."

The cops were ready. All four at once crashed through the flimsy door, screaming, "Police, get your hands up."

The caught men all went for their weapons. This wasn't going to be a cake walk. One of them got a shot off.

At the same second Detective Alfred Watts fired into the foot of the man who was cupping the grip of his 38 revolver. It never left its holster.

A shot fired from the pistol of the tall skinny man who stood by the old metal desk.

Ping!

Smart son of a bitch aimed for Angus's neck, missed his jugular, but took a nasty bite out of his shoulder.

Angus resisted the urge to grab at his wound, kept his gun aloft.

Alfred got another shot off, clipped the man's hand and the Glock flew into the air, hitting the dirty wall and just missing a hole that revealed gray wooden slats.

The remaining men abandoned their guns and reached for the high ceiling.

Officer Tony Sirico was confidently reciting their Miranda rights.

Officer Judith Heinz and Alfred Watts were making delicious rattling noises. The metal cuffs signaled bad news to the miserable recipients. They were clamped on wrists that'd been yanked roughly behind bowed backs and snapped in place with loud clicks that screamed success.

Angus was on his Rover, not possible to keep the jubilant note from his voice. "Captain Sloane, Angus Clark here. Takedown point one. Four men apprehended, all alive and cuffed."

There was a pause while Angus listened. "Yes sir, at least a dozen children. All appear healthy. Will wait here for vans. Recommend medic to be on board." Another short pause. "Thank you, sir."

Angus took a gander at his shoulder. Bright red and wet. He smelled the coppery scent of his own blood. The sharp sting now asserted itself.

"How're you doing, Angus?" Judy was eyeing the spreading crimson that stopped just short of the vest that kept it corralled and may have saved Angus Clark's life.

The van's sirens bellowed as they screamed into the back lot.

"I'm okay. Judy, go check on the kids please."

She left after patting Angus's uninjured shoulder.

The doors slammed open, aides and auxiliary personnel came in on a trot. They were carrying six-packs of water and what looked like wrapped po'boys in baskets.

Angus followed the route Judy'd just taken to the room where the kids were still shrunken into the corner.

The older girl Angus discovered later was named Chrissy Brindisi. She was facing the group of children, murmuring soothing words of comfort. He heard her say, "We'll all be okay now. We'll go home to our families."

He stood aside as the new arrivals set the baskets of food in front of the children and opened bottles of water.

Chrissy jumped right in, unwrapping the spicy scented po'boys and handing them out with napkins under them.

Angus thought of Sophie again. *Wow, she's right. Food is very healing, works miracles.*

He knew he had to get his shoulder examined, but all he wanted to do was go home. Home to Sophie.

CHAPTER 69

Clyde and Monica knocked on the purple door of a well-kept white stucco house.

In the front yard, squatted a child all alone. The child wore blue coveralls and a white tee shirt. Bits of straight black hair peeked out from under a straw hat, like a buried whist-broom. The kid twisted to observe the visitors. The ruthless afternoon sun caused the big brown eyes to narrow into slits.

Monica smiled and said, "Hola muchacho."

The boy ignored the greeting and went back to drawing in the sand with a pocketknife.

The purple door swung open and an attractive, thirtyish woman in a blue and green formfitting dress exclaimed, "Monica. Come in, come in."

"Gracias, Leticia. My friend needs to sit. Okay?"

"Si, of course. Señor, sit in this comfortable chair." She waved her hand toward a large brown armchair.

Clyde was wilting fast and welcomed the overstuffed corduroy chair she offered. He sank into it and was acutely embarrassed to be so weak in the company of two such beautiful women.

Monica took over the situation. "Leticia, this is Clyde Boudreaux."

Clyde raised his hand then dropped it.

"We need to find a place to hide. My friend is from the States. He was beaten almost to death by those assholes that hang with Jerome Rodriguez."

Leticia moaned. "He's bad news."

Monica nodded and said, "El asesino."

"So, you understand we had to leave. We have a little money but need to borrow more. Clyde has friends with means, so it will be paid back, with interest."

Clyde sat up at the mention of his name and interjected, "Yes, I can

191

get more money. Those bastards took every cent I had on me. Now they want to feather their nests with my blood."

Leticia bit her lip, then said, "I would want you to leave as soon as possible. The child you just met is my daughter."

At this, Clyde and Monica looked quizzically at each other.

Leticia continued. "I know. I dress her in boys clothing to keep her safe. She's only allowed where I can see her, and she never talks to strangers. Monica, you know what I do for a living. I hate it, but it's the only way I can provide for me and Lily."

Monica tilted her head and put her hand out to touch her friend's arm.

Clyde was totally awake now and addressed his benefactress. "You'll get every penny back, double or more. We'll leave as soon as it's dark. We don't want to endanger you or your daughter. If you can and are willing to help us, we can use enough money to tide us over for a few days."

Leticia said, "Let's eat now. I have a customer due at nine-thirty tonight. I make sure Lily's asleep before they come."

The plan was taking shape.

Leticia jumped as though struck by a bolt of lightning. "Lily." She bolted to the door, pushed it open with brute force. The sun poured into the room, filling it with daylight.

The little girl who'd been reveling in having more time outdoors than she was accustomed to, knew her fun was over. "Que pasa, Mama?"

"Nada, nada."

The girl allowed her hand to be taken and brought speedily into the casa. Company during the day was cause for curiosity, but Lily held her tongue.

Speaking in Spanish, the mother told the child to wash her hands and then help set the table so everyone could enjoy a nice meal together.

Lily's eyes sparkled. She'd never seen a colored man before. Being color-blind, he looked bright red all over to her. It was a remarkable sight.

As she laid out the plates and forks, she kept stealing glances at him until her mother reminded her it was impolite to stare.

There was leftover chicken, amazingly fluffy rice and spicy pinto beans. None of the dishes matched; neither did the tall glasses that held the icy cerveza.

Lily had cold milk in the same type of beer glass.

It was a pleasant convivial meal, despite the underlying atmosphere of danger and intrigue. The dishes were all piled into the deep aluminum sink; one of Leticia's greatest treasures.

Lily proved to be a very engaging child and delighted everyone when on her own, she gave Monica and Clyde hugs and voiced her fond farewell. "Adios Monica, linda mujer, y adios mi amigo, rojo hombre."

Tucked into her twin bed with the storage drawer underneath, Lily slipped easily into undisturbed slumber. The right of every child.

"Did you take a taxi here?"

"Yes, but is there a bus where we're going?"

"You can take a bus almost to the door. Can you walk a bit Clyde?"

"Yes, I feel a lot stronger after the rest and good food."

Always the charmer, Clyde.

"All right, here is where you have to go. Tell them I sent you and pay them upfront."

"How far is it from here?"

"You'll arrive at the hacienda in about forty-five minutes. Some of the buses are old school buses. Doesn't matter. Only two things matter. One, keep your money securely taped to your body but have your correct bus fare already in your hand. Two, don't talk to anyone, no matter how friendly they seem.

"Clyde, you're a red herring." They all laughed and broke the tension. "Seriously Clyde, keep your hat low, hide your hands and say little, or better, say nothing."

"Got it. Thank you so much, Leticia. I'll get your money to you as soon as possible."

Monica and Leticia hugged for almost half a minute.

"The bus stop is less than a quarter of a mile up this road. God speed."

The pair trundled off. The fine meal did give Clyde an energy boost that felt like a minor miracle.

The bus ride was uneventful. Monica and Clyde ignored the curious glances; in some cases, suspicious gawking.

It was dark when the duo tapped on the door of the address Leticia'd given them.

They soon realized they'd be sharing a double bed.

Neither minded.

CHAPTER 70

Stale beignets and instant coffee in Mandy Rose's kitchen was as good a place as any for Mark to broach the subject he wanted to discuss.

From Mandy's perspective, she wondered if she'd already told Mark too much. His handsome Robert Redford face looked serious as he swallowed the recently dunked beignet. She steeled herself for the questions she knew were coming next.

He jumped in. "I want to be sure I understand. So you actually, after helping this Clyde fellow to escape a mental institution, brought him to an illegal entry point into Mexico?"

Mandy's back tightened. Her voice raised, she threw down the half-eaten pastry and said, "I told you, those two aides, or whatever those creeps were, said they were going to murder him the next morning. What else could I do?"

Mark wanted to be fair but had to give his honest appraisal. "Well, you could've called the police."

"No, I wasn't going to do that. I went there because I had to see him, make sure he was okay."

"And was he… okay?"

"He was after he got out of that horrible dungeon."

Mark twisted his jaw, not sure how to go on. *What have I got myself into*? What he said was, "Mandy, are you still in love with him?"

"I don't know. I don't know anything anymore. I only knew I couldn't leave him there."

Mark took a breath. "Can you tell me again how he got out of his cell?"

"I can't explain it any better. I had his Voodoo charm, his gris-gris, and I pushed it through the slot in the cell door." Mandy's face became still. "An unearthly light spread through his cell. I could make out his rumpled cot. Clyde's face shone like an angel's. He took it completely in stride when that heavy metal door just floated open like a gossamer wing."

"Then what happened?"

"Then we ran. And one more thing. There was a young woman who also saw all of this."

"So there was a witness?"

"Yes."

"All right, we have to decide what to do next. Is there any way you can contact Clyde Boudreaux?"

Mandy answered, "Only if he calls Laura."

Mark took in Mandy's concerned face and came to his own disturbing conclusion. He was in love with her. "Mandy, we should talk to Laura too, in case he calls her. I do know Mexico can be a very dangerous place. He may not be as safe there as you think. If that wad of cash he's carrying gets spotted…" Mark let the sentence hang in the air

Mandy was quiet now; subdued.

Clyde, Mark… Mark… Clyde. Her head was ready to explode. She gave it a mighty shake, like a lioness chastising its cub. The clearing felt like a storm cloud being chased by a sudden wind. "We have to confer with Laura and also Angus."

Mark said, "Agreed, all this secrecy won't lead to anything productive."

Mandy felt lighter and said, "Let's do it today. Let's shower, change and head to the mansion."

Mark raised an eyebrow at Mandy's reference to her home as "The Mansion."

They had a direction now. *Would it help this mess?*

CHAPTER 71

It was the middle of the night in a small town in Mexico, and two people had just made love in a double bed.

One high window allowed a silver beam of moonlight to enter the dingy single room. The two bars on the window made dark shadowy paths on the tattered coverlet that sheltered the new lovers.

Her slender fingers trailed along the hard jaw of the man lying so close to her. "Clyde, are you sleeping?"

"No."

"Can I ask you a question?"

"I guess so."

Monica waited, then she plunged in. "What was your crime that sent you to Mexico?"

"It's kind of complicated."

"Most things are. Please tell me."

"I was in an institution." He stopped.

"You mean, you were in jail?"

"Not exactly."

"What exactly?"

"A mental institution, but I wasn't psychotic, just faking it."

He heard her breathing as she hesitated to form her next question. "Why were you there?"

Clyde's turn to hesitate.

"Clyde?"

"I poisoned a very bad woman who was involved in sex trafficking of children and organ trafficking; again of children. I changed my mind about hurting her, but it was too late. I couldn't stop it."

"Ay dios."

Monica laid her palm on Clyde's chest and felt the steady rhythmic thump of his heart. The heart of a good man.

Clyde turned to her and murmured, "Let's get some sleep. We'll talk more about this another time." He breathed in her female scent, savoring the sweet honeysuckle aroma, then pulled her to him.

The content woman burrowed in. She said to his warm naked shoulder, "Yes, tomorrow we'll talk more."

He was already in that place between waking and sleeping where all things are possible.

CHAPTER 72

Angus's shoulder was wrapped tightly, and he was handed some pain pills by the emergency room physician.

"I won't need these, Doc," Angus protested and thrust the little brown pill bottle back at the doctor, who's face showed wide eyes and raised brows.

"Not now maybe, but that shoulder's going to throb later and you need to get some sleep. The pills will help with that also."

Angus knew he'd be back at the precinct early the next morning. He wanted to interrogate the men who had been holding the children captive. "Goddamn sex traffickers," he said to himself.

"What?" the young doctor exclaimed.

Angus figured the doctor'd heard his mumblings, so he hurried to explain. "This should not be discussed. Please honor that."

"Yes, of course."

"We're closing in on some very bad people, part of a child-abduction ring. You may've read about it in the papers."

The doctor's face got a bit gray. "I understand. I won't include any of that in my report. My wife has been very nervous about the news. I have too."

"Thanks, Doc. I've got to get home now."

"Yes, you do. I want you back here or at your personal physician's to have that wound checked in two or three days."

"Okay, Doc. Got it. Thanks for the pills." Angus pulled his ripped and bloody shirt over his shoulder.

Sophie would be waiting up for him and worried. He left the brightly lit emergency room. In the darkened cab of his truck, he turned the ignition key and flinched.

Maybe he would take one of those pills.

CHAPTER 73

Sophie had not waited up for Angus.

Around midnight, she'd piled into bed, guilty about how drunk she'd gotten. She woke in the morning, a sour taste in her mouth. Her breath was military latrine strength. She jumped out of bed and rushed into the bathroom to correct the odor situation.

"Thank God for toothpaste and scented soap," Sophie crooned to herself as the hot shower pummeled her bowed head and body while the steamy wet rivulets cascaded down and revitalized her. She added to her original prayer, "Thank God for water too."

With a thin terrycloth towel turbined on her head, she donned her favorite Victoria's Secret robe and padded back to the bed to see if Angus was awake yet.

Still under the sheet, on his side, she gently shook the lump that was his shoulder.

He yelped, "Ow!"

Sophie sprang back.

Then as the sheet slipped off his shoulder, she gaped at the bandages and the dark red blotch. "Angus. Oh my God, what happened?"

Still sleepy-eyed, he pushed up on his good arm's elbow. "I'm fine Sophie, just grazed."

"You were shot?" Sophie paled.

"Yes, a bullet grazed my shoulder." He quickly went on, "We got them Sophie. They had children."

Then he said, "It's not serious. I'm fine. I need coffee and maybe a bite and I have to get down to the precinct. There were three stings last night. Today we'll talk to these pieces of crap. Not sure how many kids were in the other holding places. Our place had thirteen. All fine, eating po'boys, then off to the hospital to be examined. We'll need you to help Laura and Cassy sorting out where all these children go. You know some of the parents.

Sophie was still in shock.

199

Chapter 74

At the headquarters' holding area, there were fourteen traffickers; all neatly tucked away in cells kept for such purposes. There were twelve men and two women.

Angus walked through the front door, saw Captain Sloane's office door ajar, surmised Rick was waiting for him.

Two officers seated in the squad room jerked their heads in that direction, and one added, "He wants to see you now."

Angus nodded and headed into the chief's office.

"Sit down, Angus. We have a pile of sleazebuckets to talk to. I want you, Jensen and Blatchley to use three rooms. Divide them up, not the way they came to us. One from each sting."

"Understood."

"How's your shoulder?

"Ah, it's nothing."

Captain Sloane raised both eyebrows but didn't argue.

A knock on the now closed office door produced a junior officer who proclaimed that interrogation room number three was ready for Officer Clark.

Angus was eager. He asked Sloane if he was going to observe from the darkened side of the glass.

Rick got up, nodding.

"Let's go."

Detective Sloane stood in the dark area and prepared himself mentally to watch Angus do an interview. The well-lit interrogation room had a slight musty odor and the newly snagged perp sat at a slate-colored table. His hands were cuffed and folded in front of him, catechism style. To show his disdain for the proceedings, he leaned on the back legs of his chair, balanced in midair.

Angus entered, looking bored, with a file folder of papers in his hand. He plopped the papers down with a sharp smacking sound.

The perp's eyes dilated.

Angus sat, still looking bored. "Do you know what you're doing here?"

"Can't hear yah."

"Shut up. I'll tell you what the fuck you're doing here, you piece of shit."

The man cocked his head to one side and set his jaw. His eyes darted to a spot on the ceiling. "This dump needs a paint job."

Angus jumped up, knocked his metal chair over with an ear-shattering clang and banged both hands down on the table. His reddened face jutted forward, closing the space between him and the vile human being sitting across from him. "You were going to sell those kids to the highest bidder, you heartless bastard." Angus was pleased when spittle from his mouth shot out and landed on the perp's lower lip.

The cuffs rattled as the man lifted his hands to blot away Angus's spit.

Angus stood now, switched gears, a tactic meant to unnerve a person, keep a subject off balance. "What's your name?"

"Jimmy; as if you didn't fucking know."

"Jimmy, do you want something? A soda or maybe a coffee?"

Jimmy's adrenaline slowly came down from the peak load of hormones that'd flooded his body.

Angus taunted him again. "Hey, you want a tissue, Jimmy? You're sweating like a hog."

The subject scowled, swiped at his sweaty brow. The man's mouth was dry as the Sahara. "Could I have a cup of water?"

"If you say please."

"You motherfucker."

"Hang on, water coming right up."

Behind the glass window, Sloane noticed Angus getting water from the cooler and remarked, "Keep him on the fence, Angus."

Angus tilted his chin up and went back in. "Here you go, Jimmy."

The man cupped the Dixie cup with both shackled hands and emptied it in two large gulps.

The cup sat on the table.

The two men went to their corners.

Angus went on attack again. "There are fourteen of you here at our lovely resort. One of you… only one of you… is going to save their own ass by telling us what we want to know.

"I'm getting sick of your company Jimmy. You're a lousy conversationalist. I'm throwing your fucking ass out and bringing in one of the lovely ladies in your group. You know how women love to talk. One of them might be interested in being friendly and having a nice chat and saving their own pretty little ass. Yeah, get the hell out of here."

Angus stood to leave and said, "I'll get someone to escort you back to your accommodations."

"No. Wait."

"What, Jimmy? Why should I wait?"

"Wait, will I go free if I talk?"

"Free? Don't know about free, but you might see life outside a cell before you're bald and all your teeth fall out."

"You mean, I have a chance to get out in time to have a life?"

"Yes, Jimmy."

"Is that a promise?"

Angus crossed his fingers behind his back and intoned, "Promise."

Jimmy started to talk.

Angus wanted it all in writing. He slid the file over to James. It contained empty sheets of lined paper, two black juicy pens, ready for action. "Let me take those cuffs off you so you can write more easily."

"Can I have some more water?"

"Sure Jimmy, all the water you want. I'll be right back. "Keep writing."

CHAPTER 75

Monica rubbed the top of Clyde's head and chirped, "Orange curls, pretty, pretty."

He said, "My piece of shit father was white."

"Oh, that explains the green eyes too, right?"

"Guess so."

"Well, as adorable as those tangerine curls are; they have to go. I'm thinking of a more traditional black."

Clyde felt his own head and frowned. His crowning glory.

"Are you sure you can get money from someone in the States?"

"Yeah, pretty sure."

"Pretty sure doesn't cut it. We need damn sure, honey."

"Let's get out of here and rack up some miles. Somewhere where I can get to a pay phone." Clyde went over Laura's Rover number in his head.

"We can get lost in Reynosa, and I have friends there who can hook us up with a coyote."

"Monica, you forget, we're both US citizens. We don't need any fucking coyote."

"You're right." One deep nod.

Then she shocked Clyde with her next proposal. "People always get married to become citizens. There are other reasons to do it. I think we should get hitched here in Mexico to have a marriage license with new names on it. Well, your name to be specific. We'll be Mr. and Mrs. Clyde Garcia."

"With cash in our hands to grease things, that legal document will enable us to slip across the border without a lot of questions."

"But I'm a fugitive. I don't want to go back to that disgusting mental hospital or to jail."

"No, honey. Clyde Boudreaux is a fugitive. Clyde Garcia is a newly married man."

"I don't know, Mon. How will we get the money from the States?"

"In a word, wire transfer."

Clyde wore a worried frown but agreed to everything; dyed black hair, a wire transfer and a wedding.

CHAPTER 76

Reynosa was a bustling city. Most of its people were brown-skinned Mexicans.

The bus that took Monica and Clyde to their destination was crowded and dirty; full of tired and cross workers, some of whom gave Clyde sharp glances, meant to cut. Meant to draw blood.

They walked the rest of the way to Luna and Paulo's apartment.

Clyde's stomach was in knots.

The knock on the door brought an attractive ponytailed woman who let it open only part way, allowing the chain to sway in front of her ruby-colored lips. "Who's there?"

"Luna, it's me. Monica."

The latch was unhitched and the door showed a smiling woman who called out, "Monica."

They went into a small living room with worn but clean furniture and an oriental rug that only covered the center of the room. Everything was immaculate. There was a picture of Jesus Christ with his heart on display in his chest. The heart was very red.

There were also dos niños who stared unabashedly at Clyde who was now getting used to this treatment. The two children seemed pleased with this unusual company.

Monica told her friend as much of the story as she thought she needed to know. Her friend listened, seemingly without judgment.

The black dye job was accomplished easily. Luna had some on hand. She explained that her gray hairs were starting.

She also offered the use of her telephone to Clyde.

When told of the wedding plans, Luna was ecstatic and wanted a fiesta to celebrate.

"No Luna, just the ceremony and as soon as possible."

Clyde chimed in, "And a glass or two of red wine."

Luna laughed. "Que rico."

The wedding would be that evening. Everything was going as planned.

He asked if he could use the phone now. To say he was nervous would be a gross understatement. Clyde was biting the inside of his check; a habit he'd picked up from Mandy Rose.

Ah, Mandy Rose.

CHAPTER 77

It was late afternoon when Angus asked Laura to contact Mandy Rose and her friend, Mark Johnson. "Ask them to come here to the mansion, Laura."

Cassy, overhearing this, spoke up with an obviously loaded question. "Laura, I assume I'm included for this meeting?"

"Of course you are, Cass."

Cassy folded her arms across her chest and turned to face Sophie. "Will you be here for Arriona when she gets back from school?"

Sophie was dealing with her own feelings of rejection. She was also aware that her drinking was getting out of control again; that produced magnified self-pity and resentments. She answered Cassy laconically, "Sure, I'll be here."

Unbeknownst to anyone, Sophie'd attended her first Alcoholics Anonymous meeting and came home loaded with pamphlets she'd scooped up from a green velvet card table after the meeting. She told herself she was not in denial. She wanted help with her addiction.

Sophie had gotten more than a few stares as she'd dropped a twenty-dollar bill in the AA collection basket. As she did so, she noted coins and George Washington's face in there but let the twenty drop anyway. She so did not want a repeat performance of the prejudice shown to her at the church meeting for Caregivers of Abducted Children. "Rich bitch," still echoed in her mind and heart. Embarrassment about her wealth had begun to plague her.

Laura, back from her phone call, watched as Sophie agreed to be home for Arriona and wondered if her mother was trying for a do-over.

Cassy gave Sophie a hug and said, "No hotel trips today, right?"

Sophie giggled, sounding like a guilty teenager.

Laura stated flatly, "They'll be here in an hour.

The meeting was set.

207

CHAPTER 78

Laura was never certain how Mandy Rose would respond to anything, so she used the house phone to make the call. She sat on the stairs with her face turned toward the wall. She knew using the Rover would be cause for comments. Her face only registered mild surprise, a slightly dropped jaw, when Mark Johnson answered Mandy's phone.

"Hello, Bokum residence," his smooth male voice pronounced. He stood there still naked-chested from his recent shower.

"Mark?"

"Yes, is this Laura?"

"Yes, hi Mark. Listen, we're having a meeting here this afternoon. Can you and Mandy be here in about an hour?"

"Wait a minute, here's Mandy."

Mandy tightened the damp pink towel around her midriff, unaware it was rather short for other's viewing.

"Was that the phone? My sister?"

"Yes, here, take it." He extended the handset to Mandy and felt his groin quicken. He did not want to leave right away. This he knew.

Mandy lifted the phone to her ear, and Mark observed the towel rising with it. He barely heard her agreeing to go to the mansion.

When she replaced the receiver into the base, he came up behind her and loosened the knot that held the towel in place.

It dropped to the floor.

His hands found her now exposed breasts, two perfect globes. He reached down between her thighs, inserted his fingers deep into her and rocked them back and forth. She moaned with pleasure.

His free hand undid his pants and they joined the damp towel. Next his navy-blue jockey shorts completed a neat pile.

He wanted more.

She flung her arm around his neck as he lifted her and carried her back to the bedroom.

208

Laying her on the heap of rumpled sheets, he looked at her and admired her beauty.

Anticipation of another delicious bout of passionate lovemaking made them forget all about hurrying to the meeting at the mansion.

They couldn't get enough of each other.

CHAPTER 79

Laura was hanging up the house phone when she thought she heard a ringing coming from her pocketbook.

The purse was resting on a club chair where she'd flung it earlier. The quizzical look remained while she dug her Rover from beneath various sundries in her pocketbook. She wished there was a case for it to make it easier to grasp.

The ringing stopped when she picked it up and answered. The quizzical look morphed into alarm. She had to listen very closely as the voice was faint, but she knew who it was.

"Let me get something to write on and a pen. Hang on." She was now frantic, lest the call be disconnected, a common occurrence with these Rover phones. "Okay, go ahead. What's the address?"

The pen was running out of ink. "Damn it. No, I'm not making excuses. Just hang on." She purposely didn't utter his name. It would take thinking to decide how to handle this. "Okay, this pen works. Go.

"Ah ha, okay. How much do you need?" Pause. "That's fine. Not a problem." Pause. "I'll talk to Mandy later. She's on her way here." Not mentioning she wouldn't be alone. "Okay, hang in there. It might take a day or two." Another pause. "Yeah, you too."

The connection went dead. Clyde had hung up.

Laura continued to sit on the bottom step of the staircase. Her Rover was still live, the red light still blinking. She looked at it, expecting more answers it couldn't give. She snapped it off and dunked it back into her purse, then she realized her name was being called repeatedly.

"Laura? Laura?"

She clamped her lips shut and got up to answer the call of family.

CHAPTER 80

Dr. William P. Romero wished he'd never heard of Clyde Boudreaux. He would've looked the other way if Blade had snuffed the Black bastard out. Sam was afraid of his own shadow but did whatever Blade told him to do.

Romero knew there were certain other instances where back building "residents" disappeared. The medical laboratories salivated when he provided them with unidentified cadavers. And they were willing to pay a lot for their new quiet guests.

Clyde Boudreaux would've been a perfect candidate. Young and healthy, not to mention, slim, not buried under mountains of adipose fat, making dissections more difficult.

The good doctor sighed heavily. *That ship has sailed.*

Thinking of boats made him angry all over again. His hands balled into fists and his reddened face glowered with resentment. His thirty-foot cutter was in pristine condition, waiting for Captain Romero to shove off for foreign ports. He wanted a full pension. Not making it unscathed to his retirement date was not an option.

An escapee, especially one with a murder rap hanging over his head, would cause the powers that be to use that as an excuse to bump him early and cut back severely into his benefits. Time to put a call in to his childhood friend; His Honor Thomas Grady.

Old Tom owed him one. *'Bout time he collected.*

The scheming psychiatrist left his office and entered Mabel Casner's office. Dangling from his fist were the master keys to the file cabinets.

Mabel's office was mostly dark. Even with such little light, it was obviously the personal space of a neat freak. The reddish-brown desk boasted a quiet gleam on its surface, courtesy of the soft silver beam that floated in from the full moon. Nothing cluttered the desktop. Even the many-buttoned desk phone had a well-polished sheen.

211

Dr. Romero inserted the key into the little round disc. He heard a soft click. Satisfied, he pulled the metal drawer to himself and fingered through the alphabetized mylar tabs. He murmured to himself and the insistent moon beams. "As, Bs. Should be right here. Fuck, he's not here."

He slapped his forehead, said so loud he made himself jump, "Of course, he's in the 'other' file she keeps behind her desk." He went there.

He recalled other times when names were removed from that "other" file; names nobody ever asked about. Names Mabel conveniently dismissed from memory. Mabel liked the finer things in life, a good, mostly honest woman who enjoyed driving nice cars and dining on caviar and champagne.

He could count on her.

There it was, he found what he'd been looking for. Clyde Boudreaux. He read further. "Hmmm, not yet thirty years old, born right here in the great state of Louisiana, much better than up north."

The file got plucked out, not just the guts, but the whole damn file. It would go home with him and make a tidy bonfire.

Spoken aloud, he said, "This guy disappears; all will be fine."

He shoved the file drawer closed. The clang it made spoke of endings.

Chapter 81

Mandy Rose and Mark pulled into the circular drive at the mansion. With the T-Bird still idling, Mandy turned to Mark and said, "What did that creep Jake mean when he called you an Indian giver?"

Mark gave a hearty guffaw and admitted to Mandy that a while back he'd told Jake it was okay to ask her out.

"What?"

"That was before we, you know… we got to know each other."

Mandy glared at Mark.

"I'm sorry."

She said with a hint of humor, "Sometimes I think all men are idiots." She puffed air out through her lips and said, "All right, let's face this."

Laura reacted to the sound of the car in the driveway by charging to the front door. She was already there when Mark pulled the door open. He stepped aside to let Mandy enter before him.

Laura gave a head jerk and said, "Hi Mark." Then she grabbed Mandy Rose by her shoulders to hold her in place.

"Go over there, into the kitchen, Mark. I need my sister upstairs."

"Okay, Laura. I'm gonna say hello first to—" she never finished that sentence.

"No, say hello later. Upstairs, now."

Mandy saw the look on Laura's face and didn't resist.

They heard everyone else greeting Mark. The sounds of voices faded the farther they got to Laura's bedroom.

Laura took no chances. She slammed and locked the bedroom door.

Mandy's eyes were huge now. "What the hell Laura?"

The Watcher kicked in, bringing a necessary calmness and sense of peace to Laura. The Watcher had been with Laura since she was able to talk. She relied on it to always hold an overview to any situation and shed light, not easily surmised, by mere humans.

The disturbing nature of the phone call from Clyde eased as the younger sister opted for simple clarity and a need for discussion without exaggerated drama.

"Mandy." Laura peered directly into Mandy Rose's questioning eyes.

"Yes, Laura."

"Clyde just called from Mexico."

Chapter 82

"Damn it, Mandy. They're waiting for us in the kitchen. I don't think we should mention we heard from Clyde."

Before Mandy could respond, Laura tightened her face and said coldly and calmly, "And what the hell is going on with you and Mark?"

Mandy retorted, "None of your Goddamn business."

"It is my business. Mark knows things about Clyde. Now you have pitted them against each other for your lily-white ass."

Mandy Rose's face blanched to cake flour white.

Laura had never spoken to her this way before. She felt betrayed and strangely still.

Laura took the two steps needed to get to her sister and wrapped her arms around her. Spoken softly, but with crystal clear clarity, she said, "I'm sorry, Mandy."

Mandy tried not to cry but bawled anyway.

A knock on the locked bedroom door caused them both to jump.

It was Angus.

He spoke to the door without trying the knob. "Please come out, girls. Come downstairs. We can all brainstorm and come up with a plan; maybe something you never thought possible.

Laura swallowed the frog in her throat and answered, "Give us a minute. We'll be right down."

Ever the gentleman, Angus answered, "Okay fine, see you in a bit."

"Mandy, I'm thinking we should trust Angus and come clean with what we know."

"You mean about Clyde too?"

"Yes, I do."

"But, Laura, he's a cop."

"I know that, and maybe you've forgotten, but Cassy and I are cops too."

Mandy lifted the edge of the bedspread and thoroughly wiped her face, even blew her nose. Then she patted her cheeks, to try to look more normal, less afraid.

"Go splash some cold water on your face and meet me in the kitchen."

"Okay, Laura."

Minutes later the only one seated in the kitchen was Sophie who held Arriona in her lap. The child sipped lemonade through a pink bendy straw. She watched the adults.

All eyes turned to Laura and before anyone could speak, she exclaimed, "Mandy Rose will be right down. We have lots to tell you."

Angus, who stood with his hands on a chair back, nodded and said, "I do also."

Mandy Rose appeared, her face a bit pink and shiny, but not wanting to appear weak, directed, "Let's sit and get this going."

She pulled her chair next to Mark, which didn't go unnoticed by anyone, except for the lemonade sipper, who couldn't care less.

Everyone expected Angus to start, so he did. "This is what I know. At least in this area, the lists we've acquired have no more children noted to be sacrificed for their organs. We got all the little ones held at the winery to the hospital; all are recovering nicely, some faster than others. There were two children already deceased when we got there, pending possible location of their parents, we're holding their bodies, which are being autopsied. Officer Victor Hugo was shot during that takedown and died instantly." He looked pointedly at Laura and Cassy and said sternly, "He wasn't wearing his body armor, his vest."

Their faces were stone as they shook their heads.

Sophie looked at Laura and hugged Arriona tighter until the little girl lifted her straw and it dripped into the tall glass of almost gone lemonade.

Angus went on. "Now the lists show some first names. We're not sure if we have a complete accounting, so we cannot jump to conclusions. However we have to face reality. We found two Hannahs. One, by our best interpretation, was put into the adoption category relatively early on. Hannah number two was earmarked for trafficking, again not organ harvest trafficking.

Sophie's face went white. She worked her jaw up and down to maintain her emotions.

Arriona chose this exact second to bellow sweetly, "More lemonade, please."

Sophie slid her off her lap and whispered, "Go ask Almadine to pour you some more."

"Can't I stay here with you all?"

"Not now dear, go find Almadine."

The child left her empty glass with its pink straw and scampered off to find the maid.

Sophie noted the hurt look in the little girl's eyes. So did Cassandra.

Angus continued. "We're matching up names of kids taken around the same time as when our Hannah disappeared. We have to rely on some of the parents and caretakers to remember exact dates when their children were taken. This isn't always possible due to the mistrust of policemen by both women and men."

Now he looked at Cassy, who said, "I've been interviewing parents for that information. I've narrowed it down to a list of twelve kids taken in the same time frame as Hannah. Some of them are hazy on the dates. It appears there were two female children named Hannah, snatched from their homes within approximately the same two weeks."

"Thanks, Cassy. Have you anything to add to that, Laura?"

"No, nothing to add."

Angus waited half a minute before he went on to the next issue. "Now it's time to address the subject of Clyde Boudreaux. There're many questions surrounding this young man's story. After he was accused of murdering Bertie Bergeron, the woman who worked with the traffickers at the Leprosarium, he was taken into custody. Still recovering from the bullet wound he received from Felix Guidry, now incarcerated, Clyde Boudreaux had a total mental breakdown. The story seems to be that he managed an escape from the state mental hospital.

"Before I go on here, I want to make something perfectly clear. The case against Boudreaux consists only of circumstantial evidence. Ms. Bergeron's car was found behind Clyde's house. It's true that lab tests show minute traces of poison in a glass found on the counter in the Boudreaux house. Yet, there is some doubt concerning the substances contained in the glass. Absinthe was definitely identified. It cannot be proven that the woman was ever in Clyde Boudreaux's house or more explicitly, ever drank from the glass in question. The woman's body has never been recovered. And Clyde Boudreaux has never admitted to knowing Bertie Bergeron, much less murdering her.

"His mental state after being apprehended, necessitated his commitment to Bingham Mental Institute. Why he was relegated to what is called 'the back building' cannot be fully explained. I suspect it may be related to prejudicial practices brought about by residual racism still alive in the state of Louisiana. This last statement stays in this room. I bring all this up in hopes of getting a clearer picture of how this man escaped from a locked down mental facility."

He now directed his gaze at Mandy Rose. They locked eyes.

"Yes, I helped him get away from that barbaric hellhole."

Angus's face softened as he asked, "How did you do it?"

She spoke in a clear voice that rang with truth. "The two cretins who work in that back building are racist brutes. They planned to kill Clyde the next day, and since the door to the ward in the back building was normally locked on Sundays, they left it open when they left that night, so they could get back in on a day they normally could not."

"And so you went in there to that back ward?"

"Yes, yes I did. Clyde was lying on a filthy mattress in a cell. The whole place smelled like an open grave."

Angus spoke very softly. He didn't want to interrogate, just to question. "How did you get the cell door to open?"

Mandy Rose looked down to her right, then lifted her chin. "I can tell you what happened. I can't explain how it happened."

"Go on."

"Clyde practices the ancient art of Voodooism. He comes from a long line of spirituals. His grandfather was anointed a Houngan by the most-high priestess. This fact didn't save his grandfather from being lynched by a crazed mob of whites, fearful of his 'magic' though.

"Clyde was gifted a very powerful gris-gris, an African amulet; like a charm, passed on to him from his beloved grandfather. He had this in his possession already when he witnessed his grandfather being lynched. The men wanted to hang him also, screaming, "String the boy up too, right next to his grandfather.

"A white woman present at this abomination pleaded his case and stopped the mob from killing the young boy. Clyde always thought his life was spared because of his gri-gris nestled in his tattered pants pocket."

Everyone sat without moving, mesmerized by Mandy's story. They were stuck to their chairs as though struck by a thunderbolt.

After a slight pause, Mandy continued. "I was disheartened by the heavy metal cell door Clyde was behind, but I knew he set great store in his grandfather's gris-gris, which I had with me.

"I would say that was by mistake but I know better now. They surely would have taken it from Clyde and not given it back to him. I took it because I knew Clyde valued it so highly, and I just wanted to keep it for him."

Everyone held their breaths, waiting for the story to continue.

"I went close to the big iron cell door. I saw a slot, almost like a mail slot in the door. I tightened my fingers on the lip and pushed. I knew if I could get it open, there would be an exposed area, big enough to put things through.

"I called to Clyde and he answered. He looked so grateful and happy. I held the gris-gris firmly and pushed it through the slot. The interior of the cell began to pulse with light and I heard a buzzing sound like a million bees and that big heavy metal door just floated open. Hard to believe, but true.

"And that's what happened. Clyde and I took off and headed west. I got him some different clothes and shoes. He was very stable mentally, not the least bit psychotic. We drove for two days and I dropped him off where he could walk into Mexico. I gave him a pile of money."

Mark listened intently to this monologue, fascinated by Mandy Rose's grit and loyalty. *Did she still love Clyde?*

Angus said, "Have you heard from Clyde since you left him off?"

It was Laura's turn to finish the narrative. She stated succinctly. "Today."

Angus's face featured a fly-catching open mouth. "What?"

Mandy jumped in. "I had him memorize Laura's Rover phone number."

Angus said, "What did he say?"

Laura said, "More like what did he want."

"And what did he want?"

"Money, he needs money."

"Did he say why?"

"Yeah, he wanted to come back home. He was in danger of being kidnapped and held for ransom."

"How the hell would he know that?"

"He was beaten and robbed and left for dead."

Angus said, "Yeah. And?"

"And a woman and her cousin took him in; nursed him back to health. The cousin, a young man, a fugitive himself from the States, was plotting to grab him, in cahoots with the creeps who beat him nearly to death. They planned to make him tell them who'd pay for his release and safe return. They likely would've murdered him anyway after they got the ransom money."

"This is mindboggling. How does he intend to get back over the border with these dangerous men after him?"

"That's why he needs the money, Angus."

"Yes, but his name will be on the watch list at the Border Crossing. They'll detain him right there."

Laura now looked straight at Mandy Rose. She knew she hadn't disclosed this next bit of information.

Mandy steeled herself for whatever Laura was about to say.

"You see, he now has a different last name and the legal papers to prove it."

"C'mon Laura," Angus said kindly. "Stop stalling."

"He has a marriage license with his new wife's last name as his."

Mark stared at Mandy Rose as she went pale.

Angus wondered how he ever lived before he got entrenched with this unpredictable, astonishing family.

"Will you send him money?"

"Yes, I'd like to see his name cleared. He is, after all, Hannah's father, and we may be close to finding her."

"True." That's all Angus could think of to say.

Sophie was coming apart at the seams. She wanted a drink in the worst way.

CHAPTER 83

Dr. William Romero had no intention of allowing the recent debacle with this Clyde character to blight his almost-perfect work record. Retirement was around the corner. No one and no thing was going to screw it up.

The phone rang in Judge Grady's palatial home. His Honor Thomas Grady was sipping single malt whiskey from a Glencairn glass, contemplating how in his opinion it was a grave disservice to drink this fine single malt from an inferior whiskey tumbler.

He scowled at the phone as though it had it in for him.

The judge's wife, Thelma, was visiting her mother, who was in Hospice with end stage esophageal cancer. The death-watch.

He uncrossed his legs, still tall and limber, and strode across the room like a man in his thirties. Mina appeared also and he waved her away. "I have it Mina. I told you to take the rest of the day off."

The maid nodded, shouldered her over-sized pocketbook, and slid away, lest the phone call interfere with her newly-discovered free afternoon.

The judge's contented face soured when he heard Romero's voice. Judge Grady wasn't too thrilled to hear from Dr. William Romero. The doctor had the goods on old Tom Grady and the judge didn't want to be reminded of it.

He faked a cheery, "Hey, what's up Bill?"

The good Dr. Bill told the good Judge Tom exactly what was up. He went on, "I don't need to remind you, Tom, you owe me. You owe me a big one."

The judge countered, "I know, I know I do. Where is this Clyde Boudreaux guy now?"

"In the wind. The amazing detail in this, which 'could' make the wheels greasier, is that Doctor Harold Bokum is the father of the young woman who purportedly helped this young man escape from Bingham Institute, but since he's in jail right now, it could make it worse."

"How is all this possible, Bill?"

"Apparently Old Bokum was involved in the trafficking scheme."

"I mean about the escape?"

"That is the hundred-thousand-dollar question. Nobody sane has the answer."

"Bill, this is a real sticky wicket. Send me the guy's file, and I'll find loopholes to make it go away. Send it by courier."

"I knew I could count on you."

The rest of the judge's single malt was gulped and a new pour replaced it. He sat back down and rubbed his neck, already formulating a legal strategy.

CHAPTER 84

"Señor Clyde Garcia, I think I like your hair better black than those cinnamon curls."

"I can't get used to not being Clyde Boudreaux. With the name Garcia, people will tag me a Latino."

"And what's wrong with that, mi espouso?"

Clyde wrapped his arms around Monica and kissed the top of her head. Her shiny black hair smelled like orange blossoms and vanilla. "Nada, mi espousa. Nothing is wrong with it."

On the previous phone call, Laura had told Clyde a substantial amount of money would be ready to be picked up the following day. She was using Western Union. It would be deposited in Luna and Paulo's account. It was agreed that the couple would keep ten percent, or two thousand dollars. The remaining eighteen thousand dollars would be divided between Clyde and Monica; to be on the safe side. Mexico was a dangerous place. Anything could happen.

The wedding had taken place in the home of Luna and Paulo. How legal it was, was debatable. But they had a piece of paper saying they were husband and wife with the last name Garcia.

They all sat scrunched up together in the doll-sized living room and watched the old black and white Philco television.

Clyde wasn't following the inane plot. In his mind's eye he saw Mandy Rose. Relived how she thrust him out of the car. He thought about his newly discovered daughter. Would he ever see her? Hold her? Mandy'd told him she'd inherited his orange curls and green eyes. That made his whole body smile.

He winced as he recalled the beating he'd suffered. Almost died. Monica had saved his life.

The last idea that popped into his head as he dozed on that crowded couch was, Where is my gris-gris?

CHAPTER 85

Cassandra feared a schism had developed between her and Laura. Since graduation from the academy, they saw each other less and less. All natural, she supposed.

Cassy had her own life, hadn't told Laura about Willow. Willow was one of the first parents to be reunited with her child.

Her baby girl had just been snatched. Angel was among the children being held in the Industrial Park building where Angus had led the sting. These were some of the luckiest kids, not subjected to any abuse other than the trauma of being taken. The terror they experienced would affect them all, some more profoundly than others. They'd been heading toward a new and sordid existence in the cruel world of sex trafficking. Children used for the pleasures of perverted adults.

Cassy and Arriona enjoyed the company of Willow and Angel. There was no male in the equation.

Angel and Arriona were the same age and could be overheard comparing notes.

"I don't think you need a daddy."

"Nope," Angel concurred. "But," Angel delicately added, "they do make money and that's a good thing."

Arriona put her finger on the side of her tilted face and encapsulated her personal experiences in life. "I used to be poor, poor as dirt. That's what my mama called it, poor as dirt. Now I have Sophie. Mama and I live in her big castle and we have lots of money."

Angel tilted her face to match Arriona's and innocently asked, "Where did all the money come from?"

Arriona picked at something caught in her tooth and answered truthfully, "I don't know."

"Are there any men living in the castle with you?"

"Yeah, there's Angus, but he's a cop and my mama says cops don't make the big dough; they just want to protect people and put the bad guys behind bars."

"Like those bad guys that took me and the other kids and put us in that room. We were hungry and thirsty and there was no place to pee or poop. It was awful."

Arriona sat up straight and took a bit of reflected glory. "Well, that was Angus who got you guys out of there."

Angel's eyes bulged, filling one third of her tiny face. "That was Angus who rescued us?"

Shoulders squared. "Yup."

"Wow, he's a hero. Can I come over to your castle and tell him thank you? My mama said he has a place in heaven for sure."

"Let me ask my mama. You could come over and meet Angus, and we could have a tea party with Sophie too. I call her Gramma Sophie."

All of this chatter was absorbed by Cassy and Willow who listened in, ears pressed to the bedroom door where Angel and Willow slept on a double sized mattress.

Angel said, "Let's go ask our mothers when we can go over to your castle."

The two mothers scurried down the short hallway and fell into the plastic padded kitchen chairs. *Thunk, Thunk.*

Soon four females surrounded the dinette table that served as a division to the living room. Question asked and answered.

Cassy knew she couldn't keep her love affair with Willow a secret any longer.

Arriona would surely spill the beans.

CHAPTER 86

Saturday morning at the mansion, everyone, including Mark, sat at the breakfast table, a good time to compare notes and finalize the next tasks to be undertaken.

Angus was still favoring his "no bullet hole" arm as he chug-a-lugged more coffee.

"I'm keeping everything I've learned about Clyde under my hat for now. I'm not sure how long I can do this. The department is not too concerned about his departure, not considering him a danger to others. Some of them applaud what he did in killing that evil woman, if he did indeed kill her. He never confessed and there's no *corpus delecti*. That means no concrete evidence of a crime, such as a corpse. This also changes the picture for his so-called escape. It would be considered leaving a hospital against medical advice, commonly known as leaving AMA."

Mandy Rose interrupted this diatribe. "How does that affect me? You all know I helped him get out."

Angus squelched the smile that threatened his lips. Laura let hers bloom.

"A lot depends on what he did or does as a result of being freed from confinement."

Cassy asked, "How many more hidey holes are you planning to take down, Angus?"

"We're enlisting other law enforcement agencies to get involved. This putrid blight is legion. Yesterday we made contact with Interpol. A lot of these kids are passed around to other countries. Very disturbing is the fact that videos are becoming more popular as a vehicle to keep these perverted creeps entertained." Angus was always careful not to use profanity when Arriona as in company.

She'd had an awful scare with Big Carl and heard some profoundly lewd remarks from his vile mouth. Sophie cried when her little darling asked what an "untapped virgin" was and why she was one of those. How do you explain such filth to a little girl and protect her innocence? These guys should be shot or at least castrated.

Laura said, "What about dear old dad? Is he getting a pass?"

"No, his cooperation providing those names was helpful and will be considered when his parole hearing comes up. He won't be out any time soon. Your mom and I have an appointment with a divorce lawyer next week."

Mandy Rose and Laura watched as Angus's face took on a rosy glow. "And," he went on, "with your blessing girls, we'd like to plan a spring wedding."

The smiles this proclamation produced was answer enough.

Laura spoke first. "That's great. We kind of suspected this might happen."

Mandy Rose piped up. "We're all for it. Welcome to the family, Angus."

All these happy exclamations weren't lost on Arriona, who now added her little high-pitched voice. "A wedding. Yahoo! Can I invite Mama's lady friend, Willow, and my kid friend, Angel?"

Conversation screeched to a halt. All eyes telescoped to Cassy whose mouth had dropped open.

"Uh, I've been meaning to tell you all about Willow."

Arriona said, "Yeah, and Angel."

Everyone waited for more.

"We've been seeing each other. She's wonderful and Arriona and her daughter, Angel, have become good friends."

"Why didn't you tell me?"

"You've been so busy, Laura."

"Yeah, busy. Not dead."

"I know. I guess I wanted to keep it all to myself for a while; see where it went."

"And where has it gone?"

Sophie interjected, "Ease up, Laura. You always push too hard." Sophie cast a caring glance at Cassandra and asked the same question with a different attitude. "Are you two serious?"

Cassy took a cleansing breath and answered, "We're talking about moving in together."

This was the first time Arriona had heard this.

She declared, "I'm not leaving Sophie and Angus, Mama."

Laura and Mandy Rose could have predicted this same sentiment from their mother.

She didn't disappoint. "Well, you could all live here. We have plenty of room, don't we Angus?"

The man was taken by surprise but recovered in record time.

"Sure, the more the merrier."

Arriona crossed her eyebrows and said to everyone's delight, "Who's Mary?"

Laura, all softened now, said, "That means more people living here have even happier times together."

Laura rose and went over to her dear friend and hugged her, whispered something in her ear that made Cassy swallow and swipe at an errant tear.

CHAPTER 87

"Who was that on the phone, Luna?"

"It was your cousin. Pablo wants to know if I've heard from you."

"Oh God, what did you tell him?"

"That I hadn't heard from you in months, but Monica, I don't trust that little bastard. I never understood why you sacrificed your own life to bring him here. This is a good time to explain it to me. His crime was violent. He was accused of shooting that old man, not just robbing the liquor store."

Luna stood bent toward Monica. A look of fear made her pretty features darken and tighten up; her lips now pencil thin as she awaited Monica's answer.

Monica's complexion paled and her eyes drooped with threatened tears. "Lo siento, Luna. First, I agree with you. It wasn't smart. I no longer trust Pablo. I helped him because he's my mother's sister's son. Familia."

Luna wagged her head in understanding. She knew "family" was everything in Latin culture. "Si, comprendo. But Monica, what about now? I can't have trouble here. I have children. I'm sure you understand."

"Of course I do, and I can't guarantee Pablo won't come here. He stands to lose a lot of money if he doesn't produce Clyde. The hombres he's hooked up with are muy malo. Very bad indeed."

Clyde, who'd been dozing on the couch, was awake and heard this exchange. He said, "We have to leave here right now. We can't stay here tonight."

Relief shone on Luna's face. She said, "I'll fix you some burritos to take with you for later. You should avoid any bodegos."

Clyde was already pulling the bundle of their few belongings out from behind the couch.

Monica hugged Luna. She was looking around the living room to make sure nothing incriminating was left behind. These guys were bad, not stupid.

Paulo came through the door and observed the frenzied activity. "What's going on?"

Clyde answered briefly and Paulo nodded in agreement. He offered the name and directions of a cheap room to spend the night. "I'll meet you at the bank at nine o'clock sharp. It's better if Luna doesn't go. He'd recognize her, but not me." Then he added, "Get out of Pablo's clothes, leave them here and take pants and a shirt of mine."

Luna chimed in, "Monica, leave your dress here too and wear one of mine; pick a style not like yours."

Clyde's face crumpled. "I'm so grateful to you both. I never would've believed total strangers would help me in this way."

Paulo waved his hand, knuckles out. "Get going… por favore."

Luna said, "You're helping us tambien. The money you're giving us is needed and appreciated."

Little Paulo, up from a nap, stood rubbing his eyes with one tiny fist while the other hand dangled an almost bald teddy bear. "Mama, are we gonna get some money from Tia Monica?"

The adults all looked at each other and realized the children had to go elsewhere.

Paulo said, "Paulito, you and your brother are going to stay at your friend Jose's house for a few days."

Luna was already on the phone making the plans.

Paulito screeched, "Yupi!" Then swinging the almost hairless bear, he bolted to tell his brother the good news.

With everyone on the same page, soon the niños were dropped off at Jose's house and Clyde and Monica were busy paying the clerk for one night at the dreary hotel.

Paulo was headed back home where Luna waited alone, pacing and chewing on her already butchered fingernails.

A hot night, she nevertheless, felt a cold draft on her neck.

CHAPTER 88

Angus caught the "cornered" look on Sophie's face as her curls came loose from their bindings. She seemed to be hiding behind the cascading locks. Her eyes flitted from one daughter to the other, then rested on Arriona who was busy folding napkins into smaller and smaller squares.

Sophie felt guilty about taking Arriona to the hotel where that child molester chased her and said nasty vile things to her. They should get her some counseling. She said, "I'll be right back," and left for the staircase before anyone had a chance to respond.

Laura thought, Too many bathroom trips.

Mandy Rose stared at her mother's retreating back.

Cassy frowned as she observed Arriona's compulsive behavior.

Angus let Sophie go, then without a word to anyone else, followed her path. Up the stairs he went, only yards behind her. He watched her go into a spare guest room. Hesitating about being caught, he poked his head around the doorway; saw her dig behind a seldom-used Ethridge chair. It offered a great hiding place for what she sought.

He almost cried when she sat on the floor, her fancy silk dress jacked up over her knees as she cradled a bottle of Gray Goose in her lap.

Vodka now had replaced gin. Angus knew vodka held the best reputation for the most odorless alcoholic beverage.

She faced away from the door and was slanted to one side, so absorbed in getting the cap off the bottle, she didn't hear Angus approach.

"Sophie."

The woman jumped and the bottle flew; a waterfall of expensive vodka soaking into her lime green skirt then bouncing on the shirred wool carpet, a yawn of clear liquid that continued to empty in place.

Sophie's head whirled, her hair flying, an ugly snarl distorting her features.

"How dare you spy on me!"

Angus knelt and spoke in a soft, gentle voice. "Sophie honey, how can I help?"

Her fury was not to be defused. "You can help by leaving me alone."

He reached to touch her exposed knee and she slapped his hand away. "Get out and leave me alone."

"I won't ever leave you alone… I love you."

Laura and Mandy Rose hovered outside the door in the hallway, shocked to hear their mother so angry and in so much pain. They didn't interfere with the drama playing out before them.

Angus had obviously succeeded in getting Sophie into his arms. They heard their mother sobbing quietly and Angus's soothing words. "Sophie darling, you've been through so much. Let me love you. Let me help."

In a final burst of energy, she picked up the bottle and flung it across the room. Hard. It reached the wall where it smacked and clattered then dropped and lay empty and dead.

Little hands pried their way between the two sisters and a small form darted into the room to join the two adults still seated on the floor, their slightly chubby bodies melded.

Arriona patted Sophie's cheek and crooned, "Don't cry Grammy Sophie… please."

Sophie enfolded the child until she plopped into the center of their arms and legs and all three were at once replenished.

There was nothing so healing as a child's pure love.

Laura and Mandy retreated to the kitchen where Cassy and Mark waited to find out what had happened.

Cassy, ever the voice of reason, said, "Maybe it's time Sophie went to some AA meetings."

Alcoholism was rarely as much a secret as the alcoholic imagined. There was denial on everybody's part.

CHAPTER 89

Bang. Bang. Bang.

Luna knew that wasn't Paulo at her front door. She stood frozen, petrified, staring at the door as it shook under the constant pummeling.

Her voice was a soft croak. "Quien es?"

Bang. Bang. Bang.

"Quien es?"

A gruff male voice said in Spanish, "Open the fucking door."

Now the lower portion of the door quaked with loud thumps.

"We'll kick your fucking door in if you don't open it right now, you stupid bitch. We'll shoot your husband in the head if you take too long."

"Where is my husband?"

"Dead, if you don't open up."

Her heart stopped. These bad hombres meant it. "Si, si." She wiped her eyes and opened the locks that were meant to keep her safe. All three locks slid to the open position. Before the fourth lock was unchained, the door burst open, knocking her to the floor.

"Ow!" She landed hard on her coccyx bone; hands still suspended in front of her.

"Where's my husband?" she shouted up from the floor.

"Shut up you stupid whore." The room was full of men, all ogling her. She yanked her dress down to cover her thighs and tried to stand up.

A huge rough hand clamped on her shoulder and pushed her back down. "Stay where you are, sweetheart."

"C'mon, we don't have time for this Manuel."

"I won't take long. Did you see those panties?"

"Yeah Manny, I want a turn too."

Luna's eyes bugged and her chin quivered. "Please don't do this. Leave me alone. Tell me what you want."

"I'm lookin' at what I want." The man's eyes focused on her upper thighs, and his lips were wet with lust as he undid the huge silver Rams Head buckle on his pants.

Luna went onto all fours and scrambled away as fast as she could on her hands and knees.

The unbuckled man was delighted. Coarse laughter escaped his protruding lips.

"Leave me alone. Tell me what you want from me."

His big boot clamped down on her raised buttocks. He dropped his pants and put one fat sausage finger between her legs and pushed it inside her.

She screamed.

"Goddamn it, Manny. Leave that bitch alone. We need her talking, not passed out."

The other men had searched without coming up with any evidence of Clyde Boudreaux.

Manny said, "Aw shit, look at her. She's ready."

Diego, the undisputed boss, shouted, "Fucking leave her be, and pull up your Goddamned pants."

"Okay, miss, we won't hurt you if you tell us where the Negro is. He's traveling with an American woman."

Luna turned over on her butt and yanked her skirt down over her knees, all the way over her ankles. Her sobs were fewer now as she tried to form words. "Yes, yes, they were here."

"Bueno, and where are they now?"

"No se."

"Whaddya mean you don't know? Either you answer or I'll let Manuel here finish what he started."

Luna stalled, hoping Paulo would return and see the busted door and get help. "All I know is they were going to stay at a hotel tonight."

"Porque?"

"Because they were scared of you."

Manuel said, "She's stalling, Diego. Let me help her remember." He hadn't done his buckle back up yet, and his hand went to it now. He leered at her, rape in his eyes.

Manuel backhanded her, and her lip burst open. Blood, new and bright red, trickled down her chin.

Diego snapped at Manuel. "Stop wasting time. We need information. What hotel?"

"No se."

"Ah, there's a thousand shitholes they could've gone to. Do they have money or did you give them some?"

"I had no money to give them."

"How do they plan to travel with no money?"

"The Negro can get money from the United States."

"C'omo?" Manuel was tired of these negotiations. He took a step closer to Luna and yanked her dress up until her thighs and panties were exposed. He stepped on her dress to keep it where it lay. Manny then held his middle finger up and waggled it toward her.

She hyperventilated and gasped out four words, "There's a telephone number."

Manny wasn't ready to give up his fun. He reached down and pulled her panties aside and jammed two fingers hard inside her.

She screeched; a blood-curdling sound.

"Stop, I'll tell you everything. Please stop."

Diego took over. "What's the telephone number and don't fucking lie, 'cause I'm gonna dial it right now."

"It's on the last page of the tablet in the drawer over there." She pointed to a child-size accent table painted aqua that had one drawer with a knob on it.

Diego dove for it, yanked the drawer open so fast it fell on the floor, scattering its contents, which included an old-fashioned lined tablet.

With the last page in his hand, he went to the rotary wall phone and dialed.

No one made a peep while he listened, his fat head pressed into the handset.

His eyes rounded; two shot glasses with brown bottomed sludge.

He did not look happy as he slammed the phone back in its cradle so hard it cracked. "This is a fucking cop's phone. An American cop. A fucking cunt cop."

Diego shouted, a rough growly sound, "Salgamos de aqui!"

Manny cast one more lascivious glance at Luna who was balled up in a knot on the floor, knees tucked in and blanketed tightly with her stretched dress.

The creep kissed his middle finger and licked it; enjoyed watching her cringe.

"C'mon, we have to put distance. I ain't getting mixed up with no American cops."

Sorely disappointed about their loss of a ransom windfall, they knew they had to make tracks. They left the broken door hanging on its ancient hinges and piled into their rust bucket, a sixteen-year-old Ford Galaxie.

After it threatened not to start not once, but three times, it fired up sputtering and complaining. Four overweight Mexicans weighed heavily on the collapsed shocks. But luck was with them, as often happened to evildoers, causing some to doubt the existence of a loving God. Nevertheless, off they went, not a penny richer.

Paulo rode in on their exhaust as they passed each other on the road.

When he saw the gaping doorway, he barreled into his house, not even shutting his car door. He fell to his knees when he saw his beloved Luna sitting on the floor, weeping and smoothing her dress down over her shins, again and again as she tried to anchor it under her toes.

Paulo cried with her.

He vowed revenge.

<h1 style="text-align:center">CHAPTER 90</h1>

Sophie kissed Angus lightly on his lips, and Arriona applied more pressure to her snuggled head, then said, "Let's go downstairs and join the rest of the family."

In answer, the grown man and the little girl pushed up off the floor and pulled Sophie up by her hands.

All three descended into the kitchen where chatter has morphed into a heavy waiting silence.

"Glad you're here, Mama." They avoided any talk about what had just transpired upstairs. "Laura and I are going to drop Mark off and go to the after-hours Western Union. Clyde needs that money fast."

Ever the astute lawman, Angus left the kitchen, preferring not to hear the plans for aiding and abetting a fugitive. He never sat down, just kept walking.

Not so with Sophie. "Use the family account, not your personal ones. How much money does he want?"

Laura answered, "Twenty thousand."

"They might need more. Send them thirty."

It wasn't lost on Mandy Rose that her mother said "them" not him. *Could her mother be relieved Clyde was married?*

Was she relieved?

Mandy glanced at Mark, sitting at the table, hands in his lap under the table, face shiny and captivated; lower jaw sunken. *This family's like a spiderweb; get too close, you're moored, unable to move on. Stuck. So why did he want to stay?*

"Okay, Mama. Makes sense. Thirty, it is." Laura directed her gaze at her sister. "Ready, Mandy?"

Mandy tapped Mark's shoulder and to his great discomfort, his lowered jaw had produced a rivulet of drool. He backhanded it, pushed the chair out and stood, aimed his answer to the whole room. "I'm all set."

"Let's take my car. I'll bring you back here later, Laura."

Laura read between the lines. Mandy didn't want to go back to her apartment any time soon.

The sisters had to talk.

CHAPTER 91

Mandy's T-Bird lurched into her and Mark's apartment's parking lot.

Mark, riding shotgun, gave Mandy a peck on the cheek. Voice raspy, he said, "Will I see you later?"

Mandy stared ahead through the windshield and answered, "No, not tonight," then she added, "I'll be staying at home."

He thought, Home? *I thought this was your home.*

Peeved now, he shoved the door open and almost slammed it shut on Laura's leg as she exited the back seat, maneuvering to the now vacant front seat.

She yelped, "What the fuck, Mark?"

"Oh Christ, sorry Laura."

Laura roared and said, "Ah, my sister has that effect on men."

Mark tried to save face. "No sweat, catch you guys later."

Laura pulled the door shut before Mark even started walking. She and Mandy widened their eyes at each other.

"Boy, you sure can pick 'em Mandy. I have to hand it to you though, at least they're all good-looking."

"Shut up, Laura. We both picked Clyde Boudreaux."

"Again, fucking stunning."

Mandy got quiet, let her mind roam over her recent sexual encounters until Laura commented, as though a mind reader, "Jesus Mandy, I hope you're not pregnant with another of Clyde's babies." She pinned Mandy with a deep and direct stare. "Or, one of Marks?"

For the second time, Mandy Rose said, "Shut up, Laura."

"Let's hit the Crab Shack after we send the money off to Clyde. I should say Clyde Garcia."

Both laughed, letting steam off, a motley mix of emotions better camouflaged with mirth.

A reality too complex and painful would have to faced.

239

After sending the money off to Clyde Garcia, they headed to the Crab Shack. The parking lot was overflowing with cars packed so tightly there would be dings discovered in the morning on vehicles new enough for it to matter.

A big old green pickup was leaned on by elbows that also held silver flasks being tilted toward greedy lips that didn't want to pay the Shack's whiskey prices. Those elbows straightened when Mandy and Laura became visible in the moonlight.

Laura hooked her arm into Mandy's crooked elbow and said, "Pay no attention to those assholes."

The wolf-whistles rang through the cool night air, competing with the Cajun music that escaped the restaurant's doors and windows.

"Don't look at them… keep walking."

The shout was unmistakable. It was Jughead. A taunting bellow. "Well, if it ain't the gold-dust twins."

Followed by the booze-addled miscreant, "Yeah, Randy. They're out slumming."

Laura stopped abruptly, turned to face all four of their hecklers. Mandy stopped too.

Laura reached into her pocket and pulled out her badge. She held it up, and it sparkled silver and pink from the moon and the neon lights.

Two "holy shits," one "holy fuck," and one wide open pie hole struck dumb.

"What were you saying, boys?"

"Uh, nuthin'." "Just kiddin' around." Then whispered, "I told you she was a fucken cop now."

"Did you want to tell me something, guys?"

"Nope, have a nice night."

"Yeah, have a good time."

Laura slid the badge back where it came from and looked around at other patrons within earshot who were now a fascinated audience.

Two girls in short black cocktail dresses started to applaud and were joined by enough others to break the musical sound barrier.

The boys pocketed their flasks and tumbled into the pickup, making a last statement by peeling out of the parking lot, throwing gravel like a great noisy rooster tail.

The delicious aroma reminded both women of how hungry they were.

No sooner were they seated at Laura's usual VIP booth than Babette dropped coasters in front of them. She looked at Laura and said, "The usuals?"

They nodded in unison.

Mandy's mouth watered in anticipation.

Soon well-made rye and cognac Sazeracs, full of kick and muscle, put wet rings on the brand-new coasters. The distinctive scent of absinthe was unmistakable. Only for VIPs.

Two steaming crab cakes lined up for each sister. Babette grinned and said, "You gals looked hungry."

"Got that right."

"Two more Sazeracs in five minutes?"

"Perfect. You always know exactly what we want."

Babette beamed and slipped away.

They sipped and ate until the first crab cakes were crumbs and the Sazeracs showed the bottoms of both glasses.

Two more of the voluptuous drinks appeared.

"Mandy, while you were 'away,' taking Clyde to Mexico, I spoke with some of the kids who'd been taken and their mothers. In only one case was there a father involved, but he was very helpful.

"As I believe you're aware, there were two girls taken named Hannah."

Mandy stopped drinking, put her glass down. A cold and lonely feeling overtook her. She hadn't dreamed about her daughter in months and was accustomed to life as a childless woman. No ties. What would this investigation uncover? A damaged child? Her mother seemed content with Arriona. She was almost through with school; wanted to continue for a more advanced degree.

Oh God, what is the matter with me?

Laura poked her sister on her knuckles that lay like a dead fish by her glass.

Mandy jumped back into the present. "Sorry, Laura. What were you saying?"

"Mandy, level with me. What's going on with you?"

"I don't know. I feel empty inside. The only time I feel alive is when I'm helping someone else and forgetting about myself. It's like I don't really exist. Like I don't matter, don't count."

Laura's face clouded with concern. "Didn't the counselor you saw help at all?"

"I was too ashamed to tell her that my own father used me as a sex toy. It still feels like it was somehow my fault. Somehow I did something to make him think it was okay to do those things to me."

"Oh Mandy, I'm so sorry."

"Yes, I know you are. I know Mama can't totally face those ugly facts. She's never asked me to tell her about what happened. I feel sickened that she went to see him in prison."

"Mama's not a very strong person. She grew up with money and devoted parents who gave her everything, even let her marry Daddy when they knew he was bad for her; only after her for money and social status."

"Why did she have to go see him in prison?"

"She needed and got names to help find those responsible for Hannah's and the other kids' kidnappings."

Mandy's face softened, and the hard lines around her mouth faded with love. She said, "You sound like a cop."

"Hah! I am a cop."

Mandy said in a small, almost child-like voice, "Why did Daddy only molest me? And even softer, barely discernable, "And not you?"

"Think about it, Mandy. Later on when I came along, he was already abusing other little girls, so maybe he had no need to bother me. You must try not to make his monstrous behavior personal about you. He's an evil man, guilty of cruel and hateful acts committed against innocent and vulnerable children. As far as I'm concerned, he can rot in jail for the rest of his life. Mother should have no compassion for him and no desire to give him any money, not one red cent."

Mandy's cheeks glistened with tears; she reached out for her sister's hand.

"You're so strong, Laura."

"You're stronger than you think you are, Mandy. Maybe talking to a different counselor; one you feel you can completely trust will help. You've got your whole life to live."

"I do, don't I?"

Laura's face grew serious. "Maybe forget about men for a while, concentrate on yourself and what you want."

Mandy laughed. "It used to be you who had a parade of men at your door, the tables have turned. You don't even date anymore, and I'm going through men like Grant went through Richmond."

Laura gave a sly smile. "Well, there is this one cop… cute as hell. I think he's Creole. Oh my God, Mandy, he's so hot."

Now they howled. The laughter was cleansing and Mandy interjected, "No, I don't think I'm going to give men up."

Laura slapped her forehead and said, "What was I thinking?"

The laughter was drawing looks from nearby tables.

They laughed harder when they saw Babette bringing over their third Sazeracs.

CHAPTER 92

The foursome met under a blazing yellow sun in front of Paulo and Luna's bank.

Clyde choked back a gasp when he saw Luna clinging to Paulo's arm. Luna was in the middle of the ocean and Paulo the lifesaver. Her puffy red eyes spoke volumes.

Monica ran to her. "Que ha pasado?" Both women teared up as Luna gave a sugar-coated account of her horrific ordeal at the hands of the would-be kidnappers.

Paulo shook his head, his face hollow-eyed and drawn, as his wife poured out the short version of the disturbing encounter. Monica and Clyde knew details were being hidden.

Clyde's intestines clenched, and his bowels threatened to go loose right there on the sidewalk.

Monica said, "Let's get this done so you can get home and start to feel better."

The bank teller's brows knitted as she listened to the request for thousands of dollars to be withdrawn and almost deplete in a matter of minutes the recent deposit from the States. She said, "One moment please," turned and used the in-house phone to call the bank manager over to certify the transaction.

The chubby man who'd been called in wore a black suit that matched his black hair, which he parted down the middle. His weirdly tiny hands sported a ruby, set-in-gold, ring that flashed as he moved papers around and wet his thumb to turn over others.

He looked hard at Paulo and Luna, then spread his palms out and lifted them in acquiescence. He nodded toward the teller without a single hair on his head moving, not even a whisker.

The teller's face relaxed. She was glad to have this confirmation; if there was a problem, she'd lose her job. She looked at the paperwork and

244

looked at Paulo. "This deposit is for thirty thousand dollars, and you said you want to withdraw eighteen thousand. Is that correct?

Paulo's eyes bugged. His head swiveled toward Clyde, who stood elbow to elbow with him. "Did you hear that, Clyde?"

"I did." Clyde grinned. "Paulo, leave three thousand in your and Luna's account and withdraw twenty-seven thousand U.S. for us."

The teller debated about calling over Chubby Black Suit again but felt confident all was copacetic. A striking beauty with bright red lipstick, she watched Clyde's face, the best-looking hombre she'd ever laid eyes on. "Would he be staying in town?" She flipped him a look under lowered eyelids.

Knowing how to play the game, Clyde licked his bottom lip. He knew you caught more flies with honey than vinegar.

The pretty teller pulled stacks of currency out from hidden drawers. They made slapping noises as she piled them up on the counter.

"Do you want a canvas bag to hold all this, Señor Mendez?"

"Si, gracias," Paulo answered.

"For this exchange to American, there is a bank charge."

"Bueno, no hay problema." Paulo reached into his pocket and handed over the correct amount in pesos.

Finally the transaction was completed.

Paulo and Luna had three thousand dollars in their account. Clyde and Monica had twenty-seven thousand dollars; all in the requested American currency.

After the Mendez's left, Clyde led Monica to a darkened alleyway. He gave her almost half the cash. They each stuffed the bills in the homemade pockets improvised by Luna, using the needle and thread they'd bought at the bodego near the hotel.

Everything was green light.

Chapter 93

A block from the bank was a gasolinera that had two old coches for sale, parked face front on the side of the squat building. One was an ancient Willys Mexicana and the other a Gremlin hatchback that appeared to be in decent shape.

A cash deal was accomplished with little paperwork and a full tank of gas thrown in as a bonus.

Clyde knew damn well he'd been taken to the cleaners, but the ugly little car was exactly what he wanted. It would not draw attention.

Both hungry and thirsty, they drove their little Gremlin into the first taco stand they saw and bought one taco each and very large ice-filled Coca Colas. Pulling out the map, they were ecstatic to see they'd cross the border in less than three hours. They had the vehicle papers and their marriage papers, both proclaiming them as citizens of the United States of America.

Mr. and Mrs. Clyde Garcia headed to Texas.

CHAPTER 94

Morning climbed through the mansion's windows, spreading exposure like the tell-all tabloids in the drug store's magazine racks.

The gathering around the table was unusually mute with the exception of the resident chatterbox, Arriona. She seemed not to notice she was a solo act at the breakfast table, not pausing to wait for comments.

Angus stirred his coffee and said, "We've now found parents of twenty-nine children. Group counseling meetings have started at two different church basements. Some children will require individual counselors." His head bowed slightly. "Sadly, some victims are not to be reclaimed."

Head up again, he continued. "There are, as we've noted, two Hannahs to be followed up on. Both are approximately the same age. One, we believe has been 'outsourced' to, I'm loathe to say but Washington DC has enough proof to postulate, traffickers in Japan. Not one hundred percent certain yet?"

Angus was being careful with descriptions as Arriona was still sitting with them. "The other Hannah." He took a long sip of his coffee. "We've as yet unverified information that she was sent to New Jersey. We don't know if that was for trafficking purposes. This Hannah was quite young when she was deported from the Leprosarium, so we have hopes she was sold, black-market style, to adoptive parents."

Sophie clutched her throat and made a strange guttural sound that caused all eyes and ears to focus on her.

Arriona vacated her seat and scurried over to Sophie. She patted her shoulder as she tipped her little face into Sophie's, grave concern overtaking her youthful features. She pursed her lips and made soothing *tsk tsk tsk* noises.

Sophie released her hand from her own throat and encircled the child and pulled her up onto her lap. She rocked Arriona rhythmically and regained command of her uprooted emotions.

Angus said calmly, "We're working night and day. Soon we'll have more definite answers. We'll be coordinating with DC precincts to do takedowns in two different facilities being used for illicit trafficking, concerning minors."

Mandy, Laura and Cassy all wore pained expressions, eyes slitted and downturned mouths fixed to set jaws. Only Sophie had salty drips that gathered on her chin.

Angus continued, intent on getting all of this out. "We'll be sending someone from ours and other squads to some of the different locales where we believe children have been 'adopted' illegally."

"Aside from Hannah number two, there are other children who were dispatched to New Jersey and have been adopted by families living there. We will have someone from our squad go to DC and give intel for the scheduled takedowns there.

"None of these assignments promise to be easy. Takedowns never are. These are exacting details. It's not a walk in the park to tell people who believe they are the adoptive parents of a child, who they love as their own, that the child was not put up for adoption but was taken for the sole purpose of making money by unscrupulous baby snatchers.

"We'll be moving fast. Word may already have leaked to these traffickers, and they'll change venues to avoid apprehension." He took another sip of, now cold, coffee. "Carl Edwards is being wrung dry. He won't go free but will be rewarded by serving a sentence in a faraway prison. So far Big Carl claims no responsibility for any violence but admits pedophilia. Says he's sought psychiatric help for this addiction in the past, to no avail.

"But Carl is a fountain of information. His cooperation will be instrumental in corralling dozens of insiders, not to mention as many malfeasants whose names will be shocking and familiar to the general populace once all this is made public."

Mandy Rose's mind wandered. *When will Clyde reappear? Is he really married? Does he love me? Or her?*

Chapter 95

Monica patted Clyde's thigh. "Why is this line so long?"

"Dunnoh, Monica. Maybe it's a good thing. Shoo us through without a hassle. Do we have any of those burritos left that Luna gave us?"

"Let me see." She leaned over the back of her seat and stretched into the backseat where the grease-stained paper bag lay on its side. She rummaged around inside where they'd also stuffed the empty taco wrappers. There was some watery cola left in both of the cups.

Clyde observed her rounded rump as it steadied on the seat near his face. And remembered Mandy Rose. Mandy reaching back for his Jordans. He dreamily recalled what they did that day. He pressed down on his male hardness to relieve the pressure.

When Monica flipped around, she had a slightly bent burrito in a clinging wrapper held high. She laid it on his lap and was instantly aroused by the hard mound that tilted the burrito on a slant.

"Wow, Clyde." She pulled the burrito away and dropped it on the floor. Next she reached under the steering wheel to unzip Clyde's pants and free the swollen member. She stood it straight up and stroked it. Then she wet her fingers to make a more slippery ride.

Not to be left out, she slipped her free hand between her own legs. Always smart to wear a skirt, she thought. She massaged herself in the way she knew would produce enough juice for a very satisfying experience.

Clyde's eyes drooped. His head tilted back in passionate response to the up and down motion of Monica's slender fingers.

Not a moment too soon, the man and woman reached delicious heights of passion, fed by the taboo nature of Monica masturbating Clyde while masturbating her own self with him driving. They moaned together. His pleasure sounded deep and throaty, hers high and feminine.

When Clyde regained his composure, he saw that they were at the border station to the United States and were next in line. "Get the marriage papers," he said.

They rolled into the slot next to the border patrol station. There was one man inside the little building and one outside who was armed.

Monica peeled off two one-hundred-dollar bills and handed them to Clyde along with the marital documents.

The guard, a tall spaghetti in a dark green uniform, looked inside the Gremlin and took in the open fly on Clyde's trousers and the white leavings that were still shiny wet and doubled over for a better view. His buttons clicked on the partially open window.

Monica's skirt was jacked up and her face was flushed and moist. The interior smelled like sex.

The patrolman smirked and winked at Clyde. He eyeballed the recently dated marriage license; noted that they were both US citizens and went no further. He kept tucked the two hundred-dollar bills into his back pocket, returned the certificate of marriage and said in English, "You two need to get a motel. Congratulations on your marriage. Drive safely."

He tipped two fingers to his cap, bobbed his head and motioned them on.

Chapter 96

Popping another French fry from the huge communal bag where Monica and Clyde had dumped two large greasy salty orders, she talked around the tasty treat. "I don't understand. You said this Felix character was a lowlife. The one who kidnapped the kids, maybe even including your daughter."

"And that's still true. The night Angus and the family invaded the Leprosarium, it all happened very fast. The whole damn police force arrived to recover the children still kept there. They arrested a bunch of those creeps and found Felix in the home of Mandy Rose's parents' house. Her father was shot and dying."

"Did Felix shoot the father?"

"No, Mandy Rose did."

"Did she get arrested?"

"No, it was self-defense."

"Lucky for you."

Clyde rolled his eyes. "I never spoke to Felix again after that. He's in jail now."

Monica licked salt from her lips and said, "Oh, so what is it you want me to do?"

Clyde continued at his own pace. "That's where we come in, Monica sweetie."

She stopped chewing, uncrossed her legs from where she sat in the motel armchair. "I still don't understand. Why would we talk to him?"

"Not we. You. You will talk to him."

Monica leaned forward, resting her elbows on her knees, holding her head as though it weighed a ton. "Okay?"

"Mon, he's the only one who will have inside information about where some of the children were transported and for what purpose."

"You mean for sex?"

"Some kids were sold to be adopted, some little ones were sold for sexual purposes and the last use they had for these children was for their organs to be harvested for people who needed transplants."

"Oh, God." Monica's face crumbled.

"Yes, I know, it's awful."

"Why will he tell us, I mean me, anything?"

"Because he's a fat disgusting pig who loves junk food and a chain smoker who has no funds. The cops took all his assets."

Monica opened her mouth and said, "Ah."

Clyde said, "That's right. We do."

"So we get information and he gets money?"

"Yes, we'll deposit it in his commissary account. I'm dead certain he's hurting real bad for some extra crapola to make his time there easier."

"Is he the one that killed that baby girl?"

"Yes, one and the same."

"But Clyde, he doesn't know me."

"When he hears a woman's name is there to see him, he'll approve the visit; won't care if it's a mistake."

"When do we do this?"

"We'll have a nice meal tonight, no fast food, get a good night's sleep, and you'll see him in the morning."

Monica would've done whatever Clyde asked her to do. Her only worry was whether he was still hooked on that Mandy Rose person.

CHAPTER 97

Detective Richard Sloane said, "Good morning, Angus." Rick's hair was shaggy, in need of a trim. Everyone on the force was doing extra overtime, sometimes without pay.

Angus looked drawn as he seated himself in Captain Sloane's office. He didn't bother removing the file folders from the chair, just plopped down on top of them. One small nod was all he could muster.

Some more of the sludge that served as coffee would help.

"We have some addresses where some of the adopted children are now living. Only the ones that were sequestered in the Leprosarium are being followed up on from our office. The number of taken kids is beyond belief."

Angus had this intel; anticipated what Rick Sloane was leading up to.

"One child, a female child, is alleged to be living outside of Rumson, New Jersey. Information gathered insinuates this child could be Hannah Bokum."

Angus kept his face neutral.

"We'd like to send someone there to the house to investigate. We won't send Laura Bokum for obvious reasons."

"Of course." Angus still had on his cop face.

"Cassandra Allain's name has been brought up. We feel it's better to send a woman as this is a very sensitive mission. Thoughts?"

"Yes, Rick. Cassandra. Cassy's a good choice. She also has a daughter who's around the same age the Bokum girl will be now."

"And," Sloane added, "we can't spare our more experienced officers right now. They're needed to continue ferreting out these pockets of filth where children are waiting to be rescued before they get moved. I don't need to tell you, time is of the essence. So, you'll take care of telling Cassandra, Angus?"

"Yes, consider it done."

"Her flight is booked, leaving tomorrow. I'll get you the exact details."

Angus pushed his palms on his knees to rise, leaving all the files he had been parked on, pancaked. He left to go home, determined to give Cassy as much time as possible to prepare for her mission. *Would Hannah be coming back home?*

"Oh Agnus, one more thing."

Angus twisted back to listen.

Sloane finished up with, "A team from DC's going in to take down another hidey-hole where kids are being kept. This place is used for servicing the perverts. Story is old prison cells and mattresses. The other Hannah, or who we think is the other Hannah, who's around the same age is purported to be there."

Sophie's face flashed in Angus's mind's eye. He said nothing to Captain Sloane, just dipped his head and left, closing the door behind him.

<h1 style="text-align:center">CHAPTER 98</h1>

Mabel wore a new fuchsia dress. The color complimented her wavy silver hair. She'd also applied considerably more make-up and was delighted with the effect. She looked dazzling, if she did say so herself. The ruby lipstick was the crowning stroke. Yes, indeed. And she didn't feel the least bit guilty about the scent of blackmail that clung to her much overdue relationship with Dr. William Romero.

After all, they'd both get what they wanted.

Clyde Boudreaux's personal and confidential file was now non-existent.

She patted her hair in place and rubbed her naked ring finger, which she hoped would soon have a healthy diamond engagement ring to fill the naked spot.

He did look dapper in his dark blue suit, white shirt and striped red and cream tie.

The restaurant they dined in was top shelf. On the outskirts of town, not to attract observation, though there was no Mrs. William Romero to be considered.

Her delicious thoughts were interrupted as the good doctor spoke. "We have everything arranged. Clyde Boudreaux won't be acquitted due to a diagnosis of legal insanity. So that negates any need for a postponement of trial and/or a lawyer to convince a jury that the crime committed holds a not-guilty verdict by reason of insanity."

He went on as he sipped from an elegant glass of tawny colored port. "There will be a closed-door judgment with His Honor Thomas Grady presiding. Just a one-line notice in a single newspaper."

"What about Blade and Sam?"

"They've been clammed up. They won't say a word. Neither of them wants to lose their job. They love what they do. And nobody would believe a word Rosie says, especially when she starts spouting that gibberish about the door magically opening. My guess is those two idiots left it unlocked, just like they did the outside door."

"Billy…"

He was revolted when she called him that. He felt his gorge rise.

"What about Dr. Harold Bokum? How much does he know?"

He swallowed the foul-tasting bile. "Don't worry about him. I've got him all taken care of. And you too, my dear."

CHAPTER 99

"Okay Mon, you understand what you have to say?"

"Yes, Clyde."

"You have the money for his commissary account, right?"

"Clyde, we've been over all this a dozen times." Monica widened her eyes and nodded.

"It's not you. It's me. I just want to make sure Felix gets it. We talked about 'you know who' at my house. He knew her. That's when he tried to bring me into the kidnappings and the Leprosarium."

"Yes, I know who 'you know who' is. That Bertie woman. But you never admitted anything to Felix; never said you actually…" Monica stopped and swallowed a lump the size of a prune, then softly said, "murdered her."

"I never said whether I even knew her, this Bertie Bergeron. And I never confessed to killing anyone, not then, not now, not even to you."

"I know."

"So, most important, see if you can find out who knew what and admit nothing, other than that you know me, and convince him you'll be putting some money from me, in his account today. Tell him I'll keep sending something. He'll go for that."

They parked the Gremlin and Monica got out, smoothed her pocketbook to check the bulge the two paperbacks made. She wondered about the titles Clyde'd picked out for Felix. Both fiction crime novels.

Her stomach roiled and she retasted her onion omelet. Bad choice. Should've fasted.

After a brief sit-down on a wooden bench, the lady in uniform looked at her and crooked her finger for Monica to come forward to the desk.

The lady was a cop. Her uniform looked starched. So did her blonde hair. "What can I do for you?"

Monica froze.

"Yes, miss, what're you here for?"

All the information poured out in one nonstop regurgitation.

"Whoah. Okay, and what is your relation to Felix Guidry?"

"Cousins, first cousins."

Officer Cohen raised one eyebrow and made a tiny noise in her throat. The noise said, "You're full of crap."

"All right, Mrs. Garcia, leave your pocketbook in one of those lockers." She pointed. "Lock it up with this key." She slapped it down. "Bring the key back to me. Your books and money will be processed after your visit with Mr. Guidry, your uh, cousin."

Monica hurried to do as she was told; returned and held the key out to the bored looking woman who took it and reached under her counter for a button, which she pressed. She cocked her head in the direction of an oversized gray metal door that opened on command.

Monica tasted her breakfast one more time.

Inside the visitor's room, she was patted down by a female officer who looked as though she'd rather be home, drinking coffee and watching the soaps.

The metal chair she sat in was between two women, one Negro and one Latina. Both were engaged in very lively discussions with the men who sat opposite them, leaning on their elbows and listening intently; eyes filled with emotions that defied easy definitions.

Oh my God, that's him. It has to be. He wasn't as fat as Clyde'd described him. His jet-black hair stuck to his forehead, and his uncommonly plump lips glistened. His coarse features scrunched in bewilderment when he saw the only waiting visitor seated with hands folded on the long table was a looker.

He'd been given the name and "relationship" of his guest. A somewhat gruesome smile appeared, and his mind formed three words. "What the fuck?" He went to the obvious place and plopped his still overly large body down.

Before he had a chance to speak, Monica whispered, "Clyde sent me."

He took a deep breath and when he expelled it, the fetid air challenged Monica's gag reflex. She kept her language simple, as per Clyde's instructions. "Clyde wants to leave you some cash to help make life here easier."

Before he could question his good fortune, she finished up. She wanted out of here. "Clyde wants information you may have about anyone who could be a danger to him."

"Well lady, Clyde never did do much of nothing. What's he worried about? 'Sides, ain't he in the nut house?"

Monica thought it best to say as little as possible. "Clyde said you and he were childhood friends, and he wanted to help you out."

"Holy shit. Really?"

"Yes, really. He'll leave money in your account on a regular basis. He asks that you never discuss him with anyone."

"Holy shit! Don't he want to know about his kid?"

"Yes Felix, all that you know. Please."

He liked her saying please to him. "I'll tell you about New Jersey. Those early kids, 'cluding his rug rat, all went to rich bastards in New Jersey." His eyes shone. "I made a good bundle on those." His fat lips broadened into a smarmy grin.

He told her the names he was familiar with but added that they didn't know Clyde.

"If you think of anything else, write it down. And if we understand each other, I'll be going now."

"Wait, wait. Will you visit again?"

Monica looked into the eyes of the kidnapping baby murderer and saw a vacancy that cried for comfort, pleaded for someone to care.

She patted his big meaty hand and let her hand stay still for a few seconds, then she pushed away from the table and answered his question. "Maybe, I'll see." She blinked to clear her vision and held her arms close to her body as she dashed back to the gray door. She could feel his eyes on her back. It made her sad.

She stopped short at the door as the gray button from this side was pressed to let her out. Once inside the Gremlin, she collapsed into her seat.

"Are you okay, Mon?"

"Fine."

"You don't look fine. You look pale." Clyde reached over and rubbed her back in small circles.

"I'm okay. That guy is pathetic. I feel sorry for him."

"That's because you're such a good person, not because he deserves your sympathy."

"You didn't see his face."

"I'm sorry you had to do that. If it makes you feel any better, I'll make sure he has plenty of money for whatever he needs in there." Then Clyde added, "Within reason."

Monica wiped her face with a pink tissue she'd pulled from her purse that so recently had been tucked into a prison locker.

She set her lips and promised to do some soul-searching about her life. The second thought that flashed like orange neon was, "That poor Felix."

CHAPTER 100

"But Cassy, you've never met Hannah. You won't know if it's her."

"Uh, Laura, I have photos and the date she was taken. The Leprosarium lists are pretty specific on where these kids were to be relocated. And you know you're not selected for this assignment because of the close family connection." Cassy threw her arms up in exasperation with her friend. "Christ Laura, don't get suspended your first month on the job."

"I've thought of that. No reason anyone has to know I went to New Jersey. Right?"

"Damn it. I'll know." Eyes blazing, she said, "You're not gonna drag me into anything because you're so fucking stubborn."

Laura knew Cassy was right.

The scraping sound of footsteps caused both women to turn toward the open arch into the kitchen.

"Mama?" And. "Sophie?"

"Yes, my dears. I heard all of it." Sophie sent a bolt of maternal authority straight to her daughter's eyes. "Laura, stay here. No one has jurisdiction over me."

Laura countered, dreading the answer. "And what does that exactly mean?" As if she didn't know.

"It means, I'm going to New Jersey. While you two have been bickering, Angus called and we have a street address where a child called Hannah was taken and still resides. The timing is accurate." After a pause, Sophie repeated, "I'm going. Cassy, is your flight booked?"

Cassy cast a remorseful glance at Laura but answered, "It's tomorrow, around one p.m."

"Give me the itinerary, I'll get the same flight."

Sophie and Cassy walked together through the arch to complete their arrangements.

Laura gritted her teeth while she watched their backs.

CHAPTER 101

"Laura, looks like it's me and you tonight."

"Don't you want to pick Mark up?" Laura didn't bother to squeeze closed the smile that blossomed.

"You know I don't." Mandy Rose put the back of her hand to her forehead in an imitation of a Southern belle's fainting spell.

They both laughed and felt like high school mean-girls.

"Shit, let's break out some of the new duds we bought. Things've been way too serious around here. We're young and free. We deserve some fun."

Together they climbed the ornate gold staircase, ignoring the sounds of their mother who was in her room packing for the New Jersey trip.

"We both look good in this," Mandy Rose said as she held up a stretchy red dress that barely kissed the top of a kneecap."

Their closet bulged with clothes.

"You look better in it. Let me see what's back here." Laura pushed some quilt-coated hangers to one side and pulled out the black and white romper dress that still had tags hanging from it. Tags that could double as artwork. "Oooh." She put the short dress up to her bodice and did a little kick.

"I think *I* want that one."

"I'll take the red one then."

"Never mind, I want the red one."

"Mandy, you can't make your mind up about dresses any easier than you make your mind up about men."

"You just may be right, sister dear."

They both stopped as they became aware the phone had been ringing for quite some time.

They heard Sophie pattering down the long staircase to answer it.

The amount of silence that permeated the house was deafening, and they looked at each other.

Laura's Watcher kicked in. "Something's wrong."

They followed the path their mother had taken. The older woman slid to the floor, the receiver still in both hands. She turned and raised her eyes just enough to view both daughters surrounding her.

"What's happened?"

"What's the matter, Mama?"

"Your father's dead." She paused. "Murdered!"

CHAPTER 102

The New Orleans airport had three people aboard destined for New Jersey.

Two women sat in first class; Sophie'd bumped Cassy's economy ticket so they were seated together. It was a full flight.

Unbeknownst to them, a handsome Black man sat with legs folded and knees cramped in a middle seat in the back of the plane. The name on the ticket was Clyde Garcia.

He'd told Monica he could only get one ticket as the plane was completely booked.

She'd accepted being left behind without complaint.

Cassy'd never flown before. She held onto the arm rests until her hands ached. Sophie stroked Cassy's knuckles.

Cassy stared down at her own knees, not moving an inch, as though it might rock the plane, causing a crash.

Sophie tried soothing words, but Cassy held tight and watched her knees.

The airline hostess approached and bent to Cassy. "First flight, honey?"

Cassy nodded.

"Perfectly normal. Can I get you something? Glass of wine maybe?"

Cassy shook her head, then twisted to look up at the concerned face. Something in the kind brown eyes relaxed her. She felt her neck release and her hands loosen. "I'll be fine. Thank you."

The rest of the flight was smooth, very little turbulence. Neither of the women ordered wine.

In the back of the airliner, the handsome man with black hair and orange roots slept peacefully.

CHAPTER 103

"News travels fast, doesn't it?"

Laura noted Mandy Rose's face. It looked like she'd just sucked a lemon. "Pay them no mind. We're here to enjoy ourselves."

The Crab Shack was jumping, as usual. When the sisters made their entrance, a barely discernable hush blanketed the full-to-capacity dining area. The patrons seated at the bar, backs to them, continued with their usual banter.

Mandy Rose and Laura had excellent hearing and easily picked up the undertones. "Harry Bokum."…"Murdered."…"Heard he got knifed."…"In prison, right?"

Babette hurried over as soon as they'd slid into their booth. The waitress said, rather loudly, "Assholes, there's no shortage. The usual?"

"Yeah, keep 'em coming."

Laura took her badge out and let it make a clunking sound as she plopped it on the table.

The decibels in the room took a turn for the worse.

She picked the badge up… and dropped it again.

Shoulders pivoted back to their tables where they belonged, and customers went back to their former conversations. Some continued in whispers.

Mandy tapped her fingers on the table and waited to talk while Babette dropped off the Sazeracs and crab cakes. "Is there something wrong with me?"

"What do you mean?"

"I mean, what the hell is the matter with me?"

"What do you think is the matter with you?"

"I have no feelings."

"Sure, you do. You love Mama, don't you?"

Mandy paused. "Yeah, of course I do."

"Okay, what else?"

"I can't stick to a decision."

"Maybe you have too many choices."

"Yah think?"

"I do. I also think that being molested by your own father caused you to push down your feelings so you could disappear while he invaded you."

"I'll tell you, Laura. I feel nothing that he's dead."

"A little secret, Mandy, I'm glad he's gone. It'll be better for Mama. No need for a divorce and she can marry Angus sooner. I wonder if someone paid to have him capped."

"Capped?"

"That means murdered."

"Oh. Thanks, Laura. I feel a bit better."

"One more thing."

"Yes, what is it?"

"This is hard to say."

"You don't have to tell me."

"I want to."

"Okay, what do you want to say?"

Mandy drew her hands into her chest and balled her fists, tears streaming unchecked down her cheeks.

Laura waited, unsure of what was coming, but knew it was something big.

Unable to look Laura in the eye, Mandy stared at the table.

A moment passed.

Finally, still looking down, her hair a curtain on both sides of her face, a soft voice made its way out of the tunnel and across the table.

"I knew Hannah was going to be kidnapped."

Laura gasped.

CHAPTER 104

While Monica was very attracted to Clyde, she was relieved to discover he wanted to go to New Jersey without her.

She was rid of her cousin Pablo, doubted he'd ever make it out of Mexico. Rescuing Pablo, helping him escape apprehension by United States authorities was done because he was family. But he'd become a drain on her. Finding Clyde half dead on the sidewalk was a new challenge. He seemed to be on his feet now.

With a car that ran and plenty of money in her pocket, she could go on her merry way. At last count, she'd had four husbands. Her immediate plan was to bring money to that poor Felix. His swarthy looks were such a temptation. He was not a threat to Clyde, she reasoned.

So Felix was all hers. She licked her lips.

Chapter 105

Laura put her forearms on the table. "So Mandy, what'm I supposed to do with that information? That fucking bombshell."

Mandy lifted her Sazerac and quaffed it down in one long swallow. "Nothing. I had to tell someone."

"Does *anyone* else know?"

"Daddy knows. Rather knew. Now that he's dead, it's only you and me."

"Still not sure why you told me."

"Who else would I tell? I trust you. You're my sister."

Laura leaned in. "What about Clyde? He's Hannah's father."

"Oh no, I could never tell him."

"Mark?"

"Definite no. He's history anyway."

"Well Mandy, we may be hearing soon if Hannah is found in New Jersey."

"I know, and that scares me."

Laura pushed her hair back off her forehead and stared at her sister. Why?"

"I can't really answer that. Feels like something inside me is missing."

Laura covered Mandy's hands with her own and said, "Let's let this play out and see what happens."

Mandy's answer was, "Don't tell Mama."

"Don't worry. It stays between us. Can you tell me how you knew?"

Mandy went dead quiet. Half a minute dragged by. She bit her top lip and said in a hoarse whisper, "I overheard Daddy on the phone making arrangements for Hannah to be taken."

Laura's head jerked back as she said, "Ah!" Then, "You've known from the start?"

Mandy Rose didn't answer.

She didn't have to.

CHAPTER 106

Sophie was a seasoned flyer, not so Cassy, so the older woman took the lead. "We have to rent a car and get some maps to find the address where Hannah may be." She added, "We hope."

Cassy's eyes were huge and dark, a bit apprehensive. "Woe, this airport is massive."

Sophie gave Cassy one of her famous maternal hugs. The two women functioned well together. Just like family. Maybe better.

"Can you watch over both suitcases while I rent the car?"

"Sure." Cassy pulled both pieces of luggage to a vinyl bench, sat and crossed her very long legs over the top of them. She'd heard the loud-speaker's warning about not letting your belongings out of your sight.

Her long brown legs caught the eye of Clyde Boudreaux Garcia.

Under his breath, he said, "Holy shit!" He recognized the handsome Black woman from a photo Laura'd shown him months ago. So striking was this woman, that there was no possibility of a mistaken identity. He was pretty damn sure Cassandra, yeah, that was her name, didn't know what he looked like as he'd never knowingly permitted photos of himself to be taken. *Voodoo beliefs*. He kept his eye on her as he looked for a map of his own.

Once in the rental car, suitcases stowed in the trunk, Sophie and Cassy took time to study the maps they'd just purchased and familiarize themselves with the controls on their automatic Ford Fairmont.

Sophie happily agreed to let Cassy drive.

In the same airport parking lot, Clyde Boudreaux Garcia was checking out his Chevy Compact, a stick-shift. He'd also bought maps. He was prepared.

The local snitches had told him years ago where black-market babies ended up. Often up north to wealthy clients, most often New Jersey. At that time, he hadn't known his daughter was one of them.

He figured the expensive-looking older blonde was Hannah's grandmother. He banked on her being in the dark about what he looked like also.

It was crystal clear why they were here in New Jersey.

Felix was worth the money he cost him. Said New Jersey right off the bat.

CHAPTER 107

The sun was setting. An army of maple trees created a spectacular panorama. A green emerald canopy closed over the street Cassy and Sophie traveled over.

Clyde was enamored of the clean crisp air that harbored scant humidity. The dark shady tunnel with slices of sunshine rippling through it was glorious, reminding him of a Winslow Homer painting he'd seen once. The overhanging branches provided a cover of sorts for his Chevy.

Signs of city life had waned. Now the houses were hidden from view by trees and stonewalls and became farther and farther apart.

There were no names for identification. The house numbers were designed to blend with their surroundings.

"There!" cried Cassy when she located a house number. It's 2001. Must be odd numbers on this side of the street. If the numbers are going up, we'll be at 2009 any minute."

Sophie's hands were sweaty. She pressed on her sternum to relieve a painful bubble. "Urp."

"Are you okay?"

"Fine, just nervous, shouldn't drink soda pop."

Meanwhile Clyde kept a longer distance between him and the Ford. There was little traffic on this road.

The driveway was long. Tall pine trees lined both sides. Protective troops. The drive curved to the right and a house appeared.

Sophie's hand flew to her mouth as a magnificent structure filled her vision. There was a steeply pitched hip roof that overlooked ornate gables. The house's exterior was a pale orange brick and gray stone combination. It was stunning. Large, manicured shrubs surrounded the entrance.

Cassy parked the lowly Ford in the cobblestone circular driveway.

The women exited, each holding their breath.

271

A rounded three-step porch of pink marble brought them to a massive oak front door with a tiny bell, almost hidden.

Cassy gulped and swallowed. Sophie pushed the little bell.

In less than a minute, a Latina woman dressed in a crisp black uniform opened the door. Her hair was pulled back severely, away from her plain but attractive face.

Cassy said, "I'm Officer Allain and would like to speak with Mr. or Mrs. Trenton."

"State the nature of your visit please."

"It's personal. I'm here from New Orleans and am only authorized to speak with either George or Martha Trenton."

The dark eyes grew suspicious. "Do you have identification?"

Sophie just stood frozen to the pink marble stoop as Cassy extracted her badge from her trousers and held it up to be inspected.

Valeria brought her face close to the badge and squinted to read every word until a noisy new voice joined the gathering. "Valeria, who's there? Is it my friend?"

Valeria made a shoving motion with her hand behind her skirt.

"Go back inside, Izzy. It's not Jacqueline."

"Who is it?"

The child ducked and popped up in front of the flustered woman in charge of her.

Sophie went down on her knee when she caught sight of the tangerine ringlets that framed the little green-eyed beauty.

One word escaped her parched lips. "Hannah!"

The child stopped; went still. Her emerald eyes widened. A primal memory. A long-neglected visual that held a treasure chest of warm and tender feelings. Longings resurrected.

The child called Isabella reached her hand out to the stricken lady as an ill-formed memory glistened near the surface of her seven-year-old psyche.

The scent of certain long-forgotten flowers tickled her tiny nostrils. She inhaled and caught her breath in remembrance.

Valeria was too stunned to do other than stand there, open-mouthed.

Izzy touched the lady's face, which was drenched in unsought tears.

Sophie reached up to enfold the slender little fingers in her own. She longed to take the girl into her arms, but other strong hands held the girl in place.

"Go inside, Izzy. Right now."

"But, Valeria."

"Now."

"But."

"Go. You have no right being here. I want you both to leave."

Not to be deterred, Cassandra replied, "Yes, actually we do. Can we see George or Martha Trenton. Please."

"Make an appointment."

The door slammed. *Bam*!

Valeria knew something of the history concerning when Isabella came to live with her employers. She never asked questions but surmised things might not have been entirely legal with the adoption. She had to alert the Trentons.

"Sophie, we have to leave. We'll come back tomorrow."

"Cassy, that's my granddaughter. That's Hannah!"

CHAPTER 108

Exhausted and hungry, the two travelers were busy spreading the Chinese take-out cartons on the one table in their motel room.

Cassy said, "I think I have flight lag."

"That's jet lag and no, you don't." Sophie cracked her first smile since discovering her granddaughter was alive and well. The strain of wanting her so much was taking its toll. She didn't think she would get a wink of sleep; couldn't wait to get her lawyers involved in bringing Hannah back home. It grated her nerves thinking of Hannah in that house. Would they leave with her? Kidnap her!

"Sophie, didn't they put forks in here? I can't use these sticks to eat."

"Me neither. Look in the bottom of the bag, they usually put both. Plastic of course."

"Yep, here they are. Kind of greasy from leaky cartons, but forks."

Bang! Bang! Bang!

"Who on Earth could that be?"

"You stay seated. I'll get it," Cassy said, loud enough to be heard through the door. "Yes, who's there?"

Bang! Bang! Bang!

"Answer me right now."

A male voice pleaded, "Don't be scared, please don't be scared. It's Clyde, Hannah's daddy."

Cassy turned and watched Sophie's face go pale as she heard the message.

"Oh my God, what should I do?"

"Let him in, Cassy."

The door was unbolted and the visitor stood there, face a perfect mask, combining anguish and hope. "May I come in?"

Cassy moved to one side, and the tall handsome man entered the motel room that reeked of Chinese take-out.

Sophie, ever the mother hen, queried, "Are you hungry?"

Clyde's green eyes shone and locked on Sophie's tired face. His shoulders sagged and a slow smile blossomed. He resisted the urge to cry as a wave of relief overtook him. He said with a husky emotional voice, "You're Sophie." Not a question.

"And, like you said, you're Hannah's daddy."

He hesitated with his next words, yet out they tumbled. "I saw her. At the door. I heard her."

"You did?"

"Yes, I followed you, parked on the property; hid behind the big van in the driveway."

"Oh Clyde, isn't she beautiful?"

Now his tears could not be stopped.

Cassy observed all this with new awareness. Why had she ever thought white people had no emotions.

Clyde pushed farther into the room and took a seat at the table with Sophie.

"We have a lot to talk about Clyde."

Clyde wanted to hug Sophie but didn't dare. He was already tugging on his shirt and feeling self-conscious at showing so much emotion.

Cassy took the reins.

"Let's eat all this good food while it's still at least sort of warm."

By the end of the evening, a plan had been agreed upon.

The morning would bring calls to Mandy Rose first of all, then Angus to notify the police department the child in New Jersey was indeed Hannah.

Finally Sophie would make calls. Calls for the best attorneys money could buy.

Lawyers to move as fast as possible to bring Hannah home.

CHAPTER 109

Still in New Jersey, the three were seated in a booth at the Urban Griddle ordering breakfast.

"I can't believe you ordered grits, Clyde." Sophie grinned widely.

The two hundred plus pound waitress resisted an eye roll and diplomatically said to Clyde, "Home fries or French fries?"

Clyde somewhat chaffed, answered, "Give me the house fries."

"No sweetie, home fries. You'll love 'em."

Cassy chuckled out loud and said to Sophie, "Can't take him anywhere."

The large waitress waited, tapping her pencil on her pad while the trio went into peals of laughter.

Orders in, coffee poured, everyone was light-hearted as the tensions lifted.

Sophie and Clyde were optimistic. They'd have Hannah back home in Louisiana where she belonged.

Cassy had a cop's viewpoint about people. Some were good. Some not-so-much. She wished they could've just grabbed Hannah and taken her without a time lag, but that's not reality. Cassy'd been tasked with making most of the early morning phone calls. Sophie would call the lawyers later.

Cassy reported as she sipped her coffee, "I got ahold of Angus. He was ecstatic. This means it's more likely some of the other kids will be found and given back to their parents."

"Did you talk to Mandy Rose?"

"Laura answered. She said Mandy was taking a shower and she'd tell her the news as soon as she finished."

Sophie's face darkened as she considered her older daughter.

Clyde too became still.

Cassy, always mystified by Laura's older sister, remained neutral,

276

banged the bottom of the ketchup bottle to smother her newly arrived home fries.

Clyde announced his intention to telephone Monica as he noted the payphone in the corner of the little eatery.

Alone at the table, Sophie said to Cassy, "I really like that young man. I can see Hannah's face in his. Same tangerine hair and emerald eyes. Of course only Clyde's roots are orange."

Cassy nodded, going so far as to say, "Yeah, if I liked men, instead of women, I could go for him."

Sophie actually hugged herself, so pleased was she with how far she'd come burying old prejudices and embracing an open-minded worldview. Life was so good, not having to carry a truckload of biases on her back. Love was love. How could that be bad?

Clyde returned, pulled his chair out and plunked down.

The two women questioned with eyes. No words.

"No answer at the motel where I left Monica. Everyone should have a mobile phone Rover like yours and Laura's.'

Cassy made a grimacing face. "Oh Clyde, that would be a disaster."

Sophie'd insisted on upgrading Clyde's airline seat to first-class on their flight. She'd also insisted on his using her law firm for his defense, with what she called, "His legal troubles."

She was anxious to contact her firm: Babina, Frisbie and Kraft.

Sophie wanted to get home and get this ball rolling. Angus was needed to provide necessary information.

Time was of the essence.

CHAPTER 110

All three passengers were tired for the flight home and a tacit agreement was made to get some extra sleep on the flight. Even Sophie slept soundly.

Clyde popped Sophie and Cassy's suitcases into the taxi's trunk, and they all piled into the Yellow Cab. Sophie gave the driver the destination; her address.

She said to Clyde, "You left your auto with Monica, uh your wife? Right?"

Clyde jutted his jaw, then answered, "She has the car and half the money you sent to us for getting out of Mexico. She's not answering the phone at the motel. Not sure why."

Sophie said, "Hmmmm," and sucked her lips into a thin line.

Cassandra, in the taxi's back seat with Clyde, twisted to face him and said, loud enough to blot out the road noise, "You think she skedaddled?"

Clyde threw his head back and cracked up laughing. "You read my thoughts, Cassy. I'll tell you one thing, she was quite smitten with Felix in the jail house visit."

"You're kidding?"

"Nope, I think she has a 'savior complex.'"

"Sophie furrowed her brows and observed Clyde."

He said, "Yeah, your daughter taught me a lot of psychology."

Still half-shouting, Cassy questioned, "Exactly what is that?"

"Some people feel good about themselves only when helping someone else. Hell… oops, sorry Sophie, didn't mean to swear. Heck, she saved my life. I would've been dead meat if she didn't rescue me. Put her own life in danger."

Sophie looked pained and said, "Tell us more about it later, when we can talk without shouting."

The group liked that idea and quietened down. The rest of the ride continued in silence, heading, without stops for the Bokum mansion.

CHAPTER 111

Sophie ran up to Angus as he was replacing the handset into the telephone base; almost knocking him over.

His strained features relaxed at her enthusiasm.

"We found her. We found Hannah."

Angus hugged Sophie and peered over her head at a tired looking Cassy and a new arrival.

Sophie pulled out of Angus's embrace and started to introduce Clyde. "Angus, this is…"

Angus interrupted. "That phone call was about you, young man."

Clyde said, "Office Clark, I'm here to turn myself in and cooperate any way I can."

Laura shot Clyde a warning look that was loaded for bear, put her finger to her lips to stifle whatever else he was about to say.

A long pause.

"Well, son, you may be the luckiest person I've ever known who was accused of murder. You must have a guardian angel."

Clyde thought of his gris-gris, now missing, hopefully being held for him by Mandy Rose. That was all he could come up with to explain Angus's statement.

"Let's all sit down and I'll explain what I'm talking about."

"But Angus, did you hear? We found Hannah."

"I did. Cassy called with the great news this morning."

"Of course." Sophie remembered now that Cassy had made the call.

Everyone took a seat at the usual table; Almadine showed up with a pile of black muffins, her specialty. These muffins had dark blackstrap molasses and pecans in them; everyone said hers were the best. She agreed.

She noted Clyde with interest. "I'll bring some coffee in too."

"Sit with us Almadine. There's good news you should hear."

At last, Angus started while still savoring the moistest black muffin he'd ever tasted. Better than Pearl's. His mother never put pecans in there.

Sophie reached over and removed an errant crumb on his lip. He caught her hand and held onto it.

"That telephone call was His Honor, Judge Thomas Grady; as you may know, the highest officer of this state."

Clyde's eyes bugged. His jaw hung loose.

"Clyde, all charges have been dropped against you for insufficient evidence. There is no one bringing any charges against you. To help understand this; A term from Western Juris Prudence, referring to the principle that a crime must be proved to have occurred before a person can be convicted of committing that crime. In other words, *no corpse, no case.*"

Clyde closed his eyes and let his head fall back, his breathing slowing almost to hibernation mode.

A minute passed.

Laura thought he was going into a trance. A Voodoo state.

Everyone waited for Clyde to return. Another minute ticked by.

Clyde's eyelids quivered; went still again.

Another thirty seconds elapsed.

His head jerked, his eyes popped open and he searched around the faces at the table, studied each one.

"Where is Mandy Rose?" His voice was deep and insistent.

Laura felt The Watcher had been in command. She too, awakened.

"Clyde," Laura spoke somewhat mournfully, "I told her about Hannah. I told her you were coming here. I haven't seen her since early morning."

"We must check her room. Can we do that?"

Clyde held his hand out behind him for Laura to take.

They mounted the huge staircase, still connected, with Clyde at the helm.

Angus, Sophie, Almadine and Cassandra watched and wondered how Clyde could possibly know the direction of Mandy Rose's bedroom.

When they arrived at the closed door, Clyde stepped away, allowing Laura to turn the knob and push the door open.

Once inside, their eyes zoomed to the bright white bedspread and the haunting ensemble that lay there.

Long dark strands of hair and an oversized pair of fabric shears with red handles lay on the bed. Next to the long tresses were short, inch-long pieces of hair. Where the scissors had been put down; droplets of red. And a smear turning black as it dried.

Clyde walked to the cream-colored dresser as Laura watched. He pulled open the top drawer where he knew women hid things. His face lit up with a strange glow coming from inside the drawer. He cried out. "Mambo, no!"

Laura went to him. "What Clyde? What is it?"

"She took it! She has it!"

Laura recalled the mysterious totem he always carried, and the glow that came from his utility room at his house where he practiced his Voodoo rituals.

She shrieked, "Clyde, the totem?"

He threw his head back and bellowed, a blood curdling sound that invaded the marrow.

"The gris-gris. She has it. She has the power."

Laura, unable to appreciate all she was hearing, queried him again. "Why did she cut her hair off?"

"Because she thought that would keep her safe. No one could use her hair to cast spells against her if she was almost bald."

"Oh my God, Clyde. We have to find her."

Clyde's face was dusty gray. He looked at Laura and shook his head. "It won't be that easy. She's gone down under."

<h1 style="text-align:center">CHAPTER 112</h1>

Angus let no time go by. He acted.

After contacting the New Jersey Special Investigation Division, a two-person task force was selected to meet the police personnel in charge of investigating kidnapping crimes in New Jersey. They would waste no time approaching the home of George and Martha Trenton.

Sophie begged to be included but was refused.

Less than twenty-four hours elapsed before four police officers showed themselves at the palatial home where a little girl called Isabella lived with her supposed parents.

Armed with an emergency junction to remove a child who'd purportedly been sold on the black market at a tender age from his or her home, two officers climbed the marble steps, unsure of what might transpire in carrying out the legal removal of a minor.

Tap, tap, tap, with a wooden billy club.

No answer.

"Did I just hear a vehicle starting on the far side of the house?"

"Christ yeah, a van heading out."

Anticipating problems of this nature, two squad cars driven by two police officers pulled out and formed a Vee, blocking the white van, and stopping it cold.

The van driver leaned on the horn. A continuous bleat sounded loud and clear.

One officer from each car jumped out and drew guns as they surrounded the white vehicle. Aware a child might be inside the vehicle, they had no intentions of using firepower.

Driver and passenger doors were covered with a few long strides. Their guns were put down against their thighs.

"What do you want? We haven't done anything. We've committed no crime."

This was a sad emotional takedown.

Officer Dean Charest, a kind red-headed father of two, leaned on the window ledge. "Sir, we have orders to remove a child from this address who was kidnapped in Louisiana and is purported to be living here with a George and Martha Trenton and is going by the name Isabella.

At that the child pressed herself between the man and the woman, a little girl with reddish curls. She piped up, "I'm Isabella."

This was awful. "Mr. Trenton, you and Mrs. Trenton are welcome to accompany us to headquarters where the child will be held until child welfare picks her up later today."

Martha Trenton held her hands over her face as great racking sobs began. She screamed at her husband, "I told you something wasn't right when we got Izzy." She reached back and pulled the child from the back of the vehicle and crushed her into her lap, then bellowed, "This is all your fault."

George Trenton laid his fingertips on his forehead and crushed into the steering wheel.

"We're very sorry, but we have to take the child. You can follow us to the station if you want."

"It's okay, Mommy. I'll come back. Don't cry."

The officer opened the passenger side door, extracted the child from the woman's arms, carried her to the cruiser and buckled her in.

The two squad cars drove slowly away with the white van registered to George Trenton sticking close behind.

Chapter 113

Sophie was wrung out with impatience and longing. She begged Angus to expedite the proceedings necessary to bring her granddaughter back to her.

Astonishingly, the records kept by the baby snatchers were accurate and complete. They agreed with the date Hannah had been taken from her crib and the police were called in. The age of the child in New Jersey was also correct.

Though the Special Investigation Division for recovering kidnapped children was under-resourced and under-staffed, this particular case would receive immediate attention. Not preferential attention because of VIP status, but this crime resolved would move the entire backlog of missing children's cases forward. The details uncovered in the case of Hannah Bokum proved entirely accurate with no glitches.

Sophie went to her walk-in closet she shared with no one and knelt in front of her ankle length cocktail dresses. She reached beneath the silky folds until her fingers touched the stupid pair of Western boots she'd bought twenty-years ago. She was not about to go horseback riding or line-dancing.

She yanked one leather boot into her lap and stuck her hand into it. There it was. The Absolut Vodka, still intact.

She removed the crackling cellophane, using her front teeth to pull it free from the cap.

Now the bottle went between her knees. She held it by its neck with her left hand and twisted the cap on the top with her right three fingers.

It made a squeaking noise, then slid.

"Oh dear, don't have a glass."

Sophie looked to her left where a humongous mirror stretched from ceiling to floor; then wrenched her head away.

She raised the bottle of vodka to her lips and felt the liquid wet her tongue.

The mirror beckoned.

Her eyes rolled over the shiny surface.

The vodka poured.

The vodka cascaded down her chin and onto her pale blue dress, turning it royal blue.

Her rounded eyes saw all this.

The mirror showcased a middle-aged over-weight blonde woman pouring liquor on herself.

She dropped the bottle.

"Sophie. Can you please come downstairs?" Angus calmly called through the open door to the bedroom they shared.

She pushed the bottle and the cowboy boot under the dresses and was happy she was in her closet where she could change clothes. Even her shoes were soaked.

"I'll be right down, Angus."

"Okay, honey. I have news about Hannah."

CHAPTER 114

Almadine had laid out a feast for everyone. Po'boys; two varieties, lemonade, black muffins and a bowl of candied black cherries and one of just-whipped heavy cream.

Around the table were Angus, Sophie, Laura, Almadine, Cassy and Arriona and the newest addition, Clyde Boudreaux. He'd dropped the Garcia name.

Arriona fidgeted on Cassy's lap. She was still a bit clingy since her close call with Big Carl at the hotel. She kept her eyes on Clyde as she tapped her mother's face with her finger.

"What Arriona?"

"I have to ask you something."

"Can it wait?"

"No, have to ask now."

"Okay honey, then we have to hear what Grampa Angus has to tell us."

Arriona cupped her mother's ear and whispered.

"Oh, my goodness," Cassy cried. "No, Arriona."

Arriona tilted her face toward Clyde again.

Cassandra felt it better to explain.

"Arriona asked if Clyde was her daddy."

Sophie smiled broadly and said, "Natural assumption."

Clyde was touched. "No, honey, I'm not your daddy, but would be proud to have you be my little girl."

The meeting was off to an emotion-filled start.

Angus said, "We're all family here, sweetie, blood or not." Then he took a long swig of lemonade and spoke. "As you know, Hannah is presently in custody in New Jersey. Her adoptive parents feel they have a case for keeping her with them. The verdict relies on our supplying proof of Hannah's parentage. The information from the traffickers matches our reports for the time she was taken."

He continued. "We must provide her birth certificate showing identification of her birth parents. All photos are helpful and all medical or dental records too. There is also, in cases of question, a new type of testing to prove family relationships.

"It's called Deoxyribonucleic Acid. Or DNA for short. This is the hereditary material in humans and almost all other organisms. Nearly every cell in a person's body has the exact same DNA.

"So, that leads us to how do we prove Hannah belongs to us. We have the birth certificate and the medical records from Hannah's primary care physician. We have her father." Angus regarded Clyde who listened intently while leaning on his elbows.

"We apparently do not have her mother but plan to remedy that as soon as we're able."

Laura nodded with a not-too-pleasant look on her face.

"As you know, Laura, we can get DNA from a hairbrush or toothbrush of Mandy Rose's."

Angus looked at Sophie. "We'll have Hannah back here with us in five to ten days, maybe less. It'll take longer if we need DNA testing. Money can expedite that process.

Sophie leaned back in her chair. "What's the matter with me, wanting to booze again?"

No one knew why Sophie shook her head. She said, "Let's eat."

Everybody dug in.

Arriona still kept a keenly appraising eye on Clyde.

There were now more black faces around the mansion table than white.

CHAPTER 115

Eight Days Later.

Clyde had his hand on Sophie's back and he spoke into her eyes. "I haven't found Mandy Rose yet, but we have some leads. I promise you, I won't give up."

Sophie snuffled and wiped with a crumpled hanky. "I know you're doing everything you can. Today's the big day, and I want Hannah to come into her home seeing smiling faces."

"Me too. I want to meet my daughter with an open heart, free of anxious trepidation. This will be hard for her. The fact that her mother won't be here adds to the complexity and stress. A child needs a mother."

Sophie thought, but didn't say, Hannah knows me better than she knew her mother.

She did say, "Hannah will remember me, Clyde. She already recognized me from the doorway in New Jersey."

Clyde took a few anxious breaths, then tapped his heart, a neurotic habit to keep his heart ticking.

The front door awaited the arrival of Hannah.

Angus sat alone in one of the big club chairs.

On the sofa, Cassandra and Arriona sat with their legs crossed in front of them; Cassy's knees bent keeping her feet close to the skirt on the couch. Arriona's crossed legs stuck straight out.

Behind the couch stood Almadine, hair all slicked back into a tight black bun at the nape of her neck. She chewed on her bottom lip.

Laura stood with her mother. Sophie was wearing an old dress that she'd worn numerous times while rocking Hannah and singing lullabies to her.

Clyde stood alone. In spite of his personal admonitions, he was too keyed-up to sit.

The room was without sound, each in their own world.

Rumble.

Breaks.

Car door one slammed, then car door two. *Bam.*

Rap rap rap.

Laura ran to open the door.

A tall woman with a straight brown bob and charcoal gray suit accompanied a young girl dressed in a two-piece navy-blue outfit with a bright white collar. "This is the Bokum residence, I presume?"

Sophie could hold off no longer. She bolted to the entrance and dropped to her knees in front of the child.

Everyone gaped.

The girl, very poised and soft-spoken asked, "Are you my real mother?"

Sophie held her arms out but dropped them to her sides as she tried to hold her tears. She said, "I'm your grandmother."

The child stayed still. Then she spoke. "My name is Isabella."

And then, sounding much older than her seven and a half years, "I guess you called me Hannah."

Sophie put one hand out and cuddled the child's dangling hand and gently tugged her past the threshold into the house. "This is your home. You were born here."

"Where are my real mother and real father?"

Sophie partially knelt again and said, "Your real mother is away right now. Come and meet your father."

The social worker observed these proceedings with a jaundiced eye. She had mixed impressions of this group. "Where is the mother?"

Sophie led and Hannah walked with an amazingly confident air over to where Clyde stood transfixed.

He peered down at the exquisite child who bore his orange curls and green eyes and her mama's pale alabaster skin coloring.

Sophie said, "This is your real daddy."

"No, I don't believe you."

Clyde and Sophie exchanged a pained look.

The social worker moved with a haughty stride into the room.

Angus decided to speak. "Miss Holloway, do you have some papers for us to sign?"

The face on the woman was crimson and tight; but she produced several pages from the briefcase she carried. "Yes, right here."

Angus gestured toward a low table where a pen was waiting.

Clyde looked stricken, slightly gray and licking his newly dry lips. He walked to the table, picked up the pen and one by one as the pages were laid out for his signature, he signed.

Miss Jeanette Holloway gathered the papers, now in disarray, and folded them into a pack and back into her briefcase. "I'm leaving now. You are, I'm sure, aware that in these situations it's often necessary for psychological counseling for returned children."

"Yes, Miss Holloway. We intend to do that and whatever is necessary to help Hannah reacclimate to her family and home." Angus then accompanied the stiff woman to the front entrance and held the door for her to exit.

They heard the car leave their driveway.

Clyde, still kneeling, spoke in soft soothing tones to his daughter.

She had her arms folded across her chest, but her head was bowed in his direction.

Laura, who knew Clyde better than anyone in this room, smiled inwardly. *He could charm the birds out of the trees.*

Cassy wondered if Arriona would get along with Hannah and how Hannah would respond to Arriona.

Laura grimaced. Dark foreboding thoughts wrinkled her brow as she thought of her missing sister, this child's mother. *Where the hell was Mandy Rose?*

Angus was optimistic that all would work out for the best.

Sophie rejoiced and hugged herself.

Hannah was home.

AUTHOR'S NOTE

Over 30 years ago, in a local writer's group, the name of a place was suggested for an exercise. It was Santa Ana. The first chapter of *Who Took Hannah* was written; then it went on a shelf for almost three decades.

Psychologists would label my childhood as abusive and accurately say I was abandoned. But it gave me the will to conquer challenges.

A small non-fiction book, *The Secrets of Skinny* was written after *Who Took Hannah* then *The Search for Hannah*.

There is a third *Hannah* book in the beginning stages now. It's never too late to start a new path. Be all you can be. You are wondrous beings.

CJ Knapp
Cjknappauthorbooks.com

ABOUT THE AUTHOR

C J Knapp was never wealthy like her protagonist. On the contrary, she grew up poor and in multi-cultural neighborhoods. She brings these insights into her story, not having to try very hard to make it real for you.

www.CJKnappAuthorBooks.com